I0838559

HIRAETH

A Novel

Blake Edward Hamilton

SPUYTEN DUYVIL
New York City

© 2022 Blake Edward Hamilton
ISBN 978-1-956005-28-8

Library of Congress Cataloging-in-Publication Data

Names: Hamilton, Blake Edward, author.
Title: Hiraeth : a novel / Blake Edward Hamilton.
Description: New York City : Spuyten Duyvil, [2022] |
Identifiers: LCCN 2021039913 | ISBN 9781956005288 (paperback)
Subjects: LCGFT: Novels. | Experimental fiction.
Classification: LCC PS3608.A666 H57 2022 | DDC 813.6--dc23
LC record available at https://lccn.loc.gov/2021039913

PART I:
THE SENTINEL

Endless (nonlocal) consciousness…will exist forever as wave functions in nonlocal space.
—Pim van Lommel, M.D.,
Consciousness Beyond Life:
The Science of the Near-Death Experience

FRIENDLY NEIGHBORS

The painted steps of the porch go down into the water. Only two remain above it. Gray-green. Tiny waves. Lapping in a quiet I'm still getting used to; my own Venetian steps. The water darkens the deeper it goes. I don't see the path that leads, serpentine, from the driveway to the steps. I don't see the driveway. The roof of the car is bleach-baked, sun-stripped, a tiny faded island with its own lapping waves. Birds find it useful.

The steps are cheap. I can see that now. The water brings this revelation. It takes the paint off of them like thin rubber, some of it dancing in jut-whirls. Underneath it is the original concrete that came with the house when we bought it. AstroTurf covers the porch, somehow impervious to the sun, the damp. It's a vague insult, the falseness of it pretending to be legitimate grass in front of all of this water. Its green is an imagined green compared to the ocean that showed up. The water out there is distilled, an unclassifiable, murky sea green appearing like a kind of volcanic rock mixed with surging ash.

I can still sit on my porch and look around like I used to. *Porch.* Nothing is more American. What is more *American* than a porch? But that's gone, too. All nations are gone. People show up here in rafts, rolling to my porch, heads bowed in some forced penitence or consideration. They want things, and they ask for them. I shut my door when this happens. I offer them my porch for a while, if they need it, if it's raining, or if the sun roars down all day for days.

A blind group comes often, an older man, two women, a boy, eyes silver-strung and wrung out, past milk-colored. Hard. I don't know how they got this way, or if it has to do with the water, but they make it here somehow. Row up in a yellow, makeshift boat, thatched and pasted, roped down with plastics and wire. They want this porch, too. It's the shade. So I give it to them. They stay quiet. I don't tell them what I think; that they're everything *Hollywood*, everything we wanted the apocalypse to be, everything we watched when I took my grandsons to the movies around the corner at the Clifton Center, next to the cafeteria and the dry cleaners. Do they know this? Do they know what they turned into?

At night, thunder hits low. It rumbles over roof peaks, a line of hopeful triangles in the water marking the spots of the houses across from mine, all at the bottom of the hill. The one right across from me is the Pickering home. The day the water came in, their two boys played in the street at the curb. I watched them. We were warned, but that's what we did anyway. We went on like there wasn't any warning; nothing's wrong, nothing's *ever* wrong, is the attitude. Entertaining demise is too cinematic—a rush of water drowning us all. Too clean. But it took them. They clung to each other, ten year-old arms reaching then yanked back, rubber, boneless, into the torrent, the gray-green current finishing them off. I imagine Diane and Tim Pickering are still down there, up against the living room windows, clutching each other in regretful positions—their children gone.

Next door to them are the Bridges. They're still in the car, down there, trying to drive away. Further along the street, the neighbors are too new. I am too old. I should be dead. Because I am old I should be dead. These are the rules we wrote for ourselves. It is *American*. To be old means to go before anyone else. My home is slightly elevated on a hill, so I did not die.

Above me hang shell-chimes, which call out in a gentle clashing from the white metal porch lattice cut in shapes of phony grapes and coiling leaves. When they are quiet, and the wind off the water slows, I hear the tiny voices of children. I understand I don't actually hear them, but their calls echoing off of the buildings are cut into this place, ghost calls.

I survive reasonably well on my own. My own children, their children, are likely dead. I do not hear from them. They have not made a thatched raft and paddled to me from their side of the world. There have been no letters, no smoke signals. Their deaths are in my breastbone, in the center, hard like a pearl. It grew there when I woke one night to thumping deep against the side of the house, thick tail thumping all along the siding. My heart is erosion, peeled apart, in my bed, in my room. Somehow the lamps outside still work. The light comes in against me, yellow-green, and makes my curtains into rags. I hold a fist to my chest. My daughter. It's all I think. I failed you. Somehow, I did this, and my heart is unmade, here, in this room. She helped me dress the windows in this house. Those rags in that light are as much hers as they are mine. Just rags now. We spent so much time scrutinizing them that they be *right*, and for no one but myself, no one but myself.

How much time we waste scrutinizing, *picking*, for *right* things.

There are nights when I'm glad the water won and left me marooned here in this house. A 65 year-old woman hunched a quarter more than a year before. I should have been raped, poached, gutted on my spread that matches the curtains. I figured as much would have happened by now. Vulnerability is the one consistent human trait, not an instinct for survival; we got it wrong. The will to survive in spite of our vulnerability might seem more basic, but there are sharks in my backyard now, big ones swimming through the holes in the fence. I have steps out there, too, and they also reach down into the water, but it's darker. I first noticed them when I realized I could fish and live off the fish. They come into the small corner made by the old, white fence that hid our air-conditioning unit. They get trapped there, so I reach in with my pot and scoop them up, easy, willing. I do this with an odd sort of joy for the first few times, but soon a pointed snout flashes out from the water, smooth, sleek, with stone-gray skin like it's part of the water, and teeth like jagged darts wedged into raw pink.

I snap back from it, dropping the pot and releasing the fish back into the water. My pot sinks to the bottom somewhere. For the first time since we bought the house, my husband and myself, I notice his shed standing in the middle of the water, white and fading. I really *see* it. I never go inside. It is a rule we had. I don't know what's in there, but I do have the keys. I want to use one of the boats or canoes that wash up to the porch to paddle over and open the shed. The shark, gnashing up at me, heralds my attention to its door. I want to know what is down there. At the finish of this week I will betray my husband's rule and go inside.

The sharks have babies. I can hear them at night, playing, thumping their bodies against the side of my house. The next day, the sun comes down in patches; I imagine cruise ships docked at light-encrusted harbors, sprawling ports. But there is just a flat horizon with a few roofs of houses breaking up the expanse of water, and low clouds speckling the sunlight.

The clouds move slowly north. A man in the center of a narrow raft paddles by. I wave to him. My mother would have said, *No, you don't want to know him. Be polite, say hello, but we don't want to know him.* The man does not respond. I don't know if he sees me. He paddles on, quiet. The birds have vanished, and the large clouds soak up the sunlight. The sky is becoming a gray wall with light-slits, their shafts hitting odd, bare patches of ocean. I sip pekoe made from used tea bags. I turn away to set my cup on the table between two porch chairs. When I look back, the man is gone; his raft, a red plank, rocks side-to-side.

The sharks are getting greedy. In the night they take a chunk out of the fence lining the perimeter that creates a boundary between our house and the Steinwitzer home. It drifts comically around the back part of our property, holes torn from it in clear mouth-shapes. Do sharks behave this way? Is this normal? There is no way to inquire, now, except for direct observation. And I've gotten as direct as I'd like with them. It goes without saying that we once had technologically powered ways of cross-referencing our own doubts by seeking answers about the world whenever we wanted; in fact, it was done at a loss we bemoaned hypocritically: simple face-to-face discourse. So, I suppose if sharks eat fences, wide-smile-bites torn right out of them, then sharks eat fences.

I make up days, now, because a calendar feels like the AstroTurf on my porch. I can't believe in it. It's the same with my name. I never hear it anymore. It's lost its purpose.

My house groans under the weight of the water. There are more sharks every day, thumping against it. Perhaps they know that I am here, walking in the damp, making tea from a propane stove that miraculously still works. Perhaps they know we eat from the same pond. Maybe they want a trade. Maybe they just want me.

Later in the afternoon, I have a visitor. A man rows up in

a yellow canoe (why are so many of these ships yellow?) He is covered by a black, mud-speckled tarp, face oil-slicked with welts like a kind of braille down the side of one cheek.

"Food?" he asks.

I shake my head. He gets out of his canoe and comes up onto the porch. He stays and sits for about an hour. He mouths the words *TJMAXX*, tracing them with his index finger along the glass of my porch table. When he leaves, he paddles west.

Close to sundown, I see a couple huddled up on the Pickering's rooftop. They've built a fire, a red-orange tremble between them, and between their improvised island and the horizon line. As the dusk deepens, the horizon turns a deeper purple, then becomes slick black, like the ink sac in a gutted octopus. The couple sees me and waves. I return the gesture. They make no signs that they want to come over and bridge the distance between the Pickering roof and my porch. They seem content, if a little weathered. I see them embrace, the man holding his mate close, head on her shoulder. My chimes clink and jostle in the wind. The waves lap the steps. A clap of thunder breaks above us, followed by stillness. Wind whips over the water, sending mist at them, then at me. Their small boat is moored to something on the old gutter and downspout.

The fire sends up yellow-red slashes against the purple-black sky. A soft creaking builds, followed by a deep moan shuddering from the house. I watch the couple fall through the roof, and the fire with them. They go almost silently, except for a tiny cry of surprise as their island fails them.

Smoke pours up through the hole in the roof, a soggy black spot, and scatters into a haze. I watch and wait for a sign of them. Their boat smacks the edge of the roof in the waves, tugging. Dashes cut across the water from the sides of my house, sharp fins making a beeline toward the noise, going under and down to find the couple in the Pickering's living room.

I get tired of the jokes when new visitors arrive. It's their way of trying to explain our mutual circumstances. That they remember the warnings that came from movies and books is a miracle to me. Like saying, *See, see! They were right*. Trauma seeks explanations. Blame is inevitable when you lose everything at the expense of others, when some *take* from others because they feel they are somehow more deserving. We all need someone to hang for taking the ground away from us, but who? Weren't we all complicit? Aren't we all getting what we deserve? Before this, we were consumed with predicting our downfall, illustrating it, celebrating it, selling it. Selling it again, repackaged. We awarded visions of it, zeroing in on accuracy. Now that we've achieved it, everyone is disappointed, naturally.

If I want to forget where I am, I remove my glasses. My failing eyes are well-adapted to the human need for denial, and I embrace it, although closing them has the strange effect of making my place more real, the waves lapping against my Venetian steps louder. While dismissing my environment is somewhat easy, I can't forget who I am. I don't have that luxury.

The end of the week arrives, or what I think of as the end of the week. Storms have increased, and many of the boats and canoes piled up around my porch have drifted away. Only three rooftops are left above the water now. The Pickering house is gone, the roof collapsed perhaps, and the one next to it is also missing. A spot opens in my center, looking at the indefatigable ocean. It should create in me a vat of dread, something to pull me down; my house will eventually end up like those. Its foundations are rotting; sharks pound against it at night.

I remove my slippers and inch to the third step from my porch. I hold the rail and reach to the beige canoe parked to the right of the railing. An orange life jacket floats inside it. My jittery fingers clasp the edge. I drag it around and up the steps where it rests against the chairs. My legs quake. My heart feels punched through. I swallow, and my hands get slick. I can't settle, and I am afraid to sit down. I force myself to listen to my breathing, which feels like the only continuity left. I follow it until my body is solid again. At the rails of my steps, something swims by, a quick slither. A deep snap somewhere, a rumble, and I watch as another house sinks, its roof splitting apart in a soup of wood-mush and ashy, sea-green foam.

There are only two roofs left, both lower down the hill

so they are leaning further underwater already. A few more rains and they'll be gone too.

I go inside to get towels to clean out the canoe.

Inside, I make the mistake of picking up an old photo album lying on the sideboard. Here are my children and here is my husband, and myself. Our faces betray a sense of all-rightness with the world. Nothing in them suggests we will be dead soon, or that only myself, of all of them, would survive. I peel back the plastic page covers, removing certain images, placing them next to me in a pile. Nostalgia can be a kind of poison, so I avoid it. I take the pictures because I know I'll need them. I put the stack on my dresser. I move around, slowly, picking the right things to take with me.

Once I have filled a plastic trash bag with these items, I set it in a chair in the corner of my room. It occurs to me that I am packing for a journey, not simply taking some things, a few feet from my back porch to my husband's shed, but I ignore this intuition. I keep arranging things.

Another deep pop rumbles underneath, and I rush outside to see if the other two houses finally gave in, but their roofs are still visible above the water. The boom comes again, this time shaking my house. The shell-chimes fall gracelessly from the porch roof and are swallowed by the sediment floating on the surface near the rail.

I feel another quake. Just then, another man paddles up to my porch, looking so much like the last one I considered that it might be the same man, but his face is unmarked, and there is a deadened look to his pupils. He ties his boat to the rail and steps onto the porch. One of his legs is cut off above the knee. He looks at me, and without saying anything, takes a seat in my husband's chair.

He can see that I'm coming back down into myself after the quake. Neither of us says anything for a long while. I sit next to him. It's almost like real company. He rubs his fingers together as if trying to remove gum or residue. His eyes lock onto the horizon line, scoping the clouds as they coagulate in black patches. He finally turns to me.

"What's got you like this?"

I don't respond.

He waits, and smiling, says, "That's okay. That's okay."

"Your leg." I point.

"Yes," he says, eyes widening, "it was there once."

I want to ask if it was a shark but stop myself. He appears reluctant to say anything more.

"A lot of people like me come this way, no doubt," he says, "and I don't want anything. Just some space. Just tonight."

I consider what he's asking. I lean forward.

"If you want to stay, you're welcome. If you want the house, it's yours. But you have to help me."

"With what?"

"I need to cross somewhere tomorrow, and I don't want to do it alone."

"The woods?"

I shake my head. I don't know what he means. I ask, "Will you?"

There's a moment before he agrees, but when he does, I leave him in my husband's chair and go inside to sleep. In the middle of the night, I wake. The sharks are banging against the side of the house, cracking windows and knocking pictures and objects to the floor. The lamps outside have gone out but there is moonlight and the curtains are almost transparent. I am aware that I am being watched.

A figure stands at the door, a solid black outline. The head is defined in space; it leans out towards me, as if sniffing the air. I notice he has both legs, and I wonder where my guest is. Did he see this man enter? Is he asleep? Are they friends, perhaps? I wait to see what he will do. The space between us is empty except for our breath. His stillness is like a prelude. He is holding things, something at his side. I can't see what it is. He backs down the hall, his eyes stay on me, and then he's gone. It is some time before I get up to check on my guest; the porch is empty, his boat missing, and then I see him floating face down in the debris. The other man has taken my guest's boat, and left.

By mid-afternoon, I succeed in dragging the canoe through the house to the back porch where I tie it up and return inside to get my things. This way, it's a direct shot to the shed from my back porch instead of risking the longer route paddling around the side of the house; less of a chance for the hungry mouths out there to take me. I grab the keys from the table. When I go to retrieve my bag full of photographs and other items, it is gone, and I know that this is what the figure took. Another quake hits, the drawers of my dresser burst open, and clothes spill. The mirror falls from it and cracks into thick shards. Another burst from below knocks the armoire over the bed, a door opening and bending backwards, then splitting off from its hinge. A final burst and the hallway slants sideways, sending down dust and insulation, pink like the shark's mouth.

The house leans, snapping under its own pressure. I get out of the kitchen, and onto the back porch. The house slants at an angle, right into the waves. The beige canoe bobs by the rail. I lean down to pull it close, so I can get in, which is difficult with the waves pushing, but I manage. I squat on my knees in the center, push off, and paddle for the white shed in front of me, resting on its own tiny hill under the water. Below me I see the face of a large bull shark, something else, too. Something larger. The canoe glides smoothly over the turbulence below. When I reach the shed, I stand up, wobbling, key in my slick fingers. The door is right in front of me; the shed was on such high ground it appears to float on water now that everything's flooded. I feel ready to tip, to fall in, and my legs quake trying to hold the canoe steady. I listen as my house starts its dive downwards behind me. I open the shed door as the forms under me knock against the underside of the canoe, teasing me to collapse, to fall in. Dry air floats out of the entrance.

I smell cut grass. I smell earth, deep cold earth. I pull myself up onto the edge of the doorway, and I see a set of stairs going downwards into something. I shut the door, and a new silence comes. Feeling my way, I start to move down the stairs, turning only once to see a small white rectangle pressed onto black, the outline of the door against the day. I continue towards the strong scent of earth. It almost chokes me the further I descend. I worry the steps will never end. I see nothing, and only feel the metal handrail under my fingers. But the steps do end.

Before me is a wood of giant trees, like ancient redwoods, stretching into smoky darkness. Their trunks form a series of immeasurable corridors. A fire burns somewhere, flinging sharp-cut shadows up the trunks of the trees. I walk closer and hear pounding, like a large axe hitting a trunk. It reverberates everywhere, all through me, even shaking the ground. The fire burns in a black metal basin standing on four pillars. Flames crack and split the branches piled inside it. Someone calls out, a human bellow from far inside the giant columns. I wait to see who will come forward. After an abrupt silence, the fire dims, and I move into the forest.

I stop before I reach the mouth of the corridor. In the basin, the fire grows again. It's as though it is aware of me. When I face it, flames reach as high as the trees. I feel oddly apologetic like I should have something to offer it.

I see the feathered, red bark of the trunks in front of me. The wall to my left appears to connect to nothing. The corridor forms an oval. The trees bow out around it. Warm light at the end seems to emit from a silver pinprick near the top of a tree there. I feel as though I've left my body behind, like it's still at the shed door, coiled up, a skeleton-treasure for someone to find, maybe.

I enter the corridor. Around me continues the intermittent, staccato chopping carried through the branches. The same voice drifts along with it, calling to someone who does not call back. I expect something to fall from overhead, to crush me. The path is covered in long pine needles. The darkness between the trees is total. I expect faces to loom out from it. The chopping continues, its echo no closer or further than before. It occurs to me that the person responsible for it is unaware he has an audience. Something about my own awareness of this translates a misguided sense of safety in this place.

The end of the corridor is now bright. The light comes from a metal lamp attached at the top of the tree. At my feet is an unspooled garden hose, an S of green over the needles—the same serpentine shape of the path to my driveway. A small trickle of water runs from its copper mouth. The silver light from the lamp above me pricks my pupils. I don't try to shield my face. I want to see what's ahead, so I just walk through it, like I'm crossing some kind of border.

On the other side of the light is a cliff edge, then mountains. They arch like exposed, blue-gray backbones. The territory has a shape like a series of alternating Ws – WwWwWwWw. Green dust floats off of the pines in the rock creases. Stars are white dapples set far back in cobalt. The horizon leaks into a lilac wash. Looking at it, I am solid. My feet root themselves. This goes forever, I think.

But it's just a wall. My hand is open, and I am reaching, and the tips of my fingers meet with the scrape of stucco—tiny, tough mounds under my palm. I drag my hand down the painted mountains. The wall goes as high as the trees. It goes so high that the painted night sky over the mountains is the real sky. Coldness carves at my center, and I move closer, testing the boundaries I imagined were here.

I get as close to the wall as I can. I stand with my body pressed against it, keeping myself upright. A febrile splintering starts somewhere in my legs and works its way up to my skull. My face is wet. My body bends itself to the ground.

My fingers grip at the needles and the soft dirt under me. I feel stones against my shins, my knees. My center is hollow. All of my weight is in my forehead, and it pulls me to the earth. A horrible quake runs up my back. Air pours out of my open mouth, a long rage-rush from my gut. I am howling, and everything streams out of me to the cold ground. My eyes and face are quick spills; it goes on until I am no longer present.

I want to know why I am here; I want to know where I am.

A small, joyful voice behind me asks, "Do you need some water?"

I lift my head and sit up. The voice belongs to a little girl. She is maybe nine or ten. I do not see where she came from.

Her white dress is almost gossamer, worn, and spotted in tiny, yellow flowers. I wonder how she found me and if she has been watching me. I wipe my face with my dirty palms. I look at the hose on the ground, thinking this is what she means. She sees this and shakes her head.

"No," she says, hands held together in front of her. "We can do better than that."

I wait for her to elaborate, but she doesn't. When I stand she urges me to come with her. I stall at first, then follow her. Where else am I going to go? Her dark hair hangs in a perfect flat line down her back. She takes me around the perimeter of the wall to the edge of a gravel walkway. A separate wall flanks it, but this one is white. A cactus in the corner of the wall leans, and reminds me of a limp prosthetic limb. The gravel walkway turns to smooth, gray pavement. In front of us is a house rising in large wooden cubes with a concrete rectangle for a base. Many of its walls are glass.

Down here, in what is presumably the backyard, the concrete spreads to a cliff edge with a view of an ocean and small islands out in the distance. Part of the house extends to a pool, like an arm. It is really just another, lower wall. The pool and this wall are also rectangular. The center of this wall has a thin rectangular hole. A small fountain pours from it. There is an identical wall opposite this one, and it does the same thing. Lawn chairs sit parallel like thin boards in sleek Zs.

A woman stands behind me. I don't see where she appears from, either. Unlike the girl, I don't feel like I've been watched. She's dressed in a gray jacket and skirt. The girl is nowhere to be seen. She must have gone inside the house. The woman's hair is black like the girl's, but it's in a tight bob. Her face is sharp and V-shaped. Her eyes express nothing. She keeps her hands folded in front of her.

"Come," she says, tired. Her voice is cold. "This way. I'll show you everything."

Without saying anything, I walk behind her across the courtyard to what she calls "light passages," tunnels with floors of polished beige wood, and we enter the one closest to the perimeter of the backyard. Its walls are white. We turn left at the end and arrive at a set of stairs. Through a door at the top of these stairs we enter the house with another long hall attached to it. This one has glass walls that stop and open up into clear air with nothing to close over it. A birch tree grows in the center of this hall with branches stretching through an open square in the ceiling. I wonder what they do if it rains.

"This is North Elevation," she says. She walks forward, her black heels chopping the floor. I'm exhausted but try to keep up with her.

A gray couch and a beige coffee table furnish the room we enter. The floors are the same concrete as the outside of the house. We move through this room to another set of stairs, and another tunnel, to what she says is West Elevation. Here the walls of the room are entirely glass looking out at the ocean. Skinny gray chairs sit in groups of four along the windows. There is a wet-bar to my left. The shelves are empty of bottles and glasses.

"Cleaning products are in here." She gestures downwards then opens one of the cabinets. A row of spray bottles sits far back inside. She lifts one out, places it on the bar. Then she drops a thick folded cloth next to it. Without saying anything, she takes me to East Elevation, the bedrooms. A small closet in the hall houses the vacuum cleaners, she says. There are two. I am to use one in the master bedroom, and the other in the child's bedroom. I am to empty both as soon as I have finished vacuuming. She calls the man who issued these instructions "The Owner." I decide not to ask her his name, or if she is his wife.

His room is a concrete box with window-walls. The bed is a single mattress on the floor. The comforter and pillows are pressed so tightly into place his bed looks strangled. Architecturally, the girl's room is the same as the last one, but facing the opposite way, with a view of the water. On a counter, there are a few glass jars filled with sticks, leaves, and stones. A white desk with a white chair faces the wall near the door. I have no idea why I would vacuum concrete floors, and I don't ask.

The woman takes me back to West Elevation with the cleaning products. She tells me she needs to see me scrub the counters. This is to solidify that I have the job. After that, I can eat. I want to ask, Am I dead? Is this Hell? What would it matter if it was? But I don't ask questions. I take up the bottle and start to clean. The mention of food rattles in my stomach, so it's all I think about, and all I want. If I am dead, at least I still have an appetite.

The woman takes a position in one of the gray chairs. She looks as though she grew from inside it, flesh and bone seeping up from the gray cloth. Her posture is just an extension of the chair. Her knees rub, softly, under the hem of her gray skirt. Her empty eyes stay on me while I spray and wipe, spray and wipe, spray and wipe, moving incrementally down the counter. I start to do the floors. My arms ache to my shoulders. I still have dirt on my face. I feel it in my skin. My back feels heavier the longer I'm on my knees. It's an hour at least before the woman tells me she's seen enough, and she's satisfied. She tells me to go vacuum the rooms and then to meet her at South Elevation where I'll be fed. I ask if I can wash my hands. She shows me the toilet without speaking.

The sun goes down, and I'm still vacuuming. I move the machine diligently around the sides of the master bedroom. Then I turn it inward, around the mattress wrapped tight in its bedding. The vacuum cleaner rolls fast over the concrete. I can't tell if it's picking up anything. The stars outside have an ugly brightness. A subtle glow indicates the horizon, and I see trees receding towards it. I stop the vacuum and listen to the soft chirrup of crickets outside. I can see the driveway coursing through dunes and cacti at the front of the house. Parked under the lights by the garage is a black, off-road sports car. The garage is its own cube away from the house.

The girl's room is quicker. When I finish I make sure to empty both dust compartments into the compressor shown to me by the woman. After I return the vacuums to the closet, I linger in the girl's room. I wonder if she is still somewhere in the house. I decide to adjust her bed, fixing the pillows so that they are full, inviting. I flatten the comforter with my palms. I sit on the edge of it. For a minute, there is a welcome stillness.

When I look up, the woman in the gray suit is there.

"You shouldn't sit here," she says. "Are you finished?"

I nod.

"Good. Then let's get you something to eat."

I leave the girl's room, careful not to touch anything as I go.

The woman tells me I have everything necessary to cook. The kitchen is a sterile landscape, like the wet-bar. An island with a cutting board stands in the middle. Upon it are finger bowls with different seasonings: mustard-yellow ginger, diced red-orange pepper, black-green seaweed, gold-brown seeds. A large, white plate in the center holds the peeled carcass of a rabbit. Its mauve muscles announce a likeness to my own shape in their curled form, the 'me' left behind somewhere. I cook it the way you cook a steak; and I eat it alone at the dining room table.

Outside, the lights in the pool come on.

I discover I have a room. I want to make a joke about tombs, but why risk it? I'm taken there after dinner. It's a cement block with concrete steps that lead up and out of it, right to the pool. I feel that I am hidden away. Maybe this is part of a process; maybe an answer will present itself. The bed is plain. A lamp on a nightstand puts out a restrained glow. The dresser is fixed to the wall. I sit on the bed. The door to the stairs remains open. The sound of crickets is loud. It fills the room. I start to notice a twist in my gut. It's been there the whole time, but I haven't felt it until now. The sounds carry it away, clearing this room of an inexplicable density.

I stand and open the dresser drawers. Jeans and white shirts are folded neatly inside. I take some and hold them up to my body. They look as if they might fit. I remove what I'm wearing and try them. They fit well enough. I take them off. Standing naked in the center of the room reveals a new kind of intent to its design. It's like a temple. Something borrowed from mythology—refined Aztec ruins, maybe—channeled, perversely, through *Architectural Digest*.

I have no desire to re-clothe myself. I want to stay this way: My body, this room. I walk up the steps through the open door, which is more like a cellar door. The pool throws light over me. The ground is warm. The sound of waves from the ocean is somehow discernible, but only when I strain to hear them over the crickets.

A cool breeze comes. My skin tightens against it. I become hyper-aware of my nudity. I won't go back down into the room, yet. I walk to the pool and slowly step into it. It's the same temperature as the concrete.

I swim out to the edge so that I am closest to the view of the ocean, and the islands. They are absent in the dark. Not even the moon is strong enough to raise their shapes against the water. But the ocean looks silvery in the night. Waves roll calmly to wherever they are called. I search by default. I look for ships, for people. Something in me wants to mark the water, to see it populated. But I'm also glad it's far away from me. When I understand there's no need to do this anymore, the tension goes away, and everything that came before it rests. I drift in the pool. Water folds itself into every part. The stars appear heavy and clotted, glimmering crustaceans in the black above me.

Something is nestled in a crevice in the wall above the pool. I see its head move in the light and freeze in the water. We lock eyes with each other. I cannot tell what it is; I cannot make out its shape. It's large, whatever it is, and its ears are hairy triangles, pointing, and ridged. It's primed for something, but not to attack. It just seems to watch me.

A yellow eye with black around it pushes into the light. Whiskers drop around a slight snarl. The confident dart of a fang pokes out from under a black lip. It's as if it's smirking at me. I realize that it's a bobcat. Its claws flex over a mass underneath it. I hear a low rhythmic growl with something tentative and potentially vicious rattling underneath. I feel only uncertainty, not fear. I feel protected. My throat is dry, tight. My legs open; I open. I know it can hear the speed of my heart. It has those kinds of ears. I know it can see me kicking under the water to keep myself up. I know it's waiting for me to make a move.

It stands. Its body almost fills the crevice in the wall. The mass of limbs under it remains still; something that was once another animal. With a quick shove the bobcat pushes it over the side. It collapses in a red and wet heap of meat. Blood splatters across the thin edge of concrete and into the water. Beside the pool, a canted deer face stares back towards the house. Its neck is loose like a swan's. Cracked ribs stretch its split skin. Its chest is a cave, diced raw. Innards on the concrete point under the moon towards the ocean.

The cat vanishes in the brush on the cliff, leaving me his gift.

I exit the pool with some of the deer's blood still on me. I walk across the courtyard back to my room, shutting the door behind me as I descend the steps. In the bathroom I wash off the rest of the blood and find a towel to dry myself. The clothes are where I left them. I put them on. Their newness is a foreign comfort.

I decide to wander the house. I go back through all of the rooms. I stop on each level and look for signs of the others. I find nothing of the woman who led me through the house and watched me clean the counters and floors. I have seen nothing of The Owner. The girl has not come back. I go to each of their bedrooms. Now that the woman in the gray jacket and skirt is gone, I stall in the girl's bedroom. I sit back on the bed the way I did before. I look to the door expecting the woman to suddenly show up, to ask me to leave, to clean something. But she doesn't come.

A strap sticking out from under the bed catches my eye. I reach down and pull it. It is attached to my bag, the one I had filled with pictures. The person who took it had the shape of a man, not a girl. Why is it here? Was it The Owner who took it? To give to the girl, his daughter perhaps?

My reaction is not anger that it was taken from me, but that it has reappeared. The bag is empty. I get down on my knees and look under the bed. I don't find any pictures and I leave the bag on the bed.

In the kitchen I discover a note addressed to me. It is from the woman, no doubt. The handwriting is severe. It is a list of things The Owner would like sterilized, including the garage and the car. The keys are in a drawer by the front door. There is no mention of when anyone might return. There is nothing that says where they went. I planned to thank the girl for her brief kindness to me earlier. If I am astonished at anything, now, it is that I should have received any such personal kindness.

I search the house until I find another bag and fill it with clothes. I grab a few other things. I try not to repeat my mistakes where this is concerned; I don't wait for a right time.

I find the keys to the car where the note said I would but decide not to take it. Something about it is false as if this whole place is a trap. I walk out of the front door and across the dusty gravel drive to the garage. Potted cacti stand erect under the portico lights. I walk up the sloping drive into the dark. As the empty house recedes behind me, the desert looms large and black. I continue with the intention of just walking. Under the moon, tall cactuses make crooked forms, taking on the color of bleached shale. Others are just shadows.

Forms leap in the sand on either side of the road. Quick darts of movement. From their sounds—specific, brief howls—they must be coyotes. Under the baying I hear a ravenous sniffing, mewling. I can tell they're tracking me. Further out, I see hordes of them, running hard over the dunes, and scattering sand. Their call is the charge I have in me, now. I understand I am following them, not the other way around; I am being led. I am careful where I walk because they collect in the road. They move around me, brushing my legs and urging me forward. One approaches, sniffs my fingers. Its nose pushes them apart. It licks and then runs on. The others follow it, and I see a shape in the distance lying upon the dunes.

My loose skin becomes a burden as I walk. It hangs on my back and pulls, the weight of it like a stone. My knees grind. I can feel the veins in my legs thumping with blood. My heart yanks against its part of my chest. My sides are slick with my own sweat. I keep licking my mouth. The dryness in my throat is a nest of spiders hatching on my tongue and cheeks. I'm worn. What body is this if I left the other behind at the shed door? Am I imagining that I have one? The coyotes have dispersed, only a few remain with me as I near the black shape in the center of the desert.

Behind it is a range of mountains, black against the horizon. The giant form to which the dogs are leading me is breathing. Sand grinds under my feet as I near it. Its breath is a restful exhalation—a *joyful* exhalation. It is the breathing of a happy child as it sleeps. I know this kind of breathing; as a mother it becomes a part of you. You remember it as a kind of ease given by you and you only— your child is *safe*, and it rests knowing it is safe. This is the gift of the mother. Hearing it rends me.

Further, I see the form has a more defined shape; it's

an elephant lying on its side. Its tusks swoop from its face like white slashes in the moonlight. The small V of its mouth droops into the sand. Its thick trunk flops and gently sweeps the ground, then rests. Its front legs and feet are still. The broad chest and stomach rises into a full arc and descends on the right into the form of a whale. They are the same creature, sharing a body. The whale is awake. It looks at me with a curious, wrinkle-lidded eye. It moves its head and body. Its pectoral fin swipes at the ground as if trying to move itself closer to me. I walk towards it. I touch the fin gently. It slows its movement and then draws me close to its face as if enclosing me in a thick, leathery wing. It seems to want this; then it frees me. I step back, my eyes straining to absorb it in the dark. The tough gray skin of the elephant conjoins in the center with the slick, black skin of the whale. Below this is a horizontal slit that peels apart, like curtains. A man emerges from inside the beast, stepping into the cold desert, holding a lit candle in his hand. He is naked except for some jewelry. His body is scarred. He wears a pack strapped to his shoulder.

He acknowledges me with a glance.

The skin flaps of the beast glisten. Black rivulets run over its live topography. Its mid-section could contain a small building. The height of it stretches upwards like a tower. I realize the man is waiting for me to make a decision: to follow him inside the animal, or to go on somewhere else. I study his face for indications of malevolence. I search him for something that would harm me. The corner of his left eye and mouth are tweaked in subtle compassion. He knows I am afraid.

Inside the beast I hear rain. It's the kind of rain you hear in the spring, outside your window. Soft. Consistent. Everything is dark; the ceiling is invisible in the black stretching above us. I smell wax instead of blood, at first. Then, as we move deeper, the metal scent of blood is in the air, like a mist. Following this is the scent of sea salt and mud. The man leads me further in and, to the right, we enter a large apse constructed of webs of tendon and muscle. It's the interior of the organism, a living interior. Thick and smooth, the bones roll above us, ribbed, pointing up into a triangular shape. They shine slick over the candlelight, a warm glow against the red and gray pumping walls. From the center, near the entrance, roll echoes of steady thunder in a beat that I know is the thing's heart, a conjoined heart, no doubt. I could feel it, black and thrumming—a leather bag full of blood, impenetrable. And all around it is the sound of rain.

The tendon-apse is filled with candles. I wonder why this does not burn the creature. The man sits on a muscular abutment, like an impacted tooth pushing through a sore gum. I do the same across from him, the fat in my back still pulling me down. My legs release. I feel myself collect. A folding-in happens, and I see myself at that moment when I entered the shed.

The man smiles as though he understands what is happening. He is the sentinel of the apse and the beast. He arranges things I can't see at the front. I expect to see an altar.

He speaks with his back to me. "You have a choice. Two options."

I don't say anything. I just let him speak.

"The world you left is gone. This one has always been."

When he says this I remember my last visitor from above, the one who mentioned The Woods. Is this what he meant?

I wait for him to tell me about my choices. He explains the first option: I can continue to walk. The desert beyond the beast is there. I can find others like me. I can wander, but it will be a perpetual dream. Others have come here; they found ways in like I did through the shed. This is a possibility. But there is one who *owns*, he says. Somehow, I escaped him. But he tells me it is not a surprise that I would encounter him after I entered the woods. He says The Owner erects houses everywhere, and then abandons them, entrapping those who stay; he plays tricks. The Owner *uses*, he says. He takes the energy from the captured, bit-by-bit. They willingly believe in his environments; they take on the role The Owner sets for them. *What happened above you,* he continues, *is because of Him. He affects the Inner and the Outer. He takes. He takes. He takes.*

I tell him about the girl, my bag. He nods. He says this is true, and that she is not his daughter. Who is she? I ask. He tells me she is him. He says she cannot be helped. I feel a visceral kind of cutting in me at this. I held some hope that I would find her and thank her, eventually, but it would be foolish. She was The Owner's rabbit-trap. My body slumps down. The heat from the candles, from him, creates a lull, and I become drowsy.

Your second option, he says, and he gestures at the darker part of the tendon-apse. I see a hollow of some kind, and something extending from it. It appears wet and soft, like intestine.

I tell him I need more information. He moves closer to me. He explains that every failure in my life is excised here, every wound, every bruise going down, down, down to places immune to sight and memory. He says that here I can take a new form; that there are interstices where the flood does not exist, and my daughter is safe from the waste above in another time and location, just as I can be. But I will have no choice in dates or placement or form. She doesn't either. I can just go. I can return. I can return to her and salvage something; I can repeat; I can do the opposite of what I didn't do. The trade is here. It begins in the hollow. If I do not choose this, he says, the desert is there for me, and I can continue to walk it as long as I might.

I ask if The Owner will find me; if he looks for those who get away, who make the choice to leave. I ask if he punishes those he finds. He says nothing, only stares at me with intent, waiting. The gravity of my decision hangs in his eyes like liquid. His face is pulled in heaviness. My decision is a decision of fate. His expression is an attempt to communicate this to me. It is a warning.

I look towards the hollow and remember my daughter.

"What of me will remain?" I ask.

He only moves his head subtly, a gentle shake. It says, *Nothing*.

I want to know, then, how I will know my daughter; how she will know me.

He only stretches out his hand, and I take it.

I lay at the front of the tendon-apse on my back. My legs extend down the hollow. It is a tube, thick like the elephant's trunk, although it is a mouth. It fits around my feet and calves and works its way slowly up the lower half of my body. This is how it chews. I am in the process of being digested. The man sits with me, holding my hand. His face is gentle. He says, *Reese*. And he smiles at me with compassion, approval for my choice just under the surface of his eyes. Seeing this I realize I should be afraid, more afraid than I am now. But I'm not. I feel myself go. I am slipping down the throat, my chest warm in the lips of this mouth unraveling me like so much cloth. It drinks me. It takes my arms, my hand pulling away from the man's, and then my shoulders, my neck. Before the darkness, before the mouth reaches over my own, and then dissolves my eyes, my face, my jaw and my brain, I try to remember. I try to remember what is important to keep, to take with me for her.

do   not   donotdonotdonot   re rererererememberrememberrememeberrememeber rememberremember re – emeber re – emember re – member re – member re re re re re re re re know 2+2 yes that's a good one, know that, know your math, green frogs, wet-green, skin-slick windows, slick-now (know, this know this know this know this know this know this coagulant co-agulant co – agulant and thick-nest, thick-web, know (now) here, know heeee re know he – (reknow) and he – rrre know he - re get it right wet brain wet-soft wet soft w[]e[]t soft – sound of eehht – eehht – mmsoh – soh – a A soft –sohf sohf sof sill sill sill girl girl gir – un – un - uh ah –ththththroat th roat th-roat throat swallow me swallowing me swallow swallowswallow...

PART II:
INTERSTICE—
NEW FORMS

Unto one side I turned me, with the fear / Of being left alone, when I beheld / Only in front of me the ground obscured.

—Dante Alighieri, *The Purgatorio*

REESE: THE FIRST

This is what I write:

Plenty of things happened in a second, and it was no laughing matter. In less time than that he watched an old woman hunched at her steering wheel, grasping it like a leech, plow smoothly into the back of a red pick-up truck carrying four yapping dogs. Time seemed to elongate when, upon impact, their tiny bodies flew out into the road, silent suddenly as if the crash had caused them to reconsider their protests. He could argue that it took at least one whole second to realize something was wrong when his mother and sister returned home from shopping at the corner pharmacy; their house was burning. They stood there in the doorway, sniffing the air, and realized that flames were eating their house from somewhere inside its walls.

The next seconds, the ones that followed the first whole one, entailed the intricate processing that takes place when you start to accept that something has happened, or is happening; in this case, that their house was beginning to be consumed by unseen flames. And then it was gone. They didn't remember it after that. How could they? It was a better house, though. Better than what came later.

Within something less than a second a garage door ran over his right pinky finger. He felt no pain, even after the tip flipped back, like the lid to a Zippo, and a jet of red gushed down his five year-old palm.

In less than a second, or within the length of a full one, his body knew before he knew that his father had died. He was stumbling through a job interview, his mouth wasn't working properly, and physiologically he suddenly couldn't function. In another second, he knew that an unmarked envelope left on his porch slid half-under the doormat was a letter from his lover telling him to fuck off. He knew that anger came from pain, and pain was caused, most often, by betrayal. This could be betrayal by your friends, your body, your leaders, your universe. The term 'seconds' was a poor choice for what they needed to describe time, to describe the increment, the moment. There was some space in a second, a breath that time strangled. What happened in it wasn't always painful, or terrible. But when it was gone, it was gone; the family deceived themselves when they said that there was a forwards and a backwards. There was neither. And it took less than a second to fully understand this, without argument, when he saw through his living room window a woman in white standing on his front porch with a box in her hands, also white, knocking and waiting for him to answer.

I'm made of limitless thresholds. I live a specter's life, never fully rooted in my body. The person I'm haunting is myself; a permanent borderland, where I want time to arrive differently than it does, and I want it to provide answers—then, events might happen so they don't end up splitting into predictable simulacrums.

I want my father to read this and to say something to me; from one writer to another; is it the start of something?

A story at least? What carries the most weight? Do I have a story that matters? My family has left the house to go on their annual drive to find a homeless person in whom to share our Thanksgiving dinner. This is their fashionable attempt at grace. When they return, I will give this to him, and ask him to read it.

MARGARET: THANKSGIVING

The plate of food the mother and the grandmother help
to fill is too much for me to eat. As they conspire over
what to put on it I sit, rigidly, at the end of the table opposite
the father, like some mismatched matriarch. That might be
a bit exaggerated, but it feels that way. And it takes me the
better half of an hour to figure out who is related to whom.
I worry, intermittently, that I smell, that they are smelling
me, or that I carry a stench from the House I can't get off,
something permanent: the way of the street.

The mother and the grandmother lower the blue and
white china dish, placed squarely in front of me on a
Pottery Barn placemat covered in white, glazed pumpkins.
My stomach contracts. Following this comes a rush of guilt
like the anxiety I used to have coming off of Klonopin six
years ago. Not everyone gets chosen, I remind myself. But
my stomach has shrunk so much that the forearm-sized
sweet potato rounding the edge of the plate seems as if it
could nurture me for the next month. The mashed potatoes
next to it appears like an afterthought, greasy with brown
gravy, which spills in shiny pools across the expertly sliced
turkey meat, a perfect, washed-out pink. The green beans
are so stiff and green, woven across each other, that I am
reminded of the tarot card I found in the yard of the House.
I use it as a bookmark: the five of wands. Depending on
whom you ask, it means different things, but most often I
hear it referred to as an uphill battle.

Nine people sit at the table, which stretches before a

wall of clear windows overlooking a lawn with children's toys piled into a red brick corner sporting daffodils and empty terra-cotta pots. The table is glazed gray-white. It is old and expensive. I study the perfect edges of it, marveling at its sturdiness, crafted beyond anything I have seen in a long time; I am used to picnic tables spotted in cigarette burns, name carvings, and trash stuffed into the holes. I have a plastic folding chair in my room in the corner. Under it, I always place my shoes and across its seat, my folded clothes. The small nightstand was once used as a dentist's cabinet. The drawers, I imagine, contained drills and picks that spent hours clawing through people's mouths. It has a smell about it, clinical, like old baking soda. Its dented, rusted surface came from the 50s, and wasn't made to last. My mattress, a twin on the floor, has supported many bodies before mine, but when I lie on it, I imagine it likes mine best. Nothing I have had, however, compares to this table, and even the family corralled here now fails in comparison to it.

To my right is the twelve year-old daughter of the son, Reese, who sits at the opposite end next to his father, who is, as mentioned, opposite me with some papers laid out before him. The mother who prepared my plate is next to me on my left. The grandmother is diagonal from her at the other end. Next to the mother is a man I have not been introduced to and who does not look at me. Across from him, in the middle, is a woman (his wife, presumably), and it is she who stands out the most. Her raven-black hair, cut short, swoops back from her head behind her ears. Her earrings sting to look at; the pert gloss of the pearls are nestled snug in her lobes. The severity of her dress cuts in sharp angles over her shoulders and collarbones, and it is the red of spilled wine, or something else, something bloody. The twelve year-old sitting next to her, and to my immediate right, admires her in silence, and sits with annoying posture, the kind that emulates others; a child attempting maturity and respect at embarrassing levels. She looks around to see if anyone notices just how tall she sits, how regal. When she looks at me, it is with a total lack of confidence. Her act fails on me because I am not of importance. My opinion does not count, but I can see through her, and she tries to hide her awareness of this while choosily poking items on her plate. I, in contrast, have nothing to hide; the House, I realized, was all over me. I smell of it, even if I do not smell of anything. My worn clothes, my skin, all of it shows my worth, and to a certain extent, my experience in life. I look down, my plate untouched, then up, catching the disapproving stare of the mother on my left. She looks quickly away. I attempt a bite of the potatoes and listen as the father at the opposite end begins to shout at his son, shuffling through the papers.

"Reese, you've got to be fucking kidding me," he says, chewing sloppily at the meat from his fork.

"I'm not sure I understand," says Reese. He sits back into his chair, rests his thin, pale hands in his lap.

"What is this bullshit about *time*?" asks the father. His rigid posture is like a barrier between him and Reese; he appears uncomfortable with this transaction taking place at the table.

"What do you mean? It's not all *right* there? It's not evident where it's going?"

"Well, it's sporadic and sprawling. It's shit."

"Oh come on."

"What is this about time and this woman? The one at the door? I expect the box is meant to be some kind of hook? Something to grab us all for what comes next?"

"You could say that's what it is. Don't you want to know what's next?"

"I think I've read enough."

The mother coughs, clears her throat. She uses the bowl of rolls as an excuse to interrupt. "Honey, you're brow beating him to death. Don't you think? How about something supportive?"

"I am supportive," says the father, eager to defend himself. He projects his shame downwards at his plate, which is almost empty.

The twelve year-old sits forward. "Can I just say something?"

"What is that, honey?" encourages the mother.

"Could you please *quit* cussing?"

It is obvious that she wants applause of some kind; she has stopped the show with her appeal at morality. She is the new morality police fashioned by their own hands. No one says anything, and the girl looks up at the stalwart, chilled figure of the woman next to her, black and red angles, appearing hopeful that the woman neither noticed, nor cares about the girl's social failure; that no one found her request truly valid. She hasn't learned, yet, that having "values" is an issue of the public, a display for others only when it is meant to convince others of something; she is a champion of no one at this table because most of them enjoy using the word 'fuck' on more than one occasion. The child doesn't understand anything of words, yet, either. Her rickety, awkward, pre-teen body settles in clothes that were picked-out for her. And she has hair that is brown, flat, and unimpressive.

"Taylor, honey, what were you telling me in the kitchen earlier?" pushes the mother; her eyes lift with false excitement. She slurps down a green bean.

Taylor, the girl, looks down and then shakes her head.

"Oh, tell everyone," attempts the grandmother. "She says she wants to be a doctor."

"Is that right?" mutters the father, looking to his plate.

"I've started studying for the SATs," she says. Her voice fills with mimicked, business-like tones. "I plan to score highly."

"A pediatrician? Right? She wants to help babies," says the mother. A strange giggle spills from her lips and shakes in the fat under her chin.

I think of what I could tell the girl about school and college and graduate work in America; my own M.A. took less than two years to complete. But what effect would that create, except to invite questions?

"I don't know," speaks the woman in red with black hair. "Why aren't you more generous with your expertise, Frank? He is your son. He wants to write, let him write. Give him your contacts. What helps him helps you. Am I correct?"

The table is stunned. Has the woman spoken inappropriately? Has she done something even worse than demand they 'stop cussing'? The father leans forward. The son watches him expectantly, his face a perfect emulation, even the thin-rimmed glasses on his pointy nose. I feel a contraction in my gut looking at him, the feeling of knowing someone without knowing them.

"I always help my children," says Frank. He quickly fills his mouth with a larger bite of something brown piled high on his fork.

The suggestion here seems to be that his son, while perhaps of some modest talent, does not have what it takes to publish fiction, but that his father, a veteran of the book publishing world, does. The other suggestion is that only by nepotism can the son have what he wants; it is clear he can publish fiction, but it isn't the kind of publishing he is after.

"I will just say," says Frank, addressing the whole table, "that no one wants to read about the homeless, the starving, the books that are books-within-books, or these goddamn Russian doll novels! People want stories. They want a goddamn story."

"A story doesn't have to be told."

"Oh don't give me that shit. People either read because they want to be entertained or to enjoy the suffering of others. There, I said it. It's been said."

"Well, after reading one of your books, I can certainly say that's true about you, Frank," says the woman in red.

"If that isn't a bunch-of-fuck." Frank slaps his Pottery Barn napkin into the pool of gravy and residue on his plate.

Taylor forces her face to turn red and folds her arms across her chest. She catches the concerned look of the mother, and then manages to squeeze her eyes closed, pained at the *fuck* Frank has just uttered. I want to tell her to embrace it; that this word above all words will eventually become her friend; that in moments of regret, of total darkness, of hourly pain, this word stood up, it lasted. I want to tell her to use the fucking thing. Instead, the specific American *need* for approval wins out. She coyly works her expressions of sadness and violation. I see that her need for approval will neutralize any impetus for her to work hard in life; that she will never become a pediatric doctor, or even a veterinary nurse, for that matter; helping animals, to her, would be too much of a task.

These will not be options for her. Her route will change soon in the next couple of years, and it will be predictable, and it will evolve and keep evolving until she is a refined, less pretty version of the woman next to her, who receives admonishing glances from the pleasantly mute man at the other end of the table.

"Well, let's all say a thing we're thankful for," suggests the mother. "One thing. You start, Joanne."

The grandmother, happy to be given a voice, takes her time to meaningfully compose herself before answering.

"This wonderful food," she says with conviction.

"Amen!" says the mother, a bit too supportively. "And, you, Frank?"

"Well, I just second Joanne here."

"All right, Reese?"

"Family."

"Julie?"

"Good wine!"

"I'll say yes to that!" The mother toasts Julie across the table, both smiling at each other in a rare, and probably not-to-be-repeated act of camaraderie.

"Taylor, honey?"

"Manners. *Good* ones."

"Yes, we should all be grateful for that."

The mother looks helpless and somehow forgets about the mute man next to her. She turns to me, instead.

"And what about you, darling, what are you grateful for?"

They wait kindly, but uncomfortably, for me to answer. When I don't speak right away, the mother grabs the chance.

"You know, I just wanna say, we have just started this trend of taking in a person of lesser means on this great day, and I think it's a beautiful one. I really do hope you're enjoying yourself, honey, and I hope you get as full as pie before we have to take you back."

"Thank you," I mutter.

She nods, and for a minute I can tell she wants to ask me how I ended up like this. The question they all want to ask. I could make them respect me more and see me as something other than The Charity. I could engross them with my stories, my tragedies; tell them how the bank took my family's home after my mother's death near the end of the Bush era; recount the moves, natural disasters, and the job that "let me go," another convenient phrase; the kinder version of a bunch of fuck.

I could tell them how long I've gone without and watch how much it would *terrify* them; that my family, all gone now, once had a table like theirs; that I sold it in the front yard for a crisp fifty bucks when the bank couldn't get rid of me fast enough. I could tell them how ungrateful I was for some things as well. I could show them, but I don't want to ruin this; the illusion that they are on the side of fortune, after all.

The mother takes my half-eaten plate and sets another of peach pie and ice-cream in front of me.

"How was it, sweetie?" She asks. "Did you enjoy your food?"

"The best I've had," I lie. "Thank you."

DERRICK

What is a gay man, now? This is something I ask myself: How have we evolved? We went from hiding in bathroom stalls (the desperate biological push to shoot with the right anatomical partner, and then, if it is the 1950s, return home to wife and children). Nothing has changed in the 21st century, except we can get married; that's a kind of validation. Yet married couples are often only married in name—the institution doesn't sit well with us, apparently. More and more, the fight for the same traditional right to have a partner of the same sex has—overnight, it seems—been replaced for a negation of standards. A gay relationship, a gay marriage, is only sacred until the apps come on, or the sex runs flat. Keeping my sexuality ambiguous has done nothing for me, not like I thought it would. Gay existence is mutating, splitting itself between slithering around in the greasy, familiar stall-shadows, and glaring scrutiny in shattering sunlight.

There is no in-between, no balance. The hunger for relationships is being whittled down through the vending machine, algorithmic screens of apps; through addiction to repression, to banal, base animal fucking. We never leave the bathroom stall; it gets into our DNA somehow— our devotion is to the panicked rush of being caught, no longer having the freedom to cloister ourselves in the warm dark with a stranger's dick in our mouth. We deny our relationships. When our sex becomes normalized, we start a new fight, which is the clamor to keep it illicit—the sad thrill of turning the straight guy. I suppose this is in me, this illicit push, when I meet Reese, an easy closet-case to spot. Repression has a hungry, mad glee about it, like a jumper on a rooftop daring you to get a little closer, so he'll have an excuse to throw himself to the skies.

Traveling from Houston, where I train as an astronaut, to New Orleans to do brief lectures at the university brings me right to the crossroads of Reese. Do I want this? Another one, like him, shoved so far down inside himself it would be exhausting just to get on the same page? I want to rebel against my own impulse to chase the guy hiding in the shadows, but the urge to push him takes over, and I feel like I'm leading him out of a dirty, fucking cave, right to himself, right to me, away from the self he built for others. And it's always this last self—the one for others—that we spend so much time trying to kill.

At first, everything is tentative. A closet-case is a dog that's been beaten, but only by himself. Everything is cliché; meeting in hotel rooms booked in advance; the occasional "friend date" in "the open," at a chain restaurant; emotional phone calls that drag on cyclically; messages in code, which is what the relationship becomes, a thing in code that can't function any other way. Our own private bathroom stall. A part of me exists in fear, and I wonder if it's the same for Reese: abandon the stall and the relationship dies.

I'm 17, and my first time with a man is in a red barn. June in Vermont in 1979 is hot, and I spend it outside mostly helping my uncle with his small farm, walking the seven miles home to my mother, who does nothing all day except knit and collect knitting patterns in a plastic folder next to her brown La-Z-Boy chair. When my dad wraps his head in one of her quilts and blows his brains out in the bathroom, she stops making quilts. Just small stitches on things, little designs to hang in the kitchen, a lopsided rose with the slogan, "By any other name..." stitched under it in black. I am tasked with cleaning out the tub. My dad's brains are soft by the drain and slide into it easily when I push them over the rim. The blood is harder. It seems defiant, as though it wants to stay. I scrub the tile and tub for three days but it's still pink where everything shot upwards or spilled. My mother bathes in the kitchen sink. I have the shower to myself; the pink is a halo around my toes. When I jack-off in the spray, the water scatters my come across the tile. If I hold my breath long enough, I get dizzy, and a kind of euphoria fills my arms, my chest. It's like I'm lifting up, out of the house. It's the closest I get to being without a body, the weight of it.

At the barn, golden hay bales lay stacked near the parted doors, unused. I take off my shirt and let the sun burn my sweaty chest. I'm turned-on by my own surroundings, by how absurdly porn-like the whole thing is; a cheap stage-set with my uncle's stupid barn. I'm hard laying there alone, open, exposed. I want to be found, for someone to walk up and discover me hard, my skin red and shiny. This is my hope. I do this every day I go out there, while my uncle is on the other side of the property. Green grass, light wind in the trees, a soft hush, and the dull clang of a cow bell behind me. The more isolated I feel, the more insistent my need is to be found. Later, I realize this is all gay life really is: pervasive hunger for someone to find us, the source of which is our own identities.

The person who finds me is a seasonal worker recruited by my uncle from New Hampshire. His jobs are whatever my uncle tells him to do. He lives in the tiny shed tacked-on to my uncle's house. He's thirty, and says he's trying to get to L.A. He asks me to move off of one of the bales so he can complete the jobs assigned to him that day. I'm annoyed because he disrupts my staging—I'm trying to be my own kill box. I'm forced back into the emptiness of the yard. He ignores me, using hooks and thick worker gloves to haul the bales back into the barn. His plaid shirt is covered in yellow strands, his white forehead slick, hair greased in sweat. His unshaven jaw clenches, and his wide brown eyes seem moody. A strange openness comes off of him, the way that he moves.

He arrives sporadically during the week. At the barn, he starts his work. Some days I help him. We don't talk much, but I can feel him building to something. It's in my stomach.

On my way to hook another bale, he gently closes the barn doors, sealing us inside, and it's suddenly very dark, and hotter than hell. I tell him there are brown recluses in here and we should probably get the rest of the bales, and get out of there. He doesn't say anything, but instead takes me by the shoulders and moves me into a corner by the doors, like he's positioning me for a photo. I stand awkwardly. Then his gloves come off and hit the floor next to my feet. His hands go right to my belt, and he unclasps it quickly, unbuttons and unzips me, and the pants leave my bony hips to settle around my thighs.

I'm hard right there, and all he asks is, *Is this your first?* And I don't get to respond because my voice halts when his fingers spread gently around my nuts, and he moves his thumb in a circle around them; I start leaking, a thin clear line like a web filament, right to the ground. He lowers himself, takes a knee, and slides his mouth around me; my legs shake, and he moves me back and forth, his tongue hitting me like he knows where to press, and I'm sort of numb in my hands. My mouth dries out while I'm standing there, watching his head move, and it just comes out of me, a sharp river, and my stomach goes flat. He gives out a soft moan as he drinks it. Then he just stands, pulls my pants up for me, and claps a hand on my shoulder like I've done something right. Without saying anything, he goes to the back of the barn where he finishes the work for that day, and that's it. I see him again later, all the way up until he leaves, but all we do is work.

I know I'm in love with Reese when he tells me he takes care of his sister's dogs; that she leaves them without food and water sometimes, and he often spends his lunch break driving across town to make sure they are fed and walked. He doesn't understand what this reveals about him; but rather than alert him to it, I keep it to myself. He asks me about my first time when I get him to have dinner six months into our affair at a rooftop bar in the French Quarter. He says we should order blackened catfish. Then, before I can answer him, he asks me if I feel guilty because he's married—because of his wife.

"You were never married," I say, and the look of confusion disappears from his face fast. He nods his head, signaling that he understands what I mean, then looks out at the horizon, at the purple light as the sun sets.

"As for your other question," I tell him, "it was quiet."

MARGARET: THE PLANT

When they take me back to the House, some regulars are gone. So many come and go that you're never sure who has died or who has just gone on another bender. I have been chastised for using the word 'bender'; things have changed again. It seems there are other, better words to describe self-immolation, drug and alcohol abuse, than 'bender.' There are the allusions to food with 'cooked,' 'roasted,' 'fried,' and 'candy-flipped.' One could be 'chunnin,' 'blunted,' 'wacked,' 'wet,' 'e-tarded,' 'jacked-up,' 'chained,' 'krunked,' 'gowed,' 'mangled,' or 'nutched.' It's so clear, aesthetically speaking, how America arrives at its language, how we avoid rendering pain justly.

By the time the grandmother, the mother, and the girl drop me off at the weed-strewn curb, I have been asked what I do when a man wants to have sex with me in a place like this? Have I been raped and, if so, what did I do afterwards? Have I given birth? Do I recall having children? Is my vagina working properly (code, I assume, for do you have blisters down there, or warts, or crabs? If they're still called crabs.) This last one is a poorly whispered question of false concern from the grandmother. She wants me to know she is reaching out. I notice her eyes scanning the barren lots on either side of the old House, overgrown with weeds. A rusted, blue barrel lies on its side in the lot to the right, a famous spot for one-on-one smoke sessions and heart-to-hearts. I once saw a few late-nighters waking up in the dewy early light propped against its shiny, blue side, a feral block-kitten sleeping like a hair-tumor on one of their chests.

The grandmother, I can see, is internally pondering the standard questions: how did I become this? Why did I choose this? Why here? And why not change it?

The only thing that hurts is that none of them—this family I'll never see again—imagine that I ask myself the same questions, but for different reasons.

Once the family has driven off, and I pass the dusty, dirt-speckled threshold of the House, the stairs to my room are right before me. The foyer walls are gray, peeling, and the one facing the front door is decorated with a picture of Christ's face beaming up towards something Heavenly. The picture is a leftover from sometime in the 70s when the House was opened anew. The door to the right of the entrance is an empty room. No one ever occupies it, a mystery to me. It was once The Office. A person at one time worked there, made sure these people were fed, clothed, paid attention to. This is no longer the case. No one checks on us. We're on our own. Perhaps it is left vacant out of a kind of unconscious respect for the people who occupied it once. In the back near the corner is an empty green file cabinet, the only thing left by the last person who came here on a daily basis.

On the right extends a hallway with a couple of mattresses on the floor and one door leading to an unused boiler. People sometimes come here and sleep for a couple of days and then leave again, never to return. The mattresses remain. They have not been moved since I arrived. That's three years now. A large, mud splattered window shines at the end of the hall. It is uncovered, and no one attempts to cover it. Near the closest mattress is a bookshelf. This remains a constant surprise to me as it is filled with books, old ones removed and new ones always replacing them. I read almost all of them. I read them again when nothing new arrives, and then suddenly more show up. That shelf is magic.

The House was built sometime in the 1920s. The stairs have a curving shape and an ancient brown glow; years of oil and hands. They creak at times, of course, when they most want or need to announce themselves: *You walk on me, but I lift you up—a fair deal, shall we say.*

The hallway on the landing, which parallels the hallway below, is also made of this wood. There are three doors upstairs. Each door opens to a room that is shared by two people, sometimes three. I have not shared my room in the last year. I've developed some kind of odd status. Perhaps because I've stayed here the longest and seen the most come and go. Maybe, in some odd way, they see it as mine now. I want to reassure them that all rooms here are shared, and I can never have it. The dust and mold, the reek of old paper and skin, unwashed bodies, rust and something indescribable left by time, all of this is ours. I want to tell them that no one will chase us here, asking us questions; only the occasional family member will arrive wanting to "feed" us, and to reaffirm their belief in their own goodness.

Above my bed is a window similar to the one downstairs. It is also uncovered. On the sill is a plant. I have no idea what it's called, but it is some kind of succulent. This is the only thing that I can claim is mine; that I won't part with it. I keep it on the right side, about ten or so inches from the corner. The leaves resemble tiny lips stained in blue watercolor with red thorns at their tips. Its shadow during the day acts as a dial. It moves across the white, chipped edge of the window.

When it seems as if the smallness of its container isn't enough to hold it, or that it's ready to go, to leave me here to find another plant to take its place, I remind it that it has to live, to continue. And when it asks me why, I say: *You have to live because I have to live.*

REESE: STATUS UPDATE

Everything is a farce.

This is what I tell myself when I'm in the middle of a lecture, and I start to disassociate. Depersonalization. This is something a person can manage as long as they don't think too much about it. Just get through the class. They can't see that you're not in your body. The last statement is an accurate reflection of the mindset of disassociation, which is a symptom of anxiety, severe anxiety. I develop this myself after being pistol-whipped and mugged six years ago. The muggers, who take a few minutes between each other to discuss the pros and cons of killing me, choose a different route. One of them holds my head away from him using the muzzle of his gun; this is to avoid splatter when he pulls the trigger. My eyes shut in preparation for this when a heavy crack meets the side of my head, bulls-eye, right on the temple, which splits open and sprays red down my face. I am confused for a while when they run off, the red-orange blood pooling under me on the concrete lit by a single sulfur lamp. It takes me a minute to realize I've been beaten with the gun instead of shot with it. I crawl up four flights of steps to a random apartment door and knock. A man somewhere in his 70s finds me curled up like a grub worm, bleeding all over his doormat.

Later, at the hospital, he tells me he waited for me in the reception area. When he approaches me, I have my first symptoms of brain fog, although I don't know it at the time. I split into three people, fractal, like light slicing an image into multiples. Blurry-eyes. He takes my arm, says he found my suitcase and my keys scattered out in the grass of the apartment complex. He asks where I am going, and could he give me a ride. I tell him yes, thank you. But I can't remember where it is parked. As he drives us back to the complex, he tells me I kept repeating myself when he first opened his door: *You said: 'I'm sorry. I'm sorry. I didn't mean to. I didn't mean to.' You know what you was trying to tell me? Think you can remember?*

The class is restless. They stare at me with gazes of sculpted boredom to show me just how much harm I'm causing them; they're trying to tell me that it's my fault. I am the temporary target of their dissatisfaction with life today. They hate me more because I thwart their utilitarian approach to education: the New Education. I make my job have meaning, and for that they resent me. To them, I should simply hold up the hoop, shut-up, and let them jump through it; they think my pedantry is insulting because it echos a dead century—a century they have nothing to do with and that doesn't apply. To them, America, survival, and 'mind,' or 'mindfulness,' are not mutually exclusive, and to suggest it is perverse in their eyes. Where's my clown suit, my party tricks, my dance routine with a bear? I should know better, their faces tell me. The educational hope of the 20th century collapsed along with the economic crash of the early 21st century, and here we are. Fuck me for wanting to keep it alive.

Earlier in the semester, I have a meeting with the dean who, irritated by yet another student complaint, finds a way to communicate this to me with a layer of deep pity in his voice, the way one speaks to a parent who has started to forget things: *Reese. We don't actually 'teach' them anymore. Come on, you know this. Let's get with it. And don't stand so solidly behind your policies, either. It only causes more of these complaints. We need to roll them on through, keep the retention rates up: Student as customer. Understand?*

Then, what's my purpose here, exactly?

I don't know how to answer that. You'll have to figure that out.

I thought I had.

Look, let's dispense with the dark-night-of-the-soul-shit. We have a ship to sail. Help sail it, or don't, but your idealism is rather depressing.

After I scribble my last point across the white board—the black marker somehow satisfying, despite the backseat I've taken to my body—the class now wants to ask questions. Nothing is really horrifying in life, or more horrifying, than being cleaved away from your *self*, and made unfamiliar to your own corpse so that when you move it is always as if someone else is moving it for you, and that person is *you*. But these kids couldn't know that. They just want their dollars' worth.

Some of them ask the same questions. Some of them have held their query until this very moment. I choose my first carefully. I do not want to start off the long, desperate dig for answers with the wrong tone. I choose a student I know will ask something philosophical, overarching.

"Does fiction really matter?" he asks. Perfect, although his tone is one that betrays its dual, under-the-belt personal attack at me (I represent fiction; therefore, do I matter?), and it also does what I want it to.

"That's a good question," I say. "How can we know? Especially when what's real and what's false are so easily interchangeable in the 21st century."

No one takes the bait to create a discussion. A girl in the front row with phoned-in shyness, and a practiced meek quality to the way she seeks to have a voice in the class, speaks: "Professor, you talk about 'getting at truth' and connecting to the audience through suffering. Is this possible if you come from a certain background?"

Another dig. The implication is that I do not suffer since I have a famous novelist for a father. The real question is: How can you accomplish these things if your life is free of real suffering, and you're spared it because of your elitist upbringing?

I tell her it just depends on the person, and I am thinking of the woman my family picked-up off the street from a homeless shelter to join us at our Thanksgiving dinner a week ago. I could mention this. I could describe it to the class, the indelible impact I still carry from it. But I don't. It's not for them. The student is shocked by my non-committed, vague response, and sits back, unsatisfied. She does not pursue it.

The overtly masculine guy in the back shares his ideas with a tone of "real-truth" in the class: "Is what we've learned directly from *you?* Or is it what you've learned from your father that you're teaching us?"

"Both," I say, too faded to be angry at the lack of thoughtfulness in the subtext.

"Why does anyone need an agent? Why does the publishing industry work the way it does? Isn't it all just by referral anyway?" Someone shouts from the third row.

"The publishing industry is a mystery," I say. "No one knows or understands why or how it works the way it does."

"Isn't that kind of ridiculous and problematic? Do you think you would be published today if your father hadn't had the connections he had and became as successful as he has, starting in the 1970s?" I can't tell if it's the same person. I squint at the room.

"Doubtful," I offer. They're surprised by this, but also relieved. They want to know I'm a purveyor of truth, also; that I mean what I say, and that all of this does matter. But I simply want them to go away. My legs are bags of gel, now. I hold myself up using the podium.

"Is publishing possible today without social media?"

"Ah, status. Status updates: Every American's favorite pastime. The obsession with others and what others are doing, selling your *self*. I think it is possible. But it will be hard to have it written out of your contract."

This peaks their interest, the real business side of publishing. I think of ending the class with a final writing task over status updates in the future, but I don't. I tell them the class is over and they leave as if it were any other.

I am uncertain if they view me as the oracle of publishing that they did at the start. Some thank me as they walk out, while others hurry off to something else. Once the corporate, clinical room with its functional gray chairs and white desks is empty, I shut off the lights and close the heavy wooden door. The end of the semester renders the campus blessedly dead.

At my office, I shut the door and sit down at my desk. I want the brain fog to stop. I look at my phone, and I have messages from Derrick asking about my day. Why is it simple questions in states like this ask too much?

I am cheating on my wife with him. Or, it's supposed to be the other way around, isn't it? But, then, I understand that it's correct the way it is. It's absolutely correct. So I return his text with an honest response. And he tells me what it is like training to be an astronaut about to take his first journey off of this planet. I can't decide if I envy him. I turn off the lights and lay back in my chair. Now that everything's dark, I can attempt to shut off the dislocation I feel; me separating from me over and over and over and over. For a moment there is no thought, but then I think of the woman at Thanksgiving—her look from across the table.

DERRICK

It's like water but without water. It is elation. It is the joy of being everything a child tries to be. To imagine it is to hang from the monkey bars, or to drift in a pool with the sun on your back. Out here, it is a procedure. Looking at the vast blackness in a book, watching actors swim in it during a film, it is the same. To step into it, is to know it. Here zero gravity places everything into relief; the universe is clearer because of how it forces us to remain within it. It freezes us into one place.

You understand, fully, how far the blackness goes, how immeasurable it is, how it reduces us. The first understanding is that it is a kind of defiance to leave our planet; but the universe is indifferent—not to us, or our narcissistic belief that it has a consciousness and is somehow aware of us, but it *is* indifferent. To be in it, like I am now, is to know what an accident it all is, its purposelessness.

I have not decided if this is a relief. But out here, in this cold nothing, everything that I am is of the earth, and everything that is of the earth, out here, means nothing. When I look at it and observe its surreal blueness, the distance perceived as height almost, I become angry. Its appearance is a betrayal; it appears benevolent, kind. But, then, I have to remind myself that these moments, these quips of thought are born of it. As far away as we get, we are still out here working for its benefit, and to learn more about the indifference that holds it.

Maybe that's why we keep seeking things, answers;

indifference is a strong catalyst. Our desperation to believe we matter launches us unnatural distances to float around in an endless lack of a response. We are our questions. Space is always its own answer. And I am embarrassed for us, for the globe below me.

My heartbreak is two things: it is for our own inability to accept ourselves, our earth-lives, and it is because I am in love with a man who is all of these things, who is my own indifference reflected back at me. When I try to tell him this, he gets distracted or turns off. Two months in this station, and I am certain when I return Reese will leave his life and make a new one. I believe this is how I will matter. My return is in one month, an odd lowering back down, through this to the blue interspace my crew and I revolve around. Time is different for us here. We are held to nothing. Our only obligation is an earth-bound one. It only exists because we want it to, because we feel obligated. We could jettison it, and flee into the blackness, drift further from the weight carried with us from our own planet, but we don't. We don't do any of that. We're *of* it; suicide is difficult, even in space. If we accepted—if we didn't hate ourselves so much—the universe might give us an answer. It might not be the answer we want, but it would be something. I accept this, which frees me from it. I do this for Reese. Because I love him, and I love us, and when I am once again bound by weight, by gravity, I will tell him that, and I will ask him to marry me, and to hover with me in all of this nothing.

MARGARET: THE RANSOM NOTE

I wake up around 8:00 AM to a woman's scream. I sit up on my mattress and lean across the sill of my open window, and I stare over the empty lot of dead grass to the corner of the street. I search the derelict intersection, and see no one. A silver car with exhaust spiraling out of its tailpipe makes a clunky push up the hill to the left, then over it, past the crumbling, ivy strewn brick of a demolished factory building. I decide it must have been the car.

I get up and walk through the musty House. No one is here. They've all scattered for the day. I never question whether they will return. We mind our own business, a quiet sort of reverence for our own hard won spaces. Downstairs, however, is a man sleeping in a pile of stained coats, snoring, which makes a sound like an empty skull dragged over tree bark or asphalt, back and forth. He is a mattress at the furthest end of the hall. I have not seen him before. I decide not to acknowledge him. It is part of the deal to leave others alone.

Outside, on the fractured steps is a brown cardboard box, inside of which is paper sacks and other cardboard boxes. I squat down and dig through the remains. The others have been here. A stale bag of croissants is left, some oranges and pears nearing rot, peanut butter, a bar of soap (from Whole Foods, no less), some water, and covered with another paper bag is a white, plastic radio and a box of unopened Energizer batteries. It occurs to me that no one but the regulars went through it; they have left the rest for me, including the radio. I feel rich and undeserving. I don't understand what I represent to them; that I get some of the better loot left by the church that comes by once every two weeks. Each time, the boxes and their contents are different. We do not fight over what's left to us. We take only what we need. I feel as though I should celebrate. I return the box and its contents to my room and leave it under my chair in the corner. I take the bar of soap and I put it in one of the paper bags with an old towel. I slip on my shoes and leave. Walking in what is now the warm spring sun, my fading red curls bounce in a breeze across my dirty face.

I walk two blocks to the south of our street. There is an empty lot far back from the curb. It's surrounded by other brick remnants, buildings either fallen to ruin or blown apart by some company looking to do something more with the land. Nothing has changed since I've arrived. In the center of this lot is a chipped water pump, painted red. I was shown this by another tenant when I first arrived, years ago. She disappeared weeks after my arrival, and I cannot recall her name. She had seemed proud about introducing me to this secret. When you live like us, she'd said, you learn to find places. We have our places, like this one.

The water pump is cemented into a square block above the grass. Black spray paint dances in curves off the corners like half-formed faces. The stiff grass moves in the wind, carrying with it old pit-fire smoke and wet earth. The base is dry. No one is here, and you learn to stop caring if they are. One must have a shower, if nothing else in life. I have learned no matter how dirty one gets, it is never comfortable enough to stay that way.

I take the soap from the bag and unwrap it. It's a solid green mass in my palm, smooth, a bar of soap I imagine costing upwards of ten dollars. I lift it to my nose and lips, and breathe. This odd, well-crafted thing sits in my hand. I wonder who the makers of this product imagined would use it. I am amazed at the weight, the scents of lavender and tea tree oils, aloe and honey, all of this poured together into this incredible, smooth round bar. I give the metal handle of the pump some lifts with my right arm. I use all of my strength to bring the water up from the earth. It gurgles forth with a hollow belch, splashing across the pavement.

I kneel and remove my thin shirt, draping it over the edge of the platform behind me. I hold the soap under the ice-cold spill of water and move it through my fingers. Its suds bloom, and I work them quickly over my skin, my cold, bare breasts. I return for more water, splashing it across myself. My skin prickles, but the scents of the bar are overwhelming, so I don't care. I feel clean just smelling it. The dirt and slime of the House rinse off me. I hold my head under the stream and scrub my hair, the bubbles drip lovingly down my face. I squeeze the rest from the knots.

Once finished, I pull the towel from the paper bag and dry off quickly and slide my shirt over my head. Now for the bottom half. The girl who originally took me here taught me that it is best to do it this way. If the police were to show, at least you weren't fully unclothed, and it beats begging your way into the bathroom of a convenient store, or a bus stop. Those, she told me, are hardly worth the trouble when you've got a place like this.

With the bottom half done, I thank the pump, and wrap what's left of the soap carefully in its original paper, which I then put back in the bag with the towel. I begin the walk back, and as if a thought has called them forth, a police car pulls up behind me, trailing me as I walk.

Eventually, it jerks to a stop next to me, and the motion of the car suggests: We're just takin' a look, makin' sure everything's fine. There is a falseness to it, the thing which all people inherently feel when dealing with the police, the utter coldness to their inquiries, the hunt for something disapproving for which they can cuff you and, eventually, systematically use to disempower you. This is the experience for many who make the House a temporary shelter.

The driver's window is down and the man squints at me. I squint back, waiting.

"You on your way somewhere?"

"Yes, sir, just back up to my house."

"You over at the shelter?"

"Yes, sir."

"How long you been at the shelter?"

"A while now, sir."

"A while now?"

"Yes, sir."

"Any problems at the shelter? You all being taken care of?"

"Yes, sir, I believe we are."

"Anyone ever tell you, you look like Susan Sarandon?"

"No, they haven't."

"You all gonna be a problem? We going to have any problems with you?"

"No, sir. No problems."

"What's that?"

"No problems, sir."

"Okay. That's what I want to hear. You have a good day, now."

"You do the same, sir."

"I surely will."

He rolls up his window, and the car crawls, a slow turn past me up the hill and to the right, back into the maze of abandoned buildings.

My heart does not thud. No adrenaline roars through me. I am still, and I know it is because I have nothing left for them to take. Perhaps that's what they look for in those of us who live in places like the House: something to take away.

Back at the House, some regulars are sitting on the steps smoking rolled cigarettes staring at the cracked ground. I move up past them and they make space for me. One nods hello, and I know him as Charlie. He looks at me with a protective glance, and I figure he saw what the cops were doing as I made my way back from the pump.

Upstairs, in my room, I fall onto my mattress, and rest my feet at the window. The dead tree at the far end of the lot waves in the slow afternoon light. Its shadows dance and dissolve across the dusty glass in the window and the old walls of the room. Somewhere outside someone has hung wind chimes. It is the only sound that comes up from the lot below. A new tenant? A gift? I listen to them and notice how they seem to connect to the movement of the shadows from the tree.

Finally, I retrieve the radio. Opening the package of batteries, I wonder when I last held any. I had forgotten about batteries, about packaging, the odd dashes of vibrant color, the plastic casing that seems to appeal to another person in another time. I remove three and stick them into the back of the device. I snap the plastic cover into place. Holding it, I am overwhelmed by its smallness, the amount of dials and switches it contains.

I turn it on and tune it. I find a classical station and listen for a minute, then place the small device on the sill next to my plant. I tune it again, finding older stations, and listen to talk-show-voices announce music I grew up with. A quick memory jolts through me. It comes like a swift pang. I should have been more aware; music is dangerous. Scents and music are binders to dead times and places.

Eventually, a news report shatters through a song. It's pretty important, or sounds important, so I listen, and twist up the volume. The latest space shuttle launched by NASA has exploded attempting to reenter the earth's atmosphere from its mission. All of the crew is dead. They read off the names: Derrick Mayers, John Brady, Christopher Negson, Joseph Stern…

The names are read slowly followed by a prayer. There is more discussion, and a further update. This comes from another source, like entertainment news. A discovery has been made that one of the crew, Derrick Mayers, has had a long-standing affair with a married man who lives here in this state. He is a college professor, and the son of the famous writer, Frank Kent. His name is Reese Kent. Neither him nor his family responded to the accusations, yet. The news changes to another story.

Somewhere, on the West Coast, a woman has convinced police and reporters that a violent stranger is holding her hostage in her apartment. This has gone on for two days. A ransom note is even tossed from the woman's balcony. It is written in crayon and demands four million dollars or a personal night with an actor famous for playing the character of Frodo in an older movie series.

When the police finally break down her door, they find her sitting on the couch, crying. The TV had been on, but no one else is in the apartment with her.

She still denies writing the note.

MARGARET: THE NEW ROOMMATE

Charlie comes to my room.

Sometimes I find him sitting on the floor against the wall cross-legged staring at the window. Other times, he leans in the doorway and knocks on the side of the doorframe, asking if he can sit in what I come to think of as his place on the floor against the wall. He is thin enough so that I can see the gentle geometry of his ribs clothed in pale, white skin. Chocolate-brown moles march up his side from under the wilted arches of his black tank top. His dark hair is shaved on one side. The rest is a deep, curly nest pouring in a wave off the top of his head. His face is a thin V, his eyes deep-set, dark, and searching all the time for somewhere to land. There is a bit of the little boy in his eyes. When I ask him his age he tells me he is 19, then later changes it to 20. I don't question this. I don't notice marks on his arm indicating intravenous drug use, but he is reeling when I see him, when he visits. He is so quiet, I sometimes don't notice he's there, and if I do, I continue what I had been doing before as he watches me with a kind of odd fascination.

He is like a roommate. I hesitate to use the word 'friend' because these kinds of friends are brief usually, and flutter from your life without explanation. Attachment is nonsensical. But I want to call him a friend if only to reward him for his consistency. He shows up. He is also forthright in his manic suffering; he does not try to convince me he is a good person, unlike some of the others that arrive that have an ongoing argument with someone who'd rejected them outright or punished them for needing to lie about who they were. This one doesn't; he's been punished for the opposite, for being too honest.

Today, he sits half-in and half-out of the light coming in from my window. Shadows from my makeshift curtains lift around his calm face, and his eyes search the room.

"Can I just…sit here? For a while?" he asks.

"Sit there as long as you like."

"I just need you to stay. If you stay where you are, I can stop."

"Stop what?"

"The roaring in my chest."

"What causes it?"

"I don't know," he says. "I don't know. It's a wave, and it keeps going one after the next. I'm tired from it."

"How long have you had these waves?"

"For a while. But not always."

"Do you take anything?"

"Yes. I take things. Have taken them."

"I see."

An hour of quiet passes. Neither of us says anything. He pulls a pack of tobacco out of his back pocket and rolls a cigarette. Normally, I would tell him to leave if he's going to do that, but I'm helping him somehow, so I allow it, and he lights one. He is strangely considerate of where he blows the smoke. I have not yet told him that it repels me, but he's taken the initiative by assuming it does. This makes me like him more, a very dangerous thing, even platonically. For I don't believe Charlie is a sexual person the way most people, drenched in Hollywood perceptions of love, are sexual, especially the post-sexual revolutionaries. I don't even think he's heterosexual; he's transcended that pro-creative binding. Unlike me, or the others who find each other in the dark outside my window, screwing feverishly against the blue barrel, or the side of the House.

I light a small cube of pinion wood I found left in one of the rooms down the hall. I place it on the sill. Its smoke drifts over me to Charlie. I listen to his breath. I can tell by his exhalation that it settles him somehow; I wonder if I knew it would have this effect prior to lighting it, that we were meant to meet, perhaps; that we're meant to help each other. I dismiss the thought.

"Thank you," he says. His voice is full of desperate relief. He means for me to know the great thing I have done for him, although I'm not quite sure what that is, yet.

"You're welcome, Charlie," I say. "How do you feel, now?"

"The waves are stopping."

"Good."

His eyes are tearful and wide as if trying to take in as much light as possible. He evades tears spilling over by lighting the withering roach held in his fingertips and taking a drag. He doesn't blow the smoke out, so much as just allows it to unfurl from his nostrils and lips.

"Do you think time ever just stops?" he asks.

"I don't know what that means."

"Does anything stop?"

"Our lives stop."

He nods.

"Well, yes. It all stops. Eventually."

"Why are you here?"

I feel myself recoil, a quick inner shrinking. I wonder if it's enough for him to register by simply looking at me, and if it creates a new boundary between us. I look at him to measure his reaction to my reticence. He appears unchanged, waiting for an answer, perhaps. I cannot read his face, so I weigh what to tell him. My story is my own, no one else's; a promise I gave myself a while ago. This way, if more is taken from me, I at least have that remaining.

"I came here the way many of the others do," I offer, hoping that would be enough. I knew it wasn't.

"But you're different," he says. "You're smart. You're quiet. You take nothing from anyone that hasn't…already been left. Why are you here?"

"Because I want to be."

"Why would you want this, Margaret?"

"Don't say my name."

"I'm sorry."

"It's okay. I just don't like hearing it."

He waits for me to continue.

"I'm here because I want to be. There are other ways to live, obviously. But I don't want them."

He appears uncomfortable with my answer, so keeps talking through drags.

"I w-would give anything to be home again. I miss my mom."

"Where is she?"

"Gone," he says, his voice quieter. "I feel like I ricocheted off of it. Like it sent me this far, you know? After that, there was…this, I guess. I don't know where I am."

He's so high, now, he stops making sense. I keep talking to pacify him.

"Well, what are your options? What could you do? You seem to want to be somewhere else more than anyone I've met here."

He says nothing, looks down. The question is a dead end; I can tell he won't tell me why, so I let the question go. Some kind of guilt fills me, and the greasy anger underneath it forces a confession from me. It's as if he's found a way, without realizing it, to extract an answer for himself from my own story. The light in the room shifts. It's the low, challenging dimness of evening; that the threat of dark is finally arriving. It reminds me of the light during the winter, how it's a lesser version of itself.

"Options are illusory. Have you noticed?" I say. "Choices are not. Could I choose a different existence? Yes. I could go back out there into America, which is a thing, an idea. I could fashion a résumé. Put my education to work; create a network of people I never see or talk to set snug in a database somewhere. I could fight for more money, so I can buy my way from where I am now. But that's all it is. Do you understand what I'm saying?"

He does not nod or say anything. He looks at me, quiet, listening, like Buddha chain-smoking on the side of the room.

"There was a time I wanted more. I wanted all of those things, and I had them. Then they were taken from me, easily. It doesn't matter how careful you are in this country, if money is to be made, then those who can make it off of you will find a way, and that's it. How it leaves you is of no importance to them. Since I had choices, I knew I could keep going, pretending to be happy, forcing myself through it because I didn't know anything else. None of us know anything else. It's all we're taught: the system and money. I would have had to start from scratch, create more things that can be taken away. To live on the margins is unthinkable to most people, like living in space. I don't want to be tethered to anything. There is nothing worth wanting or having out there in *that*," I say, and point at the window indicating the realm beyond the House.

"Sorry, I'm rambling."

"I listen to my dream," he says, suddenly exuberant. "A long dream about space, actually. A man floating out there, like you said."

"What happened to him?"

"He's still there," says Charlie. "I felt like that's what he was saying to me. It might be because I heard the news, you know? The crash?"

"What happened in your dream?"

"I just floated. I was there beside him. He was lonely and sad. When it turned light, I woke up. The hall."

We are quiet for a minute. He remains in the posture of Buddha by the edge of the doorway, and rolls another cigarette.

"You're too old to be here," he says, an unfamiliar edge to his voice, sarcasm that might reflect a buried version of him.

"Age has nothing to do with it. We're all already old."

He seems to consider this, looks around the corner, then back to me.

"My white shaving razor was stolen from me here a few days ago. Now, I will have to steal one back. Or grow a beard, and I hate beards."

"You might look good in one."

"A beard is also a lie. It says the person has something to cover up."

"I suppose you're right."

"I am right."

The room goes quiet again. I curl up on my mattress so that I have an angled view of the sky as it slides to a deep, purple-blue. I think about Charlie's dream, of the man floating up in space forever. A shiver runs across my back. I grip the side of the mattress. I can feel Charlie watching me, and it is as if I have acquired a guardian somehow. I am not used to the sensation of protection. I have embraced vulnerability for so long, I do not recognize it at first. I do not believe anything will ever happen to me while Charlie is here. I have become a kind of rock for him. I stretch and roll away from the window. I look behind me.

The spot by the door is empty, and Charlie is gone.

REESE:
THE STRANGE BLUE OBJECT

In my fingers I hold a blue, plastic object. I can't decide what its shape is. It's like a crystal that got pulled out of tune. Elongated as if melted, but retaining its original, oddly threatening shape. It's a perfect, unmarked cornflower blue. Is it a toy piece? Something my daughter, Olivia, left here once when we dropped her off for my mother to watch? What does it belong to? I can't let go of it; the thought of putting it in the trash, or leaving it somewhere, creates a hollow in my gut, a sharp drop of horror, like knowingly letting someone drown, for example.

I'm sitting at my mother's dining room table in the chair that was, as far as I know, last occupied by the homeless woman. I last sat at this table seven months ago, the exact same time. I've avoided it in a way, but only because I've been living in this house for the last two months. Derrick died in the shuttle explosion coming into the atmosphere. The press found a wealth of evidence of our life together in his house, a famous astronaut's house. My wife, Cindy, took our daughter and filed for divorce. Simple and quick. There was not much of a discussion about that decision. She seemed more humiliated by the public reaction than by my job loss due to press harassment and controversy (or, as they put it: "performance issues"), or the fact that I have been forcing an attraction to her for fifteen years. How fast things can go.

There were a few questions my wife spewed out in a

tumbling rage that appeared suddenly while I packed my things just two months prior:

You put your dirty dick up that guy's asshole? Really? You like that kind of thing, you faggot? You like fucking a place that shit comes out of?

It's got its charm, just like you.

How can you do it, Reese? How can you fuck men? Well, I want you gone. That's all there is to it. By tomorrow. Your daughter is puking in the bathroom, by the way, if you want to say goodbye. Oh, and I'm glad he's dead. I'd probably have more respect for you and be less angry if you'd just never lied to me. Why is it so hard for people like you to be honest?

All men like me want a romantic life, like in a book; a life free of people who attack us, who are our villains, who reject us, or shame us, all the horrible clichéd norms, but everyone like me has a villain, and attack is inevitable; that is the nature of where we live. I've never let myself be naive enough to believe the opposite is true, as much as I might want to. Derrick would agree with me. I think of him completely incinerated by the thin, invisible shield over the earth with the others as they jolted into the atmosphere, attempting to return home. I counter this with thoughts of him having somehow not made it back at all, that maybe he's still out there, floating forever among planets and larger, more complex solar systems.

My first meeting with Derrick consists of directions. He gives a physics seminar at my university and asks me for the quickest route off of campus. His hair, a thick, brown wave over his forehead, creates a shadow down his slim face, narrowed from an astronaut's diet. Derrick's eyes are generous, and the expression in them is always somehow unconditional. Before everything, I remember this. At his car in the parking garage, he says: *It would be worth it for me to get to know you.* The way he says: 'worth,' projects its own center of gravity, a weight that speaks to how solid he would be whenever I felt I might break. Then the subtlest intentional graze of his fingers against mine as if to say, *I know. I get it. Just let me,* and my horrified stillness as a response. Our first kiss is like drinking, like being filled. When he holds me, I am liberated from my body, from all weight.

Before he leaves in the shuttle, we make plans. Nothing has been set, however. But he is tired of me holding onto our lie, which I loathe myself for doing. I love him, not Cindy. My daughter, if I'm honest with myself at all, is just another version of Cindy, albeit a smaller, reduced version spotlighting all of Cindy's worst traits into points; a puffer fish that can't help but bloat itself. My daughter will grow into someone I will not like. I imagine the feelings will be mutual.

I have a fondness for the term 'heart' to describe the nebulous place in a person where emotions like love take place. I think it's as functional and appropriate as any. When I search for something better, nothing suffices. So when I say that my heart is carved through, as if with the metal edge of something steel and razor-like, it expresses what this gutted cavern in me feels like. It also has an echo of nerves, like an acid burn that goes all the way to my back and my lungs. It reaches to my throat where I am strangled daily. It would be less bad if I actually let myself cry, sob like anyone else, but I don't. I push it down. It's what I know, what I'm familiar with; the pressure of it in me is what I deserve. I believe the pain would make my father happy, another casualty of all this.

If he's needed a reason after forty years of marriage to leave my mother, he got one: my homosexuality is her fault. Since he's left (to "find material for the next whopper"), she comes across to me as a woman on vacation, unperturbed, but silently questioning her own mate's reaction to her son's crumbling life. He was gone long before I arrived here. He made sure of it, and flew to our condo in Florida. I imagine he'll be there for the rest of the year, if not longer. He'll do two or three books instead of one, a compensation act for the potential loss in revenue the publishers might suffer due to the press hounding him about his political stance on people like me. The way he fields the questions, I note, is promising.

Did you always know your son was gay? How do you feel about his affair with the astronaut, the one who's recently died in the shuttle explosion?

My son is my son. This country is obsessed with affairs. And where people put their genitals, like a fucking playground. Obsess about your own goddamn bullshit.

I have not heard from him personally. There are no emails of compassion or concern, no text messages asking if I'm okay, just the unflinching silence. It speaks enough. I'm not the only gay male alive during this century to experience the punishing, hateful silence of his father for not genetically growing into an idea. I remind myself of this to stave off self-pity, the last drop down. And none of this is worth self-pity. Some have had it worse. Some have been murdered. I'm too old for that, I think; it's the younger ones that bravely expose their truth and then get shot or strangled, stabbed. It doesn't matter that we can all get married now. Some fathers and mothers still want us dead, still harbor some residual indignation handed down to them from Christendom, even if God has no place in their life, like my own father, Frank, an atheist and secularist.

I wonder sometimes if it's a type of disappointment you might find at a men's club, the kind of group angry thirteen-year-olds have for friends who view a favorite video game as a total, pointless bore, while being incredulous about it. It's the failure of these men to see it from other perspectives that ultimately perpetuates this anguish. Perhaps there is a fear that if they do take a peek from our eyes, they'll see a sliver of it in themselves, and that can't be allowed to happen, never that. The thoughts of my own pubescent thirteen-year-old-self (*why would any guy want to be with a girl when he can be with a guy? If men want to be with women it must be because, on some level, they feel obligated*), remained unexplored the minute I saw my father express barely repressed rage towards an effeminate gas station attendant.

With the loss of Derrick, my wife and daughter, my father, I have come to conclusions by force: my shame is a new shame. It is not who I am that creates this shame, but that I have lived without integrity. It was my own falseness I was convinced served me; that I could get away with it somehow. This thought gains an almost physical presence the moment my mother walks into the room and places a plastic basket of my clothes, washed and folded, at my feet.

"You need to put your clothes up, honey," she says, and walks behind me into the kitchen. Dishes clank in the sink as water pours into the disposal.

"How many dishes are you going to use, Reese? Do you mind keeping one glass out and just re-using it? Have you had lunch? Do you want a BLT?"

"No, I'm fine."

"What's wrong with you? Why are you so negative?"

I ignore this statement. I stare at the strange, blue object.

"You need to clean your room, too."

"It's the guest room, Mother. Until I have a place set-up and money to move with."

"Well, you'll have to start from scratch. What are you going to move with? What money?"

"I've been living out of the house for over a decade, what are you warning me about?"

"It's the new century, honey. A lot of kids are moving home with their parents."

"Yeah, well, that's usually because they can't get a job after they just spent a fortune on their education. I'm not a kid at thirty-six."

"We all know who to thank for that. Good ol' Bushy pal."

"Oh that guy…"

"Everything is extreme, now, and I don't want to talk about it. What do you want for dinner?"

"I can make my own dinner. I'm not five."

"You want pasta, Reese?"

I say nothing. I feel as if I am being slowly shoved down into a pillow with a firm hand on the back of my head.

"Reese? What do you want for dinner? Pasta? Chicken? I'm making salad. Did you put your clothes up, yet?"

"I just want silence."

"Well, I live here, too, okay? All you ever want is silence. I want to watch TV."

"TV causes anxiety."

"I like to be informed. I don't want to watch fake-shit all day and night like you and your father."

"Movies?"

"I like to know what's going on out in the world."

"You know what's going on in the world, you just like other peoples' dirty laundry."

"What do you want for dinner, Reese? Damn it! I'm not going to ask you again."

I stall. I wait until she thinks I've left the dining room, and while holding the strange object up to my face, close, in the light coming in from the windows, I ask, "Mother, do you remember the homeless woman? The one we brought to Thanksgiving last year? Where does she live?"

"What do you want with her, Reese?"

"I don't know," I whisper, a statement only heard by me, but I *do* know.

If you're shattered at the right time and in the right place, a path can be illuminated. It's not the path you wanted, but it is arrives, like this woman. I've never met her, not really, yet I have, and it goes further than now, before either of us—some kind of cord between us. I'm convinced my answers lie with her.

The light lowers in the room. Through the windows, clouds pass overhead, thick and white. The sheen of the table dulls, and the brick patio in the backyard becomes stark under the shadow of the house. I put the object into my pocket and walk outside.

MARGARET: THE GARDEN

Charlie and I decide to start a garden. He tells me it's the only way to fortify us against 'The Outside,' although I still haven't heard an adequate explanation as to whom or what 'The Outside' is. I go along with it, and this makes him happy.

We dig a rectangular trench in the plot of land to the right of the House. It matches the length of the foundation perfectly. It takes us all day the first time to get the soil pulpy, and soft. Weeds and grass are dug up, severed, or torn free from the ground with satisfying popping sounds. I don't ask Charlie where he gets the shovels, picks, and rakes. He just arrives with things. I decide that he is perhaps better at survival than I am; I'm so content to let whatever arrive simply arrive that I never suspect there are opportunities to find things, like shovels and picks that could help me, and benefit the House.

As we work, the sun is an insistent, unflinching boil against my back and arms, my head. Charlie has burst from his usual languid demeanor and works with a kind of focus I start to adopt myself. He digs rigorously, churning up the earth, running his hands deep into it. It's as if he has a sudden purpose that has elevated him, a cord that goes straight from the center of his sternum right into the beginnings of this plot.

We take turns walking to the water pump, and haul back full milk jugs, which we use to soften the ground and dig deeper. He shows me how to create perfect mounds and lines where the seeds will go, and although we are mostly silent as this happens, I ask where he learned this.

"I spent summers on a farm once," he says. Nothing more is mentioned.

After the first two days, I am able to peer down at our accomplishment below the edge of my bedroom window. Its potential is like one of the waves Charlie describes roaring through his chest. I can see how what we've done can become something more. I imagine a kind of growth unseen in the world; plants, vegetables, stalks sprouting closer to me here in this room, aggressively seeking life. I imagine us eating from it, our bodies shimmering from everything we're given. Bright, smooth red peppers dangling over perfectly churned earth; reaching green tentacles and firm pods bearing more seeds, and the flavors that will roll down our throats.

On the third day Charlie arrives with a box of seed packets, bulbs with damp, dark soil clinging to them, and herbs in plastic boxes. He tells me the church delivered it, and I don't question him. He shows me how we should balance the garden. The herbs are planted at the far right corner. They will be out of direct sunlight, he says, and will fare better. In the center, he plants green peppers, and then moves to the far right again where we work to divide up the packets: red peppers, okra, squash, tomatoes, mint, and near the back—closest to the wall of the House, right under my window—he plants honeysuckle. Neither of us knows what we're doing, but it seems to make sense.

"When it gets big and builds up towards your window,

the wind will blow, and you'll have the smell of it when you're here."

He smiles at me, wide brown eyes like a child's looking at me with profound joy; he is excited and happy to give this to me. I thank him, smiling, and pour him some water, which he guzzles. He hands back the glass and we stand in the shade of the tree occasionally looking at the work we've done. Cicadas rip through the air, unleashing a grating whine, like old leather stretching beyond its capacity, signaling the growing heat. I look at the broken concrete and cracked mud baking beneath us, and smell the scent of dead grass, Charlie's sweat, soil, gasoline and singed leaves in the humidity.

Charlie retreats to his own languid world again and walks the perimeter of the big oak in the yard with a bouquet of dead grass in his right hand. He hums a song to himself, balancing in the spaces between the roots. I squat down, and rest against the trunk. Something black glimmers a few blocks away, then disappears among the hulking remains of buildings until it draws nearer. It's the black hood of a car, and before I see all of it near the corner of our street, I stand up and move away from the tree.

"Come on Charlie, let's get closer to the House."

Without responding, he stops his play with the oak and follows me back across the plot of land to our garden.

"Just keep working for the moment," I tell him.

He seems unsure where to start since we've done all we can for the day. The urgency in my voice doesn't betray to him that I'm nervous. He continues humming his song, lowers to his knees with a piece of grass in his mouth, which he chews as he leans over the tilled rectangle and runs his fingers gently through it as if it were a Japanese garden and the perfectly combed areas should be tended as such.

The black shape draws nearer to us as it proceeds up the block and stops about ten feet from the House. It's a police car, greased deep black in the sun and bearing its proud emblem on the stark white of its passenger side door. It stays there, unmoved for minutes, no officer rising from inside to do what it is he came here to do. It stays that way for so long I wonder if he's stopped to take a nap, and this is as good a place as any. But, then the driver's side door opens, and he emerges, a tall, uniformed dart in the light, eyes covered in black shades. His face is gaunt and white, his mouth unmoving. Despite the gear cloaking him, I recognize him as the same man who followed me from the water pump weeks ago, the same one who questioned me and knew the House. Has he been watching Charlie and I these past few days? What does he want?

He stands near his car, hands on hips, watching us as we work. He strolls slowly across the street. He looks both ways, even though the street is empty, and no cars come by for hours, sometimes days. Stepping onto the curb in front of us, he seems to wait for us to acknowledge him.

"What do you all have going on here today?" he asks.

Charlie looks up at him, squints, confused. He doesn't know who this man is, and the uniform is seemingly lost on him.

"Any of you been down at the water pump lately?"

Charlie ignores him, returns to the soil.

I do the same, and the officer steps closer.

"Since you all want to be silent, that's okay, but let me ask you, do either of you have a permit for this land? Do you own this land here that you're diggin' up?"

Charlie's humming, and I stand to carry a jug of water to him at the opposite end.

"Ma'am. Haven't we shared words before, I believe? Down the road here a bit? Didn't we have a talk about you and the other residents here not being a nuisance to the neighborhood?"

I look at him. I fix my expression so that it communicates anticipation; I'm waiting for him to continue, but I don't intend to respond.

"I don't think this is your land, lady. Not yours, not his. I advise you stop diggin' it up."

"It's just a garden, Sir. Just some plants," I say, hoping this will appease him for the moment.

He says nothing, adjusts his posture. He turns away from us, walks back across the street to his car, and leaves. The black smear of his cruiser vanishes behind the buildings at the end of the block. Somehow, it feels very close by.

When the sun goes down, Charlie and I stack our shovels and picks against the side of the House. We leave our garden and take the jugs inside.

MARGARET: THE BABBLING MAN

The House is emptier than it's ever been. A new guy comes and goes sporadically throughout the week, and he sleeps on the mattress in the hallway downstairs. We do not communicate; many of the people who visit these halls are not always of sound mind, to put it as gently as possible. Many of them bring whole legions with them when they visit; and, when they stay the conversations ensue, long ones of them babbling to the air, people all but invisible to me.

I watch them sometimes, listening for some kind of logic, a steady stream of thought. The personalities that follow these individuals are real to them, as real as myself. The new man downstairs has conversations at a whisper all through the night. He sits facing the corner of the wall, leans into it, and very intensely works to express something of importance to the figure he sees there. These conversations are a matter of importance. Sometimes the House becomes a place of supplication, a deserted hovel for those of us on the margins to come and to babble at the dark; the only place we can dig for answers, it seems.

Charlie is aware of the man and does not like him.

"He'll bring us trouble," he tells me.

At around three in the morning, he joins me on the second floor hallway where I sit watching the new man talk to the dark. Charlie stays back against the wall then slides down it so that he sits directly behind me.

"Can we make him go?"

I shake my head, but I'm wondering if it is possible. If Charlie's right, could we get him to leave before something bad happens? I believe Charlie is slightly more sensitive, psychically speaking, than he'll give himself credit for. When I look at him, I juggle the idea that the drugs were a clichéd blessing; that underneath all of the wet folds of his brain slogging through streams of potent chemicals cooked in the antiseptic, do-well walls of pharmaceutical labs, a few doors flew open as a result. I don't think he anticipated this; I think it was the opposite that he wanted.

"What is he saying?"

I lean over to speak, so as not to interrupt the man downstairs, his conversation escalating, his whole body leaning further into the corner. The entity, to which he is speaking, appears to be stubborn, or plays Devil's advocate.

"Something about burning," I say. "Fires."

"Is that all?"

"Charlie, I can't hear everything. Come closer." I pat the floor next to me. Charlie inches forward, grasps hold of the wooden bars marking the space of the banister. We are like an old aunt and nephew spying down on the weary relative while the rest of the house sleeps, if there were more people asleep in it. I glance at Charlie. His hand goes to his chest as if to keep something from entering it. His mouth stays open as he watches the man. I return my focus to the mattress below. The man stops talking, but he rocks and rocks and rocks as if dunking his head into the inky black of the corner under the window. What does he see?

What does he move to, or away from? Eventually, either because of exhaustion or satisfaction, it's difficult to say, he collapses at an angle on the bed, and then begins a long, skull-grating snore.

Charlie seems simultaneously disappointed and relieved when he drops his hand to his lap and looks at me.

"I'm worried."

"Don't be," I tell him.

I pat his back gently, and he lets me. He leans and rests his head onto my shoulder. It is a brief, but heavy sigh that shudders through him, a slight whimper.

"Charlie, it's okay. Whatever it is, it's okay. I promise."

"Promises are unkind."

I slide my hand along his spine, the nodules of it press against my palm, round and hard. His ribs assert themselves under my fingers, bony planks under cool, paper-like flesh. An insect crawls along the edge of the banister, its many segments lurching and shifting as it moves. It's too dark to see what it is. Charlie sits up, and then stands to walk to his room. He shuts his door. I go to my room and sit on my bed, my legs tucked under me.

I place my hands on the sill, glance at my odd plant next to the tiny white radio. I lay my head on the sill and look out. The night air is cool. Our street is dark, save for the sulfur lamp looming at the corner. The demolished buildings hulk in the blackness like battlements left untended. The tiny whir of a cicada rambles out, further away. A breeze pushes through the opening into my room, lifting things, a sheet of paper, my fading gray-strawberry hair.

Below, in the yard near our garden, I hear a snap, then a crunch; feet moving tenderly around the house. The sound of a person sneaking around, I suppose. It was unusual, even for the House. The sounds of those who need this place are never tentative; they come barreling through, flinging their plastic sacks and torn bags against the wall, aware of their strange noises and the reek of their skin, their clothes. There is very little consideration when it comes to that. Or they pass out so quietly in the yard flanking either side of the House, that no one hears them. This sound is different.

I, too, am tentative. I stretch upwards and lean over the sill enough to spy the plot of land below, and the garden. I see nothing. I stretch further, extending my head fully out of the window and twist right to left, scrutinizing the street and the dark spaces around the House.

When I look straight down, I lock eyes with the cop. He leans against the wall of the House, head tilted so he can watch me. I repress my startle and wait for him to speak. I even attempt to feign a sort of blindness as if I can't quite make out the figure there, which feels ridiculous and fearful as I do it. But I can see his smirk in the dark; it's enough to know he knows, and that's all he wants. Shortly after this, he moves off the wall, out across the garden, which he steps over, not out of respect, but because his legs happened to span its width. He goes around the side of the House to the front where he is out of sight. I slide back into my room and wait for the sound of the unbolted door to wing open downstairs. Nothing is locked here; anyone can come in. I wait and wait and wait, and the night carries on, and no one ever comes.

MARGARET: THE BURNING

Charlie is gone. The wind outside builds into sharp bursts around the edges of the House, the trees. Leaves clack together, producing a sound all across the yard, like thousands of plastic bottle lids showering down a metal chute. It is so loud, it only seems to escalate. The House creaks like all old houses. It moves against the wind, its boards groaning and sighing out puffs of dust. The whines and snaps of its structure are heightened now that the place has emptied, as if it knows something. I can't determine if it's the sound of celebration, or the sound of agony.

I don't think to look for Charlie until later. I check his room and his mat is in the same place, covered with a small brown towel. A few glass bottles filled with leaves, sticks, and insect corpses sit clustered in a circle near the baseboards, perhaps close to his head where he slept. A paperback book sits further away, no cover, the pages yellowed and torn. I pick it up. Whole pages are covered with sketches, drawings, and notes over the print. Lines have been drawn through the gaps in sentences like zigzag paths leading nowhere. This book, I realize, was brought here and did not come from the shelf downstairs. At the top of the page is a title. It says: *Christine.* I remember the film from the 1980s. I saw it with friends as a teenager; a car that kills. The 80s, to me, were ironically hopeful times. Everyone just wanted to have fun, as the song went, not just girls. I drop the book to the floor and move around the room. The wind rattles the glass and dust floats down through evening light, drifting up around my body as I move through it.

The room smells of Charlie, his odd chemical reek, his paper-skin. I try to sense if he's near, if he's going to return, and there's nothing to indicate that he will. The House groans deeper, and it is as if I'm at the bottom of a ship. I go outside to check the garden. Maybe he's there.

Dust whips up the dislocated steps and showers the foyer. Sand crackles against the hardwood floors. Clouds cloak the sun, and the heat dissipates. They lower, gray-black bellies clumping together. Thunderheads. A sudden cold breeze blows against me, runs across the grass over the garden. Our plants bend close to the earth or smash flat from the wind. I stand at the corner of the House, my hair moving across my face.

The street darkens. I walk to the corner of the street, looking for him. I don't know what I expect to find, but it doesn't give any better of a vantage point. I don't discover another clue, or any clues at all. The House from this distance, I realize, is completely barren. No one is in it. I don't know that I've ever known it this way; a voided structure, another building like the others around it. The street could be any street. I know I won't be here forever; that the House won't, either. When I move back towards it, it's already not the same. But I don't know why, or how.

I decide to walk to the water pump. The path is more weed-strewn; tall, lime-green plants shoot upwards in defiance of the brick nestled in the ground around them. The buildings appear weathered, ground down further into their cracked foundations. At the pump, a low ripple of preemptive thunder splits the odd silence of the street. I work the handle of the pump and kneel to sip the penny-tasting water. Its coldness is of the earth, from as far down as it can get, nurtured by the dark and the minerals below. There is no sign of Charlie here, either. I stay at the pump awhile. The scent of weather electricity and smoke thickens in the air. The smoke is stronger, like an ad-hoc bonfire some of the stragglers make around here; not everyone wants to sleep in the House.

Charlie might be gone for good. I walk back the way I came. The sky is completely without sun, now. The clouds have solidified, a gray mass promising a downpour. The wind is cold and rolls up my back. The scent of burning is stronger, heavier. The cicadas scream. I am a block away from our street. I see a sputtering black coil of smoke rising upwards over the sun-withered trees and hulking ruins. It is ink-black and appears almost like liquid. I round the corner and the House comes into view.

There is Charlie, scrambling to protect the garden. Bright orange flames roar over the plot of earth. Behind him is the tall, black figure of the cop, gas can at his feet. His pale skin shines like a greasy white stain against his dark uniform. Charlie cries for help, and the officer stands back and watches him. I begin to run towards them from the corner.

"Help me!" he screams. "Help me! Margaret, help me!"

"I'm here, Charlie! I'm here!"

I'm not halfway across the street when the officer grabs

Charlie by the neck and drags his skinny form through the grass, and then holds his face into the flames. It catches on Charlie's hair, his face blackening in the sputtering smoke.

I run at the officer. Before I can do anything, he manages to throw out a punch that lands in the center of my chest and knocks clear through to my lungs. Like a loose shard, the pain moves right up to my throat. I collapse to my knees, trying to breathe, and air won't come. Charlie's face blisters and peels to bloody red. He's screaming like a little boy, his legs thrashing under the cop. The officer kicks him in his ribs. I can tell by the way his body flattens that a rib is broken.

When the air returns to my chest, I pull myself up and run around to the back of the tree. The officer pulls out his gun and starts firing shots. He's holding Charlie by the neck away from the fire, so I've momentarily distracted him enough to keep him from putting Charlie's face back over the flames. I stay behind the tree and then run for the side of the house where Charlie stores the rakes and the picks, and I grab the pick. When I make it back, the cop is gone. Charlie is curled up on the ground, sweating. His face is a blistered, purple mass, like chewed-up black berries. I kneel down next to him.

"Charlie? Are you okay? Can you hear me?"

He nods.

"Do you see where he went?"

He shakes his head.

"Can you sit up?"

He doesn't respond. I reach under him and pull him

away from the burning garden to the tree where I prop him up. I run to get a water jug near the porch and carry it back to him. I place it between his legs and put his hands on it. I tell him to drink from it, to get cool; I tell him that I don't think the officer's gone, yet, and that I'm going to find him. Charlie nods.

"I tried."

"You did good."

"The House is going."

I turned and saw what he meant. The fire had extended from our garden to the side of the building. Its flames went quickly upward, meeting with gasoline that must have already been spilled there. They spread in a bright flash, racing at the edge of my bedroom window. I feel something drop in me, but I don't know a word for it, yet. I turn my attention to Charlie's face. I examine him. I think it looks worse than it is. The burns can be taken care of. He's worn out, but he's okay. I grab his hand, lay the pick at my side, and spill some of the water into my hand. I help him drink from it. Then I lift the jug and tilt it into his mouth. It spills down his throat and chest, which is part of my intention to cool him.

The boards on the side of the house split and burst. Thunder pounds overhead, but no rain comes.

"Please someone help us," I say to myself. Charlie squeezes my hand as if to say he hears me; that even if no one else hears me, he hears me. Someone is listening.

I feel my hair jerked up behind me and an arm comes around my throat, squeezing me until all air is cut off, and

I start to choke. I see the black cuff of the uniform. The officer's body presses into my back like a metal door.

Charlie's eyes widen, his mouth hanging open, hands reaching out like a child to his mother. I'm lifted off the ground, and I understand how light I am, how easy it is for him to accomplish this. I know he means to kill me, to crush my neck while Charlie watches. His huge brown eyes spill over with tears. A helpless cry comes from him. He tries to stand, and can't. A punch lands in the center of my back; the officer drops me. The pick is on the ground, maybe seven inches in front of me. I pull myself to it, and grab its wooden handle. When I turn around the officer isn't there. I turn again, and he has his gun pointed at Charlie's head. The smile on his face is the smile of smug indignation; he believes he is doing the right thing.

"In America," he says, "Nothing is for free. You pay for what you get here. This is not fair. It is not FAIR!"

I don't say anything. I grip the pick and hold it ready, although I don't know what I'll do with it. I'm momentarily frozen. The thunder pounds again and the officer seems unfazed by it. Wind ruffles his brown hair. His eyes lock onto my face and bore hard, conveying hatred passed onto him by hundreds of others like him. He turns his attention to Charlie.

"You faggots," he says. "You worthless FAGGOTS!"

He lowers his gun, and before he can raise it again I run at him with the pick. He lets off a shot that goes somewhere into the yard. The pick meets his Adam's apple and splits his throat diagonally, until it protrudes from the other side.

He falls backwards. A tiny fountain of red pours down the side of the handle. He struggles for a minute, attempting to pull it out. His mouth fills up and turns into a small pool of red. The officer's eyes widen at the sky. His body shudders then collapses in the dirt, his head angled at the fire now devouring the House.

I move fast, and grab hold of Charlie to pull him further into the field away from the fire. I run back for the water jug, then re-join him. His body shakes in my arms. He tells me he's cold all over. Thunder hits again, and rain comes this time, a small spatter, then more. Sirens echo over the crackle of the fire before us, nearing.

"Margaret, leave," says Charlie. He sits up, looks at me. His face is worse than I thought.

"I'm not going anywhere, Charlie."

"Please. I've got this." He nods, silences me.

"You were never here, Margaret," he says. "That's easy, right?"

He means what he says. If I go, I can tell this will make him happy. But it is not the right thing to do. How can I do what is wrong only to make someone else happy?

"This is wrong. You understand that, don't you?"

"You just saved me," he says. "That's plenty. Now let me."

I shake my head.

He tells me to go, now, before the other police come and see what has happened.

"I can't do this, Charlie. Don't ask me to."

"You killed a cop, Margaret. I've got this. I killed him. I *killed* him. Let me be the one. You can repay me later. Just go."

Without further argument, I kiss him on the side of his face, and I know that what I'm doing is abandoning him, and he can see I don't want this, but I am doing it anyway. I'm going. The rain is hitting hard now, drenching us, but it is no match for the fire around the House, which is unrecognizable now. The black corpse of the cop lies outlined by the tree, the garden devoured in bright yellow flames.

Charlie smiles at me. He stands, shaking, and walks back to the dead officer. He grips the handle of the pick in the officer's neck and pulls it out. Charlie sits against the tree and leans his head on the trunk, the pick placed across his thighs. He's not looking at me anymore; the act has been done.

I have no choice but to turn around and walk, to leave him as he wishes, but not without another silent promise to myself, to Charlie; that I will repay. I can hear the House behind me caving in, the sirens expanding. The rain sluices down the street, blackening the pavement, soaking me through, and I run as far as I can until I know I can't be seen, or found.

From the dark place in the ground I sleep in for the night, the blaze of the House burns bright in the distance; ambulance and police lights spin through gray smoke rising from the ground. The stars are weirdly absent. I think of Charlie and what they'll do to him.

I think of his bones. Frail, like a bird's bones.

PART III:
REESE—
SHARK DREAMS

These are the worst pies in London…
    —Sweeny Todd: The Demon Barber of Fleet Street

I want to find the woman. The homeless woman. My search is for her. At night, images come on strong like a viper around my neck: her *look* at me from across the table (such a horrible fucking Thanksgiving), and a feeling ripping me open. Why wasn't it clear until now? How could she know me? I want to ask. What do you know about me? How did you end up here?

June 8:

I come out of New Orleans on the bus. 6 AM. My mother left the house, went to Florida to be with dad, who is in a hospital from sun stroke. I hear nothing from my wife, my kid. I don't expect to. What's left of my money goes to them now. My car is sold. This is to fund part of this trip. I feel all of it behind me, a road of nothing.

Cold slit of 6 AM sunlight cracks the border between earth and sky. It spills white across empty fields. I lean my shoulder into the big glass window of my bus seat, pushing, so I can get closer to the light. We pass swampland, green slush rolling down the sides of the road; we're on a detour that takes us across a blue-gray bridge ramped-up in giant steel arches; long bolts of rust down its sides. The whole bus is quiet cause they're waiting for it to crack, and the bus to go under. Water beneath us rolls smooth and thick like chocolate in the bright morning. Shady cypress trees hang low. Alligators slide over each other near the banks, fat bodies grimed in earth. We make it safely, moving through more dead cypress and nets of Spanish moss and have to stop because a heavy, old mother alligator lies horizontally in the road.

Everyone stands up to watch the driver attempt to usher it away by gesturing with his hands in the air. The gator remains unmoved; its big wallop of a pale gut is sprinkled dusty brown from its travels. Eventually the driver snaps a branch from a collapsing cypress and steps towards it, fanning at its tail. People laugh when the animal turns and appears to look at him as if irritated, then shimmies forward, away, and into the brush filling the side of the road. Exhausted, the driver tosses the branch. More laughter and *hoo-haws* from clumps of leaning riders clustered at the glass. With the driver aboard, people still seek the alligator crawling its way through the bracken.

NIGHT:

I can't sleep. I've read everything I brought with me. I brought so little; only enough money to last me a couple of months (if that's what it takes), now that I'm out of work, and I didn't plan on accumulating anything on this trip, but I picked up another book once we hit a stop two hours back, so that the riders could smoke. I thought of joining them even though I don't smoke.

The single, odd light canted towards me from above resembles the lights in airplanes. It's the same with the vents, like something that would suck at you rather than give. The air comes at me stale for a while, then too cold. A woman slumps away from me towards the aisle in the seat next to mine. Her body is a puddle in the seat. She snores like a jammed zipper, and her brown, curly hair is a thinning nest on top of her smooth brow. We don't speak when she gets on and takes the seat. She seems to want to be left alone, the way I want to be left alone.

I go over my notes from earlier. The homeless woman is named Margaret. When I locate the shelter, it is a burned husk with a set of black steps walking up into nothing. Stench of carbon everywhere. The whole house has gone up. Remnants that look as if someone is building, then gets a quarter of the way, and stops. There is nothing of Margaret remaining, nothing of the people who stayed there. A cop has been murdered on site. One of the residents has been shot—the same one who confesses to killing the cop. I learn this from the man I find roaming the area, a former resident of the shelter according to him.

I spend two days combing the place to find him. He knows her. He says Margaret has a kind of fame among the old residents. There is protectiveness in this man's regard for her. His face is shattered by scars and the skin around his eyes droops purple-black, like small thumbs pushed under them. Odd blond whiskers spot the pocked skin over his chin. His lower lip slants. I can tell he debates with himself about whether or not he should say anything at all when I ask where she is; that I need to find her. And then he tells me: *She gone. She gone from here.* I ask him where and he said she left a long time ago, went to Oklahoma. Why Oklahoma? I ask him. Where? *The city. She gone there. Now get the fuck away from me.* He seems scared, like he took a risk of some kind telling me this. I offer him money in exchange for his help, but he refuses it. Just repeats his last sentence, *get the fuck away from me, get the fuck away from me.* He disappears around the corner. A strange wind picks up near the torched lot and the black remains of the house, and the trees. There is a subtle rattle in all of it. Leaves and debris scatters over the road, scratch the asphalt, then go quiet. And I leave. Later, I locate a picture from our Thanksgiving that year. I print a copy from an album on my phone. I have a city; I have a location; I have a name.

A sharp drop registers in my gut at the thought of not finding her, the dread of which saws into me.

I slide down into my seat and try to make out the black objects going past us, cities nestled far back around old trees glowing piss-yellow. Steam rises under the moon from skeletal factories jumbled together in a penumbra. Worn, slumped houses stay dark under heavy, bowed branches. Nothing is here.

I see a shape of myself in it, partially; the dark reflection of me in the window; those things we pass fill the center, where my face should be. What examples are there, now? I wonder. For myself, for what I'm becoming. Where can I look? I am untethered, rocking like a loose bone in this seat with the others here. All of us adrift on thin filaments. This is what we share while remaining quietly disparate, looking for a warm locus in the dark. Riding with these others, I grip my own uncertainty like a torch, a feeble guide. Is that what I have? I wonder if they do the same.

Someone in the far back of the bus yells at me to turn off my fucking light. It's the only one on.

The riders sleep.

JUNE 10:

We're somewhere in Southeast Oklahoma near a town called Broken Bow. The woman who is next to me departs, exiting a few stops back. The seat remains empty, now, except I can still smell her: The mix of laundry sheets and the faded stink of baby powder from under arms that haven't been washed in days. The whole bus stinks of it, actually. I only get up to pee twice, and once to get food and coffee at a stop. The taste of the coffee is like a coagulant in my throat. But I drink it anyway because it's all they have. The smell of hot bodies so close together permeates the space. A woman in the back cries into a man's side, moaning over the mechanical hiss of the bus, the decompressed air. I turn to look at them. Everyone does. She sobs, and the man looks back at us with a kind of murder in his squint. We could be watching them fuck the way he glares at us. His black leather vest is tight around his bulging stomach and the points of his sagging chest. A taut blue bandanna covers his forehead, and a white handlebar mustache hides his mouth. Faded tattoos coat his hairy, speckled arms. Probably got them twenty years ago.

No one takes the seat next to me after the woman leaves, and I am glad for this. Relieved, actually. So many lonely talkers.

LATE AFTERNOON:

We cross multiple bridges. Some are longer than others. The oxidized green of the smaller ones probably date back to the 1940s, 1950s. There is an enforced quality to the newer ones, an appearance of forethought in the structure. The older ones will fail in a flood, eventually. I imagine generations of young men fishing off the rims, lines cast out in high water, catching nothing, staring off into thunderheads and smelling the hard pack of raw earth, sand and mud. The water in Oklahoma is red, like corrupted tomato paste thickened into a muddy scab. Trees stretch onto receding hills. Bright blue sky fans over us. Clouds bulge in it, huge-white, clumped, shadows blooming stark over the glitter of river water.

The passengers thin out. Once we get into Broken Bow, it is another two hours before we stop. The driver gives us a fifteen-minute break at a rest-stop/gas station/museum.

Hanging on the walls inside are fringed, white leather jackets. Shirts with bears and deer and wolves on them are for sale on a table. Rows of leather bullwhips hang in tight circles from a shiny, metal spoke in the wall. A plastic cube of rubber snakes rests near the shirts. Boxes containing BB guns lean in stacks near an entrance that says MUSEUM THIS WAY. Glass cases at the register have blue handled knives opened and pointing into rings carved into skull and snake shapes. A picture of George W. Bush in a pink frame with a heart design is nailed to the back wall near a window behind the clerk, small cards wedged into its corners. My stomach becomes queasy. I grab some water, pay for it and leave, passing a wall full of tan moccasins in different sizes, studded in blue plastic beads.

I walk away from the bus once I'm back outside. The crunch of loose gravel under my shoes is somehow grounding. My head is hot from the sun. I push my hair back behind my ears, and it is sweaty underneath. My face is dark from not shaving. I pinch the bridge of bone between my eyes until it hurts. I walk back behind the building, past the group of smoking passengers, and find a ledge overlooking a small creek.

Thick green trees bend over it. The trickle is loud, a strong propulsive rush. I sit on the edge of the tarmac, feet in the weeds. A green dumpster to my right stinks of sweet-rot. The ground boils my skin, and it isn't long before I have to give up, and stand again. I take a few steps towards the water. I watch it fold in on itself in white crests. It is clear in parts. A Styrofoam cup bobs in the crook of two rocks with water coursing over it. Cicadas thrum overhead. Clouds cover the sun. A cold shadow follows, darkening the creek and the parking lot. There is a brisk wind. I cross my arms for a minute, looking at the water. A woman approaches me from the crowd of smokers. She is tall, bony in a denim shirt. The sleeves are cut off. Pale, flabby arms dangle from her shoulders. Her hair is a short, butch crop up her neck, curly on top, a masculine jut to her jaw. Her jeans are hiked up on her waist. She has an annoying, surliness in her gait. Sunken eyes, deep red scratches all up her arms, crusted welts. She stares for a long time before asking if I could feel something. I have no idea what she means, but I humor her. She nods at my crossed arms.

You're telling me you can't sense that?
I can't. I'm sorry—just taking a break from the bus.
From Oklahoma?
I'm not.
Well, you're lucky. A lot of sadness here.
Oh yeah?
It's a shithole, honey. A cursed state.
You're from here then, I take it?
Yes, I am. (Sounds like AH-yam)
She nods.

I don't say anything, just wait for her to move back to the group. She asks me where I'm going, if I am visiting, and comes closer. I tell her I have to get back to the bus, that we are leaving soon. She nods again, watching me. I expect her to follow and awkwardly pass me to her seat. When I see her through the window as the bus pulls away, she is bent halfway into the dumpster, reaching and digging. Not a rider after all. A local.

Night:

Later, when the bus goes quiet and everyone is trying to sleep, I wonder if the woman is right, and Oklahoma is indeed a cursed state. Sometime around 2:00 AM I wake up, hot. Sweat rolls down my neck, and I reach to turn on a vent, but air only trickles out of it. I can smell myself, and I want a shower. New people arrive on the bus at various stops when I sleep. I get up to use the bathroom at the back. In the corner seat by the door a man rests his head on his chin looking out of the window. A slumped form—man or woman, I can't tell—covers his lap. He looks frozen. The person on his lap is covered by a black jacket, their head moving subtly underneath doing their best not to seem obvious in their act.

The bathroom offers a sharp urine stench that burns right into my throat. The movement of the bus makes it difficult to stand and piss, but I manage. When I step out, I avoid looking at the couple squirming in their dark corner.

4:00 AM:

The land outside is astounding in its flatness, unending, hollow.

The seep of low horizon light etches this more clearly, when for hours it seems as if it will not alter: a ticker tape of scenery played on loop; emptiness that jerks a tooth of fear in me. You would have to push back at this with all the imagination possible. How else could you survive it? It is apparent how it could drain a person, and if you didn't have the ability to imagine, what then? I suppose you just became like *it*, flattened inside and out. A ripple of horror licks my back. Who would accept this? I wonder. Why did she come to *this* place?

We're stopping soon.

JUNE 11:

Norman, Oklahoma. 2 AM. I wake up. The bus pulls to a stop in a small alley behind a building closed for the night. The driver says it's an emergency stop—the engine is messing up, and he has to fix it, so no ride into the city. He apologizes. There are dumpsters in the corner of the driveway, weeds go high around them; black plastic trash bags bulge in a pile in the corner next to a partial brick wall. The rest is a wooden fence, splitting in places. The bus is at a diagonal position, and I wonder how it will pull out of here after we've left. Lights come on above us and all along the path leading from the seats to the door. Exhausted, slow and silent, bodies reach up to pull bags down from overhead, tugging them from under their seats. I wait for most of the passengers to depart before I sling my pack over my shoulder, and exit the bus.

Outside, the night air is humid, thick, and mixed with the odd smell of cool concrete. Soft chatter erupts to my left as the old riders move off together. Some have made friends with others; they're shaking hands, hugging, exchanging information. I watch them in the spotlight-glow of the bus. The driver moves speedily around it checking things. He wishes me a good night. I do the same.

I step around the building, walk down the drive. The street in front of me appears endless, stretching in directions that mirror each other's flatness. Two dim sulfur lamps light a closed gas station across the street. The direction to my left shows a series of stoplights. Across from me, the street leads directly into a neighborhood. White, mid-twentieth century houses with cramped garages. A bike lies half on the grass, half in the street. The rest of the houses recede into black, lit by opaque yellow porch lights, like small eyes poking between sickly tree branches.

A single car drives by, blue-silver, dark windows. It comes from the left. I decided to go that way. My legs are grateful for the walk. My bones and back speak up as I move faster, gulping down the humid air, happy when a cool breeze hits me. I walk for about thirty minutes and come to a larger intersection, then an even bigger one by the highway. Car dealerships shine in unnaturally bright light across the road.

More cars pass the intersection. The highway has a moderate stream of traffic this late at night. I walk over the bridge spanning the highway, to the cluster of shops, gas stations, and fast-food restaurants glowing garish against each other. I enter one gas station to buy junk food and water, and I drink it sitting on a bench across the street. I fall asleep, lulled by the soft purr of cars speeding by.

The humidity doubles at 8 AM, and I wake up. Behind me is a tiny mall, still lit up from the night. Cars pull in and park. Giant charter busses line up around one of the entrances. A sign in front near the curb says: MODEL SHOW AT THE MALL—FREE HOT DOGS!

The thought of free food leads me further in, and I locate the vendors who eye me with an up-down scrutiny, eyes cutting me into quickly judged pieces when I ask for a free hotdog. A woman with white curly hair—stomach and breasts pushing at her yellow top—hands me one grudgingly, and I can tell she believes she has done a good act for today: feeding someone of *lesser* means, which I read in her expression. Although I am not dressed poorly, I assume it is my backpack and general 'traveled' appearance that does this. I notice others have the same reaction: quick judgment, snide stares, fear. I'm curious what would be acceptable, as worthy of simple acknowledgement. I wonder how easy it will be for me to speak to anyone about Margaret when the reactions of the people so far have been like this. The names on the busses boast smaller towns. They know an outsider when they see one; they know difference. They seem to like to point at it.

A stream of teenage girls and mothers stand in line to the doors of the mall. They're overly manicured and emit forced professionalism, dressed in what is probably their best clothing, no doubt. The mothers talk to each other, huge dark sunglasses, the incessant bobbing of heads in agreement with whatever one or the other is saying. The girls turn back to look, then look at each other. A woman to my right asks me what I'm doing there. Mall security, I imagine. I tell her I am eating a hot dog. I ask her what this is, and she tells me it's a fashion show, a modeling contest. She says Oklahoma is getting huge and the mall is just the start, and people from all over the country are moving here just for this.

I finish my hot dog and walk away from the rising crowds booming around the mall and the sidewalks, and begin a stroll that leads me down a street parallel to the highway. The heat is thick against my back. I am already showered with sweat. My GPS tells me this direction will take me into the city but would be an absurd walk; I'll have to hitchhike, or try for a cab or an Uber as a last resort. No one's going to bail me out if I spend what I've got left, so I have to watch it.

I pass more car dealerships. Giant signs announce brands with the severity and desperation of a national emergency. They follow one after the next further down the highway. The bent necks of more sulfur lamps line the path. Warm exhaust, and what is becoming the familiar sweet stench of garbage rot drifts up in the haze and humidity. I cut through the lot of one dealership. The road I'm on dead-ends in a collapsed chain-link fence as if forcing travelers into the lot. Men in black jackets and black pants rush at me in one motion, a herd, and one even waves. He has a red, desperate face, shouting almost angrily to come in, to come in, to come in! Look at the cars! I keep my head forward. I keep walking.

LATE AFTERNOON:

My feet are blistered, sliding around in the juice of those that already burst. My socks are soaked. I manage to walk to the middle of a place called Moore, which I discover is the victim of multiple Tornado attacks. An entire city built right in the path of tornado activity. I find a Dairy Queen next to a closed church and stay there for about a couple of hours drinking nothing but water. The short blond girl behind the counter becomes annoyed with my continuous requests for refills and adjusts her black visor in abrupt pulls to demonstrate this.

A woman with three children enters and orders fries. They walk barefoot to their seat. Blackened soles dangle from their chairs. The mother tells them to shut up and eat when they start moaning about their feet. The skinny children look gloomily at their brown trays. People who come into the restaurant glance over the entire place, and stare. There's a great deal of staring, I notice, as if they are sniffing something out, digging for something. I get up and move to a table outside, deciding to finally take a cab into the city if I can't hitch a ride. The brown cross on top of the derelict church across the street hangs slanted over a peeling door. A FOR SALE sign flaps in the tall grass at the curb. On it, a grin like a razor shines from the realtor's photo.

I pull off my shoes and examine my soles. Skin, peeled and pink, bright with new rawness. I pick black debris from the creases, flick them to the ground. My big, right toenail is bent back at the corner, tearing the skin. A line of blood traces the outline of the arch of my foot. For a minute, I lean back my head and close my eyes. I hear the mother inside, yelling at her solemn children through the windows behind me. My feet pulse from the ache sent down from my thighs and calf muscles, and I realize I have not seen a city bus, a train, anything; I wonder why there is not a viable public transit system—I could have avoided this, even though I really needed the walk after the bus ride. But it isn't an option. You're on your own here.

NIGHT:

Driving north on I-35. The sun is an orange flare sinking behind buildings that mark downtown. The rest of the orange sky forms a jagged, purple-blue suture. A stream of motels and fast-food restaurants run in mirrors of each other along the highway, announced in lurid yellows and reds. An incredible brownness covers everything. The buildings, with the exception of a single skyscraper, emanate variations of nothing but brown. Spreading out from the highway is an expanse of more flatness. Apartment buildings attempt a contemporary look, but remain empty. Old tarps billow from unused balconies.

The man who offered me a ride found me stretched out at the Dairy Queen. He ate his dinner at one of the tables and spoke to me about the heat without concern for who I am, or what I was doing there, which I've noticed is the way with many Oklahomans; they will talk to anyone about anything. It's disconcerting at first. It's easy to think they would want something. I wait for him to make a request of some kind, but he just keeps rambling. I learn about his divorce, bankruptcy, and pending court case in less than fifteen minutes. When he asked me about myself, I only tell him I need a ride into Oklahoma City.

That's not far, he says, chewing, *I can take you there. What brings you here? I love New Orleans, by the way.*

I'm looking for someone. A friend. I dig into my pack and pull out a picture of Margaret. *Seen her?*

He shakes his head. *Can't say I have. This a big city though. She do something to you?*

No, no. Nothing like that.

Well, I'll give you a ride (Well, ahll giv ya ah rahd), but nothing weird about you, is there?

Just my feet.

He laughs at this, and then shows me his truck, which has giant rubber cow testicles hanging from the trailer hitch. Stickers on the back window show a poorly removed W'04 sticker, an NRA quip I didn't bother to read, and one saying something about teaching evolution in schools. I say nothing about the odd tone of these, simply grateful for his offer. In the cab it's mostly quiet, although he continues to talk about his ex-wife, about things I should do while I'm in the state, including casinos and the zoo, and the art museum if I'm "feeling uppity."

We swoop past downtown, heading further north to 36th street. When he asks where I should be dropped, I tell him the place where I'm likely to find the most homeless people. He says that's easy and takes me down to a single street called the Paseo. It resembles a weak facsimile of a street you might find in New Mexico—close, but still missing something. He drops me off at the curb, says it's a nice street all around, and a good place to start. *She'll be around here somewhere I imagine. Just have to keep looking. But it's gonna be hard with the way you're going about it, I have to tell ya.*

Although it's not the first place to look, he says there are many homeless in the area, along with "artsy types," as he puts it, and "gays, if that don't bother ya. Jews, too." His tone describes them as if they are a massive animal herd that sometimes wanders into the area from a neighboring village outcrop, rather than just regular people walking around. Is he testing me? Is this some way of passively seeing how I'll respond? It's as if he is gambling, waiting to see what I'll say so he can deem himself correct or incorrect as if some kind of binary exists to him that determines his relationships with people. He sees I don't acknowledge his sentiment, and drops it, then thanks me, oddly. For what, I don't know. A brief moment passes when I consider what he would think if he knew about me and my dead astronaut boyfriend.

He drives further north, turns left, then goes up, forward, and disappears forever beyond the lightless streets.

MIDNIGHT:

I sit at a table outside of a mildly populated restaurant and order a glass of water, some tea. Looking around, I already feel a subtle difference. No one notices me as much. I don't feel as if I am being scoured by the searching stares of others as I sit here and pull out my notes and my things trying to arrange my next move. I drink water, a cold flood down my throat, which is dry for some reason. My tongue is a thick cord. Pressure drops behind my eyes to my cheeks, the base of my skull. I listen, gently, to the slivers of chatter at the tables around me. The street goes a little further, stretching beyond an awkwardly shaped apartment complex, some other buildings drenched in pastel purple, red, and yellow. Lights from closed, sparse art galleries cut bright window shapes onto the path sloping down from the restaurant.

I go over my location, orienting myself, drawing up sections, areas I can achieve in terms of canvassing. I imagine Margaret here. Could she be just down this tiny street, somewhere back behind one of these buildings, in one of the surrounding homes? Is this enough to find her? It also occurs to me for one paralyzing moment—a sharp spike of numbness in my chest, my skull—*what if she's dead? What if she's not here at all?*

JUNE 15:

I abandon the Paseo, moving west into the city.

Most homeless women or men that I find are incoherent or asleep, or slink away in fear. I think about the sadness the woman in Broken Bow spoke about, the "cursed state." I buy many of them food, water, try talking to them. When I ask about Margaret and show them her picture, they just stare at her face, a soft longing in their features. When I go to get more water, many are gone when I return.

A woman approaches me at a bench outside of a sub-sandwich shop where I sat with an older man earlier. She is in gray business attire and has huge black hair, smiling. She holds a half-eaten parfait in her hand. Raspberries smashed in white yogurt.

I just want to say I've been watching what you're doing (watchin' wut yur doin'), and it is refreshing to see someone so kindly treating another fellow human being. Even if they're homeless.

Thank you.

Can I ask what you're doing here?

Sure. I'm just looking for a friend. From Louisiana. She might have come here.

That what you were showing them? She indicates the picture in my hand.

Yes.

Mind if I take a look?

I don't.

She's got a strong look, this-

Margaret.

Margaret? Yeah, she looks real nice. Any luck so far?

Not yet, no.

You try the Internet? The police?

Both things that wouldn't help in this situation.

I see, well, where all have you looked so far?

I tell her and she slurps her yogurt, her eyes moving over my face.

Well, don't you just have a journey ahead of you? What you think of Oklahoma?

I haven't really formed a solid opinion yet.

Oh come on! You can't look at me and tell me you don't think something! People are weird here, aren't they?

I told her about the truck driver, the mall crowd.

Oh yeah, but it's real friendly here. Real friendly. There are places for the gays to go, now. I hope you're not worried about being bothered by any of them. They won't bother you if you stay away from 'em. They're harmless, really. And it's getting more accepting here. It really is. Have you been to the Paseo? It's real artsy down there. I bet the girl you're looking for, I bet she's down there.

Thank you. I've been there.

Oh you see! Already ahead of the game.

She leaves after insisting on a hug, which I manage to turn into a gentle handshake. She looks over her shoulder twice as she walks back into the restaurant. The second time she turns around her expression is unrestricted disgust.

THE TRAIN YARD:

2:00 – 3:00 AM. I'm lost. Down by the train tracks south of where I started. Old apartment buildings, crumbled brick tenements, dark windows, orange light at hopeful looking doors. Stretch of nothing-land around these buildings; dry, dead tufted grass and waist-high weeds, burs in my socks pricking at my ankles. Hard gravel crunch in my steps. Rust scent and metal cans lining the rock bed under tracks leading away to other shadowed buildings beyond the edge of huge black trees, factory shapes, and more orange lights drifting high up in space on their edges, like astral bodies, orbs.

The stars are not visible from here; the sky is just one spread of blue-black like looking into a body bag. I see shadows hulking around buildings, movement, glimpses, their leaning shoulders, and then they're gone. I walk north again—or what I think is north—stepping on each plank under the rails as if in contest with myself.

I get further up to another darkened building (is it closed? Do people still live in it?), must have been built sometime in the 1940s, maybe earlier. Cars are parked outside, but it's quiet and windows are all black, yet I can see curtains in one shadowy window from the moonlight coating this and the entire field around me. Wind pushes the trees and a roar of leaves shatters the quiet. Then I see another shape huddled up under one of them, watching. There is a long time before we address each other and he asks me what I want. His throat is the sound of fat snail bodies clawed from dry shells. I walk near and get down under the tree with him, and I smell the hard stink of a man who does not bathe. His brown pants show the bones of his knees, one leg up, the other open. I smell shit and dirt. Dry pine needles press into my palm when I join him on the ground. I pull out my picture and use my phone light to show him. I ask if he knows Margaret, and he just stares at the picture, breathing. He turns away, then, as if in anticipation of someone else walking up, but no one comes. I try again, and he belches, shifts and says, *Why don't you just go away from here, go away from here, go on down that a-way, that a-way. If you're lookin,'* so I stand and leave him, and walk further along the train tracks.

A low sound drifts across everything like a distant train coming in and reminds me of the howl of a foghorn. The field widens the further I go, trees spreading out, the moonlight draping silver on everything so sharp I can see things distinctly. Up ahead is a small island of trees, and a group of hulking buildings indistinguishable from one another with strange rock facades lit by a rusted barrel filled with fire. Shadows dance along the building walls and the trees. The ground is pooled in orange light. A small alley divides two of the buildings that lead back to others closer to the main streets and intersections, and it's lit by another barrel.

I hear voices when I approach, laughter and agreement. I move up near the door to one of them, under the small porch roof held aloft by thin, green posts. I look around the corner. Two men. One stands by the barrel with hands in his pockets, the other leans against the wall. Another man is on his knees. The fire outlines his face and head like a crown. Two other men hold his arms back while a third stands looking down at him, holding a brick or a stone.

The two men who watch mutter to one another, and that's the agreeable tone I hear. But the man on his knees is agreeable too, saying over and over, *do it do it I deserve it do it I deserve it if you'll do it I'm better than you I'm better than you,* and the man leaning over him takes his chin with his free hand and opens the kneeler's mouth. He slides the brick into it, pushing to see how far he can get it in, popping his fist against it, eliciting a gurgling retch. Ropes of spittle pour off his face and the brick, and then he pulls the brick out, a gentle slide, and the man's head falls loose, and I get that this has been going on for hours, maybe longer, and the man is clearly drunk. He attempts talking again, calling himself a "faggot who deserves it," and begs the man for the brick.

I leave, quietly, and walk past the first barrel beyond the trees. The fire feels cold somehow. I head back to the tracks looking behind me as I go.

Further down I find abandoned train segments looming still in the dark near a blackened bridge with two tunnels under it. Rocks I kick ping loudly against their sides, and their glass eyes shine hollow under the moon. It's silent here except for the rush of tree leaves and the clink of my feet on gravel. I see nothing, but when I look at the empty windows of the train parts I think I see faces looking out at me, and then they're empty again. I stop and stare, and question what I'm seeing, until I get further down to the tunnels underneath the bridge. Here are boxcars opened up, empty, and showing nothing. I hear movement in the far back of some as if people in them hear me approach and are retracting further into the dark. Some whispering is carried from the wet echo inside the tunnels. I go further in, and at the opening, I can see the slight curve of the tunnel's cement walls rising in an arch.

The tracks are illuminated on the other side by the moon. High up on a ledge sits a group of people huddled together. A few others stand around an electric lamp the color of blue fire. Its light doesn't stretch beyond their bodies. But the faces of those on the ledge are etched in haunted expressions staring down at it with odd fixation.

Those standing hear my approach, and turn to look at me. I think of the people at the mall earlier—those huddled here know an outsider, too, although they're more hesitant in their judgments, it seems; they're giving me a chance to step forward, to ask of them something, and I can tell they know I want something. I say little, only produce the picture for them, ask them if they have seen her, know her, and they look it with clarity and concentration, a genuine interest to help me, perhaps. Each one hands it back to me with a shake of their head, a grunt. The ones on the ledge do the same. A man behind me I didn't see enter comes forward and asks to see it.

For a minute I expect him to do the same, and gladly, because I can feel my exhaustion as a palpable thing, and I want to sleep, but he looks at me, and the churning adrenaline tells me this man knows something. Or, at least that's what I want to believe. He tells me to follow him, so I do, walking deeper into the tunnel.

At the far end we stand in the moonlight. The tracks cut a smooth curve like a ladder through the weed-pillars and waist-high grass. He tells me to wait here, and then pulls a phone from his pocket, which he presses to his face, talking quick to the person on the other end with reassurances. He turns to me, and gestures with his finger—*one minute*—and then walks further off into the weeds along the tracks.

I wait, listening, and when he comes back he tells me to be here tomorrow if I want to see her; I'm numb for a second, silent, then I try to corroborate the parts of the story I have to make sure that he actually *knows* her. He reassures me, now, telling me, this spot, here, tomorrow. He says she is "being protected." Somehow this convinces me, and I tell him I'll do what he says even if it's bullshit. The man nods and disappears back into the tunnel. I find a set of cracked cement stairs curving up around the bridge, which takes me to the top. I walk to the cement railing and look out across the tops of the train sections, and the field I just walked across. I search for the glow among the odd buildings where the man and those who stood forcing a brick into his mouth, but it is dark in that direction, now. Nothing is visible.

A road leads from the bridge through more empty land, but I can see lights from a greater intersection ahead, so I start for it, and walk for about twenty minutes.

When the car comes, I don't see it at all. But I hear the childish, aggressive roar of its engine, and I don't see it pass, I *hear* it pass. And I feel it. Or I feel the metal pound of something cracking into my shoulder, something one of the passengers held outside the window as they sped past me, a shovel or a board maybe; my neck twists up in agony when I smack the ground. The engine dims to a trickle the further away it gets and eventually a truck pulls up to me, although slower, gentler. I cup my shoulder with my hand thinking how it could be worse, it could have been my head, but it feels as if it is my head with the pain going like it is.

I manage to lift myself up and crawl away from the road to the grass over the curb. From the truck comes a tiny woman in round glasses with brown hair piled on top, and a smile on her small, thin face. She walks, hunched over. Her hair is tied loosely on top of her head, which shakes free the closer she steps. She moves over to me and leans down as if to examine my back better.

I saw that, she says, *I saw what they did.*

What was that? Can you help me?

I'm gonna help ya. That's what I'm doin', I'm helpin' ya. But you gotta stop askin' about her. People know. It's small here. You gotta stop askin'. Understand?

I don't say anything and the woman tries to move me. Her cool hand presses assuredly against my neck.

She's with me. At my house.

A man told me—

He lied, whoever he was.

How do you—

Everyone knows. The right ones anyway.

She helps me to stand, and I'm hunched forward, holding myself, grimacing between short gasps.

Why is she with you?

You coming with me or not?

I walk with her to her car and slide into the passenger's seat. It's difficult to lean back. My legs stiffen like frozen planks.

You come with me to my house, okay? We get you looked at. You'll see her, don't worry. Margaret's at my house, but you gotta be patient. What you want her for anyway?

What's your name?

Ma Eldrige. And you can call me that.

THE FAR AWAY HOUSE:

July 10—Lime-green tree leaves flip and shake under the charcoal bellies of thunderheads rolling over Ma Eldrige's land. She asks me to go outside and help Tambourine cover the truck with a tarp in case of hail, although I'm not sure what defense that will provide.

The dirt drive leading from the east side of the house comes up in smooth, red spumes when we race to pull the corners down over the truck bed, tightening it over the windows. I see Tambourine struggling on the other side. He is short for fifteen. His shoulders curve inward with the shape of a wishbone. His neck is a long tube. The rest of his body spreads out thin, awkward. He combs his hair in spikes with too much gel Ma buys from the Dollar General at the intersection they refer to as town, which is called Sayter. Tambourine grunts as he ties the final notch down, and some rain starts to sprinkle us. I can see the irritation in his features as he moves to meet me on the other side and help me finish the last corner. He's worried about his hair.

This issue must be a relief for him when he says he is grateful he won't be returning to high school the following year; he's going to be homeschooled by Ma and help her with the house. He complains about the quality of the education with a forced sense of expertise. His shame is barely hidden when he does this; the deformities of his shoulders and underdeveloped ribcage gain a sudden strange etched quality as if they become bigger. I can't imagine a school here that would welcome him. He mentions women he sees when he's feeling cocky, how he's making progress with one or two in town, and then goes quiet for a week or two, staying sealed in his bedroom on the second floor of Ma's house across from the small room I currently occupy.

Due to a slip on Ma's part, I learn that he is not her son. She's too old, anyway, but he's not her grandson, either. She does not talk about his parents, or where they are, or how he came to live with her in Sayter and be called Tambourine. None of this is spoken. Attempting to question it creates a form of tension that appears to connect to the house itself, so I know not to. There are many stories here that are treated with the same silence; the house is weighty with them. The Far Away House, a name she says she gave to it as a girl.

Once Tambourine's done with his corner he runs back through the yard and up the porch steps. He yells at me, asks if I'm coming in, and I tell him I'll be there in a minute. He goes inside patting his hair, a look of confusion on his face, and shuts the door. I watch dark build in the sky. The clouds slowly stretch towards the house, the only structure visible for many miles.

The house stands parallel to a leafy oak tree on its right. Four stories, including the strange attic-studio and the basement. Its white wood never seems to accumulate dirt from the road leading all the way to a two-lane slab of asphalt that goes twenty miles into town. Black shutters flank the windows. The roof is blanketed in black shingles, and the roof over the porch is the same with a front door painted to match. Two scratched wooden chairs fill up one corner of the porch. The brown of the wood catches the late afternoon light and glows like thick honey. The white boards of the porch have gaps the width of a hand and show caked mud and old trash that fell through and remains there with the rotting leaves.

Looking at the front of it, the lights inside burn a soft candle-yellow behind white drapes as thin as cheesecloth. The lights outside are strong beats of color under the gray spilling overhead. Thunder snaps across the vacant land. Yellow-green grass ruffles in a sudden, cool push of wind.

I breathe in the smell of it, cut grass, mud-stink, the age of the house mixed in with it somehow. It is older than Ma, and as she has told me it has been here since the 1930s. She took it over when her father died in the fifties and she has never lived anywhere else. But she travels, she says, and she knows people all over, and people know her. She tells me they know her for her favors. When I ask about Margaret, she tells me that that's a favor.

Like some underground railroad for the homeless?

Something like that.

Two days after my initial arrival, Ma bandaged my arm and shoulder, rubbing a homemade mint gel on my neck, and I ate what she cooked. I asked for Margaret constantly at first, and she repeated that she's not here, yet, but will return. I remind her what she told me when she found me; that she had said Margaret was indeed there. She now tells me that Margaret is in fact staying at the house but has left it briefly; that she has to take care of some business in another undisclosed location. All of this, says Ma, is for her own protection.

Protect herself from what? I ask.

It doesn't concern you, Reese. You'll have to be patient if you want to see her. If not, you know where you can go.

I stay, and three weeks pass. I wait for her. And I help Ma with her house while I wait. It's my payment to her. She shows me Margaret's room, which is a bare space with wooden floors. A twin bed in the corner is made up with white sheets. On the ledge of the window is a tiny potted plant. Some pictures of pressed flowers hang on the wall, purple petals crinkled dry under dusty glass.

Ma says the plant is important to Margaret, and that it must stay at the window. She offers me the job of making sure it is watered, looked after. I don't hesitate; I believe somehow that this will give me insight into her, into my pull to her. It's naive, this thought, but it's something.

Ma never asks if I'm attracted to Margaret. She doesn't suspect me in some predatory way. She seems to understand my vague compulsion, my need to meet with her. I tell her about the Thanksgiving dinner, about the things that followed. I think she has an instinct for identifying men who do not want to be with women; she seems to get this about me, too, and never asks about it. I find myself wanting to tell her about Derrick—there is a part of me that thinks she will be proud, but this is because I am proud of him. Because I still think of him. My injustice to my family is also an injustice to him. I could have loved him and been my full self. Instead I chose to live divided by absurd shame and confusion, and he died loving falseness. There are too many people like me in the world, and I am in debt.

Lightening splits the gray apart. Thunder cracks. Rain blows over me. It smells heavily of earth and warm concrete; the scent carries all the way from the road. I breathe it down as far as I can get it. Tambourine watches me from his window upstairs, consternation on his face. He waves at me to come in, like he has something crucial to tell me, so I go inside.

What do you have to tell me? I ask him.

Nothin', he says, as though I am silly to ask anything at all. *Storms comin'.*

Ma has me help her with errands in town throughout the week. The Dollar General is next to a locally owned sub-sandwich shop, a tiny grocery store called *Rick's*, and a hardware store that sells mattresses and office supplies, and even has a partial garage where a local mechanic performs oil changes and tune-ups. Further up the street are a tiny library and a gas station. This makes up most of Sayter. She urges me to hurry and get the groceries from *Rick's* while she waits in the truck. I do this for her never asking why she won't come in herself. The small aisles take less than five minutes to peruse. I gather the items from her list and take them to the register. I have to signal the man from the back. He sees me but continues talking with someone I can't see. Finally he walks slowly towards me. He has a handlebar mustache and long, dark brown hair. He says nothing, only stares.

Just these, I say.

You with her? He nods out the windows at Ma Eldrige in her truck.

I say that I am. And thought by now he would recognize me.

Well, then next time you tell that bitch that if she wants something to come and get it herself.

He rings up the items, places a paper sack on the counter for me to bag them myself, and then disappears down the hall to the back.

When I slide into the truck she asks me how it went. I start to tell her about the clerk's directive, to ask her if there's some correlation here with her staying in the truck while I purchase her groceries, but I know what kind of answer I'll receive. So I leave it alone.

Parked in the space next to us is a light-blue mini-van sporting rough fades on the sides and hood from age and sun. It's larger than most vans and the tint on the windows is splitting back on itself. The open door reveals a dark interior. A woman with a pannus marred in deep stretch marks, that also hangs and jiggles from beneath her stained, white shirt, clutches a little boy from beneath his tiny arms, and shakes him so hard his head lashes about. The immense flab of her dimpled biceps swings. She appears completely unaware of her surroundings, or of others. The boy screams gutturally while she pounds his back with the flat of her wide hand. *Shut your mouth! Shut your god damn mouth! Shut-the-fuck-up!* Her hand comes down again and again, whack, whack, whack! A stream of brown diarrhea runs over the child's bare legs from the edge of his slanted diaper, as if forced out by the woman's repeated slaps. He kicks his legs in the air.

Ma backs out of the lot, impervious.

JULY 12:

The tree outside my window contains soft chirping. Wind lightly ruffles its leaves. There are three windows in my room; two face the front of the house. Another at the foot of my bed faces a tree.

I have an old wooden desk oiled to a shade like soaked coffee grounds. It has been with the house since the Second World War, says Ma. I have a few papers inside it, some sketches, and my writing. A lamp puts out a gentle spot of yellow against the bare wall, across the center of the desk, the chair, the floor, wooden like the rest of the house. I have an armoire in which I keep my clothes. Its surface glows like a polished violin but drained to a strange ivory color. I assume it belonged to Ma's father, or maybe her grandfather. The scent of old powders and leather drifts from the far back of it—behind the place I hang my shirts and pants—and is overwhelming. Small shelves line the inside of its doors, and it has slots for brushes, combs, and brill cream. A faded spot with four holes mark the interior and lacks a mirror, perhaps, or a label of manufacture.

I stand at the window facing the tree. Yellowed cheesecloth curtains brush my shoulder. I look down at the base of the oak. A thorn bush grows gracelessly from the side of its trunk at an angle. The thickness and multitude of its branches collect like a ball of twine, or a giant round seed with open pits from which tiny finches dart and bounce throughout. One falls from an opening, its wings sputtering to quickly raise itself before spilling to the ground and hopping to the shadows underneath it. Their round brown bodies scare one another, shaking the thorny leaves.

The floors in the hall outside of my room moan. The modest wood-creak one would expect from a floor like this. It's the sound of shifting feet at the threshold of my door.

Tambourine sometimes does this when he has something he wants to ask me but is hesitant to do it. He stands by the railing of the stairs until he finds the impetus to turn into my open doorway, casually, as if I do not hear him breathing, moving, working through his decisions physically. His shyness is tangential. Once he moves past it, his openness is quite natural, as if the initial silence and pensive juggling never existed. Even after two long months, this is still his way, which is no doubt due to the intentional balance I keep: my distance, and then politely listening when he has an inquiry, usually short. Ma must have told him why I am here, and that it's for that reason alone that I stay. We talk sparingly when helping Ma in her kitchen, washing dishes from that night's meal or fixing something on the house; me breaking things, doing things incorrectly, and him always following it up with a kind of unconditional forgiveness I haven't heard in another's voice.

That's okay. You're okay, he says when I break Ma's cups or when I strip a bolt trying to fix a part of her washer.

Today, the wait outside my door is longer, so I know that whatever he has to tell or ask me is of some importance. There is a weight between him in the hall and me in here. I almost become annoyed with him and tell him to just come into the room, but I am afraid that would scare him. I let him have his process.

I study the marks in the branches of the tree—rope marks from a swing, perhaps—when he finally comes into the doorway. He lets out a big sigh, as if he regrets whatever he's about to say, and then asks me what I'm doing. I'm not sure he really wants to know, or cares, but I tell him anyway and he joins me at the window. I show him the bush that looks like a hollowed out seed with birds jumping through its holes. I mention the marks on the tree, hoping that maybe he knows what caused them. He just nods, looks, and from his reaction I can tell it means nothing to him. His hair is spiked like a thick brush. His thin arms stay at his sides and look whiter in his black t-shirt sporting an emblem for a death-metal band. Purple woven bracelets cover one of his wrists. The black shirt makes his shoulders appear less distorted, and I don't know if this is intentional, I can still see the curve of them and the smallness of his ribcage as if two large fingers pressed down on his shoulders at birth, smoothing them into this rounded shape, and hipbones jutting in his black jeans like half of a bowl.

Look at that one, he says, and points at the birds. *It just bounces.*

I don't see which one he's talking about. They all appear to be bouncing with absurd giddiness from one branch to another, sometimes knocking into one another. He drops his hand back to his side but remains looking out the window.

So...I want to show you something.

I wait for him to elaborate before saying anything, but he doesn't, so I turn to him and implicate for him to continue.

Not here. Will you just come with me?

What is it?

Something I just want to show. Just come with me.

If it's a private thing, I don't want—

It's not private. I mean—

Why do you want to show this—whatever it is—why do you want to show it?

Because. I haven't shown anyone before, he says, and waits, measuring my reaction. His eyes grow momentarily glossy, hopeful, but expecting pure rejection; a wound in their braced, wide expression. The light filtering into the room from the tree and the window dapples his narrow face and dark eyes; he believes I will tell him no because everyone else has told him no and turned him away.

You're my friend, he says, although a tone of doubt in his voice suggests this is something he wants to be true and hopes that by saying it this way, it will become true.

Okay. Take me, I tell him, *I would like to see this, whatever it is.*

We move west of the house, walking into the open land behind it, and I see that it cuts into the earth like a hulking white block. The black, pointed roof shifts dark-to-light under moving clouds. Trees on the far side of the property stay gray even if the afternoon light pushes through breaks in boat-sized clouds. The house looks alone the further away we get—the only way I can describe it—and I feel a kind of relief as if I can breathe and move, finally, and haven't for a while. We stop for a minute so Tambourine can retie his shoelaces. A cool wind blows over the field, and the grass ripples, appearing like green water. I look at

Ma's weathered, historic residence and sense that it wants something; if places can desire, this one emanates an ache, while at the same time holding something in. The ground around our feet is spotted in shadow. Bright areas show red mud in worn places where grass bends back. A few steps over, and it's shadow again, only cooler, and the ground turns gray-green, sometimes blue.

Come on, Reese, says Tambourine. *We're almost there.*

I don't reply, but I assume he says this—looking over his shoulder at me with a questioning expression—because he's worried I'll turn back, or I won't want to continue this trek with him wherever he's taking me.

The grass crunches underfoot, and I catch the scent of rain coming from the south, hidden just under the breeze. The ground starts to slump downwards when we get to the furthest edge of the property. I look back at the house one more time, and it's become minuscule, nothing but a white dot far away from us, almost unrecognizable.

Tambourine steps cautiously down the sloping earth, but with a sense of practice, as if he knows this is the sort of movement you have to take in order to get into the trees. I do the same, almost slipping, surprised at how I took the ground for granted; it's less dense then it appears.

Once I make it to the line of trees next to Tambourine, I'm breathing heavily. His strange stink wafts off of him and it mixes with the sap scent of the underbrush and the trunks around us. He looks at me, amused.

Almost have a fall there, Mr. Silent? Don't die hyperventilating on me, now.

I don't respond except for a polite chuckle; I don't want him to feel bad for attempting some kind of humor with me.

He's less crushed and condensed out here than he is moping around Ma's tiny kingdom; some amount of natural confidence comes through, even if it's a bit derivative, forced. He's enjoying himself. The solidity of his movements, as he leads us further into the forest, speaks of the freedom he feels, the lack of judgment, perhaps, which I think has very little to do with my presence.

Watch out here. Snakes under these branches. Look for logs like that, gouged-out ones. Be careful where you step. I once saw a rattler in here. 'Bout shit myself cold when I heard that damn tail. Scary as hell.

A muddy trail forms over roots and stones. It leads further down another slope and into a dried riverbed smothered in dead leaves over smooth, partially dried mud, like brown wax. He stomps across it, and I follow, irritated at the sinking squelch of my feet sunk in the wet earth. We climb up the embankment on the other side. Animals leap in the branches above us.

We're here, he says.

He stands at the trunk of an ancient oak with branches like elephant tusks sloping down to meet with the ground, then rising up again. The bark is darker than the trees around it, and it has somehow cordoned off its own space. It seems as if it is soaked through with ink, or that it has drunk the entire riverbed dry behind us. The round bulge of its roots contains a pale moss sheen, and the two front roots curl inward as if these are its arms, and it's holding something in the center, which, when I look down where Tambourine stares, I notice a caved-in hole right in the center; it's black inside, but mostly made of dark mud and small rocks. It looks like something has been extracted from it, or an animal dug far down into it, and made the hole its home. I think of engorged, furry spiders the size of my palm, something fast that could jump on you, eyes without reason staring back on a furry head as it sinks in its insect teeth.

Rattlers? I ask and point at the hole. Tambourine shakes his head. He stares at the space between the two branches with an odd sort of reverence, and says, *That's where I was born.*

Before responding, I take a moment to see if he's being sarcastic, or playing a joke, but he isn't.

What do you mean? I ask.

He points again and looks at me. *I was born there.* His voice is irritated that I'm offering him any kind of disbelief or seeking an explanation.

Well, it's—it's a hole in the ground, Tambourine. Do you know how you came to be born in a tree?

In the earth, from the tree. He corrects me.

Sorry, my mistake.

Ma took me here, said she found me in this spot, and that is where I was born. Pulled up from the ground, still in my sack.

Your sack? Like a trash bag?

He shakes his head.

What, then?

Whatever sacks babies breathe in, I don't know. My sack.

You were found in your placenta?

He freezes at the word.

Or caul? Sometimes that happens, but it's rare.

Ma says she cut the cord from the tree; that it was attached here. He points at an odd notch in the bottom of one of the roots. *She said I was bobbin' and sloshin' in the pool of water down in there, tryin' to move. She said the water was red from the mud and me, and I was barely breathin'. I was purple in my sack.*

What else did Ma say?

She says I get my shape from the tree.

I don't say anything and hold back on my pressing need to challenge his story, and the things Ma has told him about how he came to be in the world. But I wouldn't be responsible for taking away from him the origin story that has clearly been provided to cover up the real one. Did Ma actually find him here, in the muddy hole of this ancient oak, floating in his placenta? Or was it just a story?

He kneels down to the ground and reaches into the hole with his skinny right arm.

How'd you get your name?

He pulls out a stack of papers sealed in a plastic bag and stands up with it, brushing off the dirt and mud caked to its bottom. He opens it up and takes out the papers.

Ma gave it to me. She says I was so thin and little when she pulled me from the earth that my bones rattled like a tambourine. So now I'm Tambourine.

He waits, looking at me. *How did you become Reese?*

My name was my mother's idea. Probably just a popular baby name at the time. How I became me is another story altogether.

I got time.

What are those you're holding?

My letters.

To whom?

I write them and leave them here every birthday.

What for?

Thanking the tree for helping me come to life, and also asking it questions.

You understand it's just a tree, right? That it can't think or speak or anything but—

He's looking at me with annoyance again, and a tinge of anger underneath; I stop myself from continuing this line of questioning. A wave of embarrassment and shame creeps through my abdomen. I start to apologize, but he's gone back to his letters, indifferent to my sense of decorum.

Why did you want to show me this?

He shrugs. *Cause I think you're cool. Just kidding. Because I wanted to. And I do think you're cool, but I wanted to. Only you and Ma know.*

His eyes lift, and I can tell he's proud of it.

Where were you born?

In a hospital in Louisiana.

That where you're from?

Yeah, New Orleans.

Ma found you, too, she told me.

She did, that's true. She helped me at a bad time.

You're here for that lady, I know.

What do you know about her?

He shakes his head. *Nothin'. She's not here enough.*

What does that mean?

He shrugs again. *People always coming and going from Ma's house. I just thought you was another one.*

Well, I am in a manner of speaking.

How long you gonna stay?

I don't know the answer to that. Until I get what I'm seeking, or I have to leave to get what I'm seeking.

Seems simple enough. But you should stay. Tambourine looks at the ground, stuffs his letters back into the plastic bag, then lowers down and pushes them back into the muddy hole.

What do you have back in New Orleans?

Nothing, really.

No family? Nothing?

Well, some family. I had a wife, and there's my daughter.

He stands there, says nothing for a minute.

Ma says you don't like girls, so I'm confused.

She did, did she?

Yeah.

Well, she's a perceptive woman.

Is it true?

In one way, yes, I don't like women in one way.

Why not? How can you be with one if that's how it is?

One of the world's many questions, Tambourine.

After a minute of silence, I notice he's waiting for me to continue. An explanation is what he's after.

I'll put it this way. A man can force himself to like something, for strange reasons. Women, too.

Family hate?

I laugh, and he seems put-off by my reaction. *No, they don't, which is what makes my case strange. I had no tangible, articulated reason for forcing myself to be in a marriage with a woman. I just did it. Lots of men do it. I didn't even feel a pressure to fit in or seek acceptance from others. It was just something I did.*

I don't get it, then.

Most people don't. Because they're usually thinking on a binary.

What's that?

The idea that something has to be one way or another with no gray zones.

Why no gray zones?

I feel like I'm teaching a class. *Because gray zones are not comfortable places for most people, let alone Americans. Black—white, gay—straight. Polarization. No in-between. We're permanently coded in.*

And you're in-between, then?

I guess you could say that.

Why are Americans like that, you think?

Because they like to take sides, and they don't know any better. Cause it's an angry place, I don't know.

I feel like I'm in-between, too. He looks off, away from the tree to the woods stretching beyond us, darkening, as the sun lowers.

What do you want that woman for?

Margaret.

Yeah.

That's another big question I can't really answer. I feel, in some way, I was born to be a part of this woman's life, but I don't know in what way, yet. I just know I need to find her, talk to her, and I think when I do that, I'll know. I'll know more anyway.

Tambourine stares at me, and I add, *Sometimes you feel like you've known someone before, like long before you were born.*

He nods. *You gotta boyfriend at least?*

I shake my head. *No. I did, but not anymore.*

What happened there?

He died. And then my wife found out and left me and took my daughter.

How'd he die?

In space. He was an astronaut. Space shuttle blew up coming into the atmosphere, and he went with it.

You mean, he could still be up there?

It's possible, but I very much doubt it.

Man you're weird.

I know. Come on, let's go.

Back at the house, I ask to borrow the truck to drive into town to get a sub-sandwich, and Ma reluctantly agrees to let me. Tambourine asks if he can ride along, and I tell him I'll bring him something back. He seems disappointed, but relieved at the prospect of me returning with a sandwich for him. I manage to grab a few things from my room, including Margaret's picture, and drive west towards the tiny intersection that makes up the town.

Lengths of empty green field pass both sides of the road. I drive with the window down, the wind ruffling the cuff of my shirt. To my left, at the edge of the field, ash-black storm clouds cloak the horizon. Cold, rain-scented wind blows from it, carrying the undertones of gravel, dirt, and the electric crackle of energy built in the belly of humidity.

The town intersection is empty, although the stores appear to be open. *Rick's* sign is lit up, glowing in red neon. A single car pumps gas at the station at the end of the road. I park at *Rick's* and go inside the empty store. A fluorescent bulb flickers at the back near a makeshift movie rental corner and crates of orange soda stacked almost to the ceiling. I wait to see if someone will come from the back. I don't hear or see anyone. For a minute, I pretend to shop, and the same man from before enters from the side door in the furthest wall, which leads to some kind of bay for delivery trucks. He nods at me. His eyes squint at the edges; he seems sheepish, as if he's embarrassed about the last time, calling Ma a bitch and giving me orders.

I grab a box of matches and walk up to the counter. He moves more boxes down the yellow hallway to the right of the counter. Zippo lighters with shining American flags, eagles, and skulls flash out at me from dusty plastic cases. Beef jerky sprouts up in a bent cardboard container in front of the register. He straightens the denim of his tucked-in shirt. His blue jeans have grease stains; they're tight on his legs, his brown, pointy boots. His sleeves are rolled to his forearms. He runs his hand through his long black hair, keeping it slicked from his brow down the back of his head. The handlebar mustache seems darker than last time, his face thinner, narrower. He notices me already, knows I'm standing at the register. But he makes me wait until he finishes folding empty boxes, shoving the bulk of them down the back wall into an older stack near the corner. He wipes his hands on his jeans, a signal that says now I'm ready to deal with you.

He approaches the counter, looks at my single box of matches. A smirk pushes up his mustache. He folds his arms over his chest.

That what you came all this way for? Matches?

Maybe.

He waits, slight impatience in his eyes.

No, I say, *it's not. Not at all. I came because I want to talk to you.*

Oh yeah?

I have a lot of questions. Is there somewhere we can go?

He drops his arms to his sides, and his amused expression flattens.

I'm Reese.

He nods. *Rick.*

The proprietor, I imagine.

Yeah, I sure am.

A gap of silence forms until he says, *Okay, let's go back this way, and you can ask your questions. Ma Eldrige send you?*

No, this has nothing to do with her. Well, almost nothing.

I can tell you now, friend, it's got everything to do with that woman.

That's partly why I want to talk to you.

Come around this way. Follow me.

He leads me around the edge of the counter past the register and through the back hall into a larger, colder warehouse with racks full of bread and boxes of vegetables. A strong oniony stench fills the room, hints of wet lettuce, and plastic. Two swinging doors with porthole windows lead to another delivery bay. The cement floor and metal-gray walls push the light to the center of the space. Two wooden desk chairs sit propped in a corner by the bay doors under a post holding different keys on it and some clipboards. One of them leans at an awkward angle. A wooden crate is used as a table between the chairs with a white plastic ashtray sitting on top of torn greasy auto-magazines. He points for me sit down in the leaning chair and takes the one opposite. He lights a cigarette, and doesn't ask if I mind, or if I want one. He leans forward and peers at me with a sudden open expression, as if he can finally be genuine now, and help me, rather than the gruff bullying guy he was the first two times.

What you got? He asks.

You ever seen this woman? I hand him a picture of Margaret.

No, he shakes his head, *no, haven't see this one. That it?*

I'm looking for her—have been looking for her for a while, now, which is why I'm at Ma Eldrige's house.

He sits back into his chair, taking a full look at me, and crosses his arms.

That woman, he says, and shakes his head.

See, I was tipped off by you when you barked at me last time. Seemed like you might have some insight, or know something?

What are you doing, man?

I don't know what you mean.

You're out here with her, and you're looking for this lady— you even know Ma Eldrige before you come here?

No, she found me when I was looking for this woman. I was attacked, and she helped me, told me she heard through the pipeline that I was looking for Margaret. She had been following me, I guess. That part's not exactly clear.

It never occurred to you to ask her.

I have asked her. I ask a lot of things. She's quite good at evading, but she knows intimate things about Margaret, and—

Well, that's all good and fine, but… We all know what she does here. Everyone here knows for the most part. She helps those 'in need'. He makes air-quotes with his hands. Smoke drifts up into the light.

Underground railroad, right?

I'm guessing, but I don't know everything. That's what I thought you were when you come in here.

I'm not.

I can see that now.

She still got the boy living with her?

Tambourine?

Is that his name?

It's the only boy there.

Well, then, that's him.

How much you know about her and that house, that boy?

I only know what three weeks will allow, and I'm only helping her until Margaret shows.

I'm not saying she's not helping the lady you're looking for, or that she hasn't passed on through, but you sure are trusting. You sure you're in the right place? You sure you know who you're dealing with?

And old woman and a young kid?

Well, I guess I don't have to say much about appearances, now do I? You seem smart.

There's quite a bit more to this. You don't know that because you're so blinded looking for your gal.

Am I in danger of some kind?

He shrugs. I'll help you, but you have to help me, too. You'll be helping me by helping yourself.

What do you mean?

Here, he pulls out a small pad of paper from his jeans pocket, and pen from the breast pocket of his shirt. He draws something on it, cigarette held between pressed lips. Then he hands it to me.

There's a house on that street. You just go past this block like the way you come but go for another twenty minutes or so. Turn left on Stone Street. The end of the block. You'll have some answers there.

I don't understand—

Just go there with some questions, you'll be surprised. He grins, and I see all of his teeth, which are oddly unblemished. The smile has traces of something else in it, and I cannot tell if this whole thing has been a ruse, part of a prank for his own amusement, or if he means what he says.

Trust me. That's the house you want.

Why can't you tell me?

I just did. Don't go there today. Go tomorrow. Storm is about to come in anyway, and they're already pumping up the tornado track on the news. You know how they love that. Everybody run for cover, ha! These folk would buy a feedbag of meth before they bought a storm shelter. Fuck.

You never answered my question. Am I in danger here?

Rick shrugs. His eyes glaze, and he stares through me. There's a rumble. Shelves rattle next to us; a couple of tools drop from their posts in the wall.

That a truck?

Earthquake. I'm exhausted. My dreams these days.

I start to speak, but he stops me aware that he's rambling, stretching one hand out between us.

Just go there. That house is what you want. Stone street. But I wouldn't let Ma know about any of this. Keep that little map I made you hidden. The boy doesn't need to know, either. If any of this comes back to me, well, you're gonna be a permanent resident of our fine town after that, if you know what I mean.

On the way back to Ma's house, the clouds are low to the ground and lightening jumps down bright flashes in the curves of purple-blue bellies. Rain thumps the car, and it's the sound of a chorus of urgent fingers beating against the roof. The wipers struggle to keep up. The road is a green blur.

JULY 14:

Two days pass since my conversation with Rick, and I am not able to make it to the house on Stone Street. The storm lasts most of the day and night, and the rain continues into today, although the clouds are breaking up and some sun is slicing through them. Ma Eldrige's yard and house are in constant shadow. She lights candles throughout the living room and dining room, including the ledge lining the stairwell, despite the lamps emitting a diffused orange glow. Old gas lamps in corners near the kitchen flutter in odd drafts, flickering down the hall leading to a bathroom, and Ma's bedroom. The light barely illuminates the white wall paneling, and dust appears to float over their sooty glass encasements. I wonder if they have been changed since the house was originally built.

Ma has asked me to take laundry down from the two lines stretching from the back of the house, fold it, and put it in the kitchen so she can sort it. After I do this, she asks me to check the boiler downstairs, the pipes connecting to her bathroom and the kitchen sink. She believes there is a leak somewhere in the house, and if I could kindly tighten the bolts then all will be fine. She says this while cleaning other things, her back to me. Ma's primary obligation since I have been in her house has been cleanliness. Her preoccupation with it is, at times, staggering. Everything must be tightened, held down, appropriately scrubbed and sanded, brushed clean of any minuscule debris.

In my bedroom, I study the gaps in between the wood and the glass panes of the window overlooking the tree. Tiny white eggs sit in a cluster trapped inside. An insect has laid them here thinking it was safe, or they fell into the gap on their own from another part of the window. They are my secret from Ma; something she can't scrub away.

Tambourine has been quieter since our last conversation. He didn't ask why I returned empty handed two days ago when I promised him a sub-sandwich. He lay in his room; his feet propped on his bed are the only thing visible through the open door. The TV on his tiny desk is turned down low. I spot Jamie Lee Curtis running around Haddonfield.

I creep around the edge of my room as quietly as I can to avoid any conversation and move downstairs to finish the last of Ma's requests before she asks me for more help, this time cooking food for the three of us. In the kitchen she hovers, bent like a crooked wire over a silver tub in the sink. She holds corn in her hands, and she is working the kernels out of them; it amazes me that she simply doesn't pick up a can of it, or maybe it's clear why she doesn't since the corn comes directly from her own backyard.

Her black hair is tied up behind her head, but strands of it still fall around her face, and she doesn't seem to notice, or care. Her glasses, redolent of John Lennon's, are fogged in the steam coming up from the metal tub. She slowly works the corn with both hands, which are tight, spidery. Her white skin is speckled, turning the color of yellow cream around the knuckles. She digs, moves up, digs, moves up. The kernels fall silently. She's only about 5'4", so the sink comes right up under her breasts, which are almost flat. Her body is a scrawny wire. Her face is pointed, always, and somewhat mouse-like. When she looks at something, she peers at it. When she addresses me, she looks down, or at something else needing attention. If she looks up at me for any reason, there is something sharper about what she says or wants done. Certain questions cause her to curl inward, making a hunch of her back, and her focus increases on something else. I know that to suggest things is a better way of asking than to actually ask.

She jerks her shoulder in my direction, doesn't turn from her tub.

You wanna hand me that knife? she asks.

Saying nothing, I locate the butcher knife on the table and place it on the counter by her. She doesn't move to pick it up.

Thank you, here, help me with this, Reese. Can you lift this out of the sink here? Just lift it out and carry it over the counter to the stove there. Just right there. Good.

She picks up the large bowl of corn and slides it in my direction. *Finish these, please. I'm going to start with the rest over here. The oven needs to preheat.*

Do I do this a certain way?

Just like I was doing it. Use the faucet. It usually helps with some water running.

I start popping kernels out of the corn under a thin stream of water over the bowl. It's quiet between us while she works in the corner behind me.

You've gotta wry smile on your face there, Reese. What's causing that?

Corn. I can't believe I'm shucking corn. Is that what this is? Am I shucking corn?

Ma laughs, and it's reedy, full of quiet judgment. *You're making something, that's what you're doing. You never make food this way where you're from?*

Well, I actually can't say, but we mostly had it made for us, or if my mother cooked it was with store bought ingredients.

No garden, then? Nothing you grew yourselves?

I don't think my mother had one, no.

What comes to mind when you think of your mother?

Drinking, mostly.

That can't be all you think of. It's your mother.

Loudness?

Well, I can tell by the way you are that she loved you.

How can you tell that?

Just something you can tell.

What do unloved people look like? I turn my head so I can see her, and she's peering up at me over her glasses with an incredulous expression.

Well, Reese, I think you have an idea of what that looks like. At least some. I see it all the time, the people that come through here. There's a surplus of unloved people in the world; people that were born on accident, not wanted, forced into whatever situation would have them. They all have a look of decision about them.

Decision? I turn back to my bowl, the stream of water.

Yeah. Like they're deciding whether or not they wanna stick around? You know? Even the ones who had married parents their whole lives.

Love is wanting someone around, then?

Oh. Well, hell, it's not that simple. No, no, not that simple. It's complicated, but it doesn't have to be.

Cruel world and all that?

Mmmm, I don't know about the world, but cruelty's a given. Especially here, where we live.

What does that mean? I look at her again. This time she's putting clumps of chopped vegetables in the tub.

Well, you might be from one part of the Bible Belt, but you haven't been in this one long.

Oklahoma?

This place will chew you up and spit you out.

Me, personally? Or just anyone?

That boy upstairs, she gestures with a handful of chopped green peppers. *He's been chewed up and spit out plenty.*

I gather that.

Can't even go to school with regular people and be a normal kid without someone choking him to death with religion.

I've heard much about the religion thing in this state.

You haven't lived it. Just last year, a kid murdered in his own backyard by four other boys for being a gay.

You mean: 'gay', not a gay.

Well, he wasn't even that, he just didn't act how they wanted. Or, who knows, but they stabbed him to death. Fourteen years old. And now their lives are ruined. And for what? Religion said so. That's what.

An ongoing problem with mankind it seems.

Well, here it's endless.

You know a woman came up to me during a break at a rest

stop when I took the bus here, and she kept telling me it's a cursed state. Any idea what she meant by that?

No, but if I were to think on it, I'd say she means the Indians—

Native Americans—

—who were sent here to die. You can't have a state free of ghosts with that kind of horror.

Why do they call it 'Native America' then, if they were sent here to die?

The Trail of Tears is an understatement in my book, Reese. Retribution comes somehow, and maybe that's why all of these folk hate their lives so much, hate others so much, and use their religion to justify it. The state is cursed like the lady said.

Where are the Native Americans here? It seems…muted, like the culture is not at the forefront where it should be.

They're here, they just mind their own. Can't say I blame them. But these small towns, you know, places like Minco, Dibble, Tuttle—and let me tell you, the Trash really comes from Tuttle—they got small minds. Lot of influx from places like Kansas, Arkansas, Texas. Small towns, small minds. You in the Big Slow and Dumb, honey. Slow and dumb.

Isn't that unfair to yourself, though? Surely not everyone's like that.

People always want to say that, and it's a poor excuse. I just bide my time in this place. I don't consider myself a part of it. Maybe why the locals don't like me so much.

I hesitate before saying what I want to say, and there's a queer silence. Finally, I let it out: *You know, Rick the other day at your grocery store wasn't the nicest when he saw I was with you.*

I'm not surprised. He's an asshole. A lot of assholes here.

He told me to tell you if you want groceries to go in and get them yourself.

Ma drops her utensils, and I turn around to see her with a hand on her stomach, a deep laugh pouring out of her.

He would say that. Yes he would. Been going there for years, doesn't change anything. He's always sweet to Tambourine, so he can hate me all he likes.

A couple of days ago, Tambourine took me on a bit of a hike.

Did he?

He did. Great country back there.

There's a lot of it.

We walked pretty far in, and he wanted to show me a tree.

Ma goes quiet, a compressed silence.

He tried to tell me he was born in it, and that you found him there. Do you know about this?

I do know about it. And I did find him there. There's not much to say about it, frankly, but that was an act of kindness that he told you, let alone took you there. He doesn't do that. For anyone.

What do you know about his parents? How did he end up in there? How did you find him?

Reese, I've gotta bitch of twist in my lower back, will you help me move this. I just need it to move it so I can ladle some of this into the oven.

I drop the corn back into its bowl, and turn to help Ma move the tub, which is brimming with bright diced, vegetables. She makes too much food—more than is necessary for three people, shoving the excess into little yellow containers in the fridge.

Okay, you've done enough, she says. *Go tell Tambourine to get ready. And wash your hands.*

JULY 15:

I tell Ma that I will run all of her errands in town, buy everything she needs, and fill up her tank. She agrees without much of a challenge, satisfied to have someone take charge. She seems convinced about my status at her house, that I'm webbed-in, and that I'll do any chore as long as it means I'll be seeing Margaret soon.

Using the map drawn by Rick, I drive directly past the intersection, past his store, which is closed, and further south. The street changes, and I'm driving under thick, heavy foliage; the trees have formed a tunnel with their branches, shading the entire street, and the tiny houses lining it. The yards are mostly mud, speckled in dead leaves. Some are bound in chain-link fences showing scattered orange and yellow plastic children's toys. One has a giant green turtle sandbox with the lid half on its back. The houses might have been built around the 1940s. The porches are darkened. Small cement steps lead up into the murk. The street continues, marked in the zig-zag of snakelike tar lines covering old gaps in the pavement. Further ahead, the houses lessen, and the left side of the road is a bare field. Multiple pick-up trucks, and a squat black Geo with shattered taillights, are parked at the curb.

The further I drive, the houses become less and, soon,

it's nothing but fields on both sides of the road with a mixture of tall, dead grass waving in slight pulls of wind. To the left is the highway just a couple of miles from the neighborhood. Tiny cars curve up, around, and away from the town far back, out of sight. Ten minutes later I arrive at Stone Street, and turn left. It's a cul-de-sac with four houses near the entrance of the road. I park near the end of it along the curb, and get out.

One house is painted gray-blue; the others are plain white but stained from the mud around their yards. More ramshackle chain-link fences ring in the houses. A plastic, yellow and red sunflower spins near a sagging wooden mailbox. The soft jingle of wind chimes drifts from one of the porches. All of these houses and streets appear derelict of people, of activity. The purr of cars from the highway is slightly audible where I stand, and I examine the map Rick made for me, searching for the location of the house he drew, and circled, as if to emphasize its whereabouts.

I walk around the truck and up the curb to the bare patch of grassy land where the house should be. The ground appears scorched, and chunks of cement fill in parts of it. Up ahead, to my left, is a man in overalls that have been made into shorts. His bald head catches the glint of the sun as he pees in the grass. He twists side-to-side, sprinkling the grass in an arc of urine. His socks sag on his ankles under legs the color and texture of cottage cheese. When he finishes peeing, he zips himself up, and then looks around with his hands on his hips. When he spots me, he waves, smiling, apparently oblivious to the fact that I just watched him take a leak. As he gets closer, I notice he's wearing black sneakers covered in burs.

Hello! He reaches out to shake my hand, and asks, *Can I help you?*

I take his hand apprehensively.

Actually, yes. My friend drew this map for me, and I'm looking for a house that should be here. Am I in the right place?

Let me take a look at that. He pulls the paper from my fingers, squints at it.

This is Stone Street, correct?

You are right, there. Yes, sir, the house you're looking for, you're standing in it.

I am? This is it?

This is it.

Well, I'm a bit confused. Is my friend wrong, perhaps? He told me just a couple of days ago that it was here.

Uh huh. Well, who's your friend if you don't mind me askin'?

He's not really my friend, to be honest. I just met him at the grocery store. He owns Rick's. Told me this house would be here.

Uh huh. Rick. Well, I'm not surprised there. What do you want with this house? Been gone a long time. He knows that.

He does? How long?

Been over a year, he says, flattening a hand over his eyes like a visor, squinting down at me, angry suddenly.

What happened to it?

Burned down. Answer my question: what do you want with it?

You live on this block?

None of your damn business. Now if you can't answer my question, I'm gonna call the god damn police—

I'm trying to find a friend, okay? I'm looking for someone. Rick said I might find some answers here.

Well, he of all people knows better. I can't guess for the life of me why he sent you out here when he knows that.

How did it burn down? Does anyone know?

The man looks away from me, doesn't say anything. When he looks up his mouth is a grim line.

I'm not sayin' I agree with what was done, but some folks want to move on, you understand. The family that lived here was long gone before that house went up. I know that, and I've been on this block twenty years.

Where did they go? What happened to them?

They weren't good people, son. They left. What they—

They left the town?

No. They moved further inward. Out to the forest.

The forest?

Yeah, old houses out there. Falling apart, but there are some of them.

Can you tell me how to find them?

He hesitates, then says, *They're gone. I don't even know who you are, or anything. I'm just out here tryin' to enjoy my day.*

I understand that, but you'd be helping me quite a bit.

All right, give me that paper there. I'll draw you a better one than Rick's.

I hand him a pen, and the map. He flips it over and begins to sketch.

You think Rick was just having some fun sending me here?

Uh, no, I don't. I think he know what he's done. It ain't funny, but he done it.

What would that be?

Rick—and don't go back to him with this, either—but he was in love with one of 'em. A smile perks his lips as if incredulous amusement fills him at the thought.

One of who?

Them. That lived here. Sissy.

Oh really? Why is that—

He real broken up about it. Always has been. But he couldn't compete. The fire, them leaving, all of it. He'd come here when they weren't even in the house anymore. Just wander around here. Lookin'.

Can you tell me what this family did?

He glances up at me, and his face is a perfect rendering of the word 'grave'. He shoves the paper and pen back into my hand, and I can feel the force of his meaty arm.

They was bein' with each other.

Being with each other?

You want me to say it again? They was bein' with each other! Understand? Now go on. Get out of here!

I'm sorry. I don't understand, actually.

Well, you dig long and hard enough and you gonna understand.

I look down at his map. I'm able to make out the forest and a single square block with an arrow pointing away from it.

What's this? I ask, indicating the block he drew.

That's Ma Eldrige's place. Stay away from it. Otherwise you're liable to be in some deep shit.

He turns away, shoulders up, hands in pockets and walks back the way he came. The abruptness of it, his movement away from me, stops me from saying anything more.

That night, Ma doesn't come out of her room. The door at the end of the hall remains shut. I approach it and knock softly, calling, *Ma? You okay?* And no answer comes. Voices mumble from Tambourine's TV upstairs. In the kitchen, multiple yellow bowls containing Ma's excess food clutter the counter tops near the back door. What does she do with all of them?

Tambourine's door is also shut. I consider knocking, but go to my room instead. Watery light comes through the part of the window not covered by the curtains. The sun drops slowly, leaving gray-white light on the floor and walls, the bed in half-shadow. When I lie down, my body releases and my eyes close. They flutter open and catch more of that same light. My breath eases and, between this place and another, I dream:

The room is a cold likeness of the room in which I'm staying, now, except the walls are green, and the light comes from an unknown source because there are no windows. Stretching around the mattress, and all the way to the open door, is a frothing body of water. Ocean water. Parts of it are clear from the light, but much of it is dark, and I know, somehow, that there are things in it. Swimming right under the surface is something big. The longer I lie there negotiating ways to get to the open door across from me—where the water seems to stop—the more helpless I feel. I have no way to make it from the bed to the door without the thing underneath swooping up and taking a bite from me. And it will kill me. I know this with a thick twist in my stomach; that it will swallow me completely. I can feel the chill of the water from the mattress, and I sit up.

I'm on my side, and I look over the edge of the bed down into the churning water. My eyes search it, and then I see the pointed head of the thing. It's right there, looking forward, waiting for me to notice it. I see its black eyes, and the length of it sliding back down into the darkness below. It just sits there, inanimate, as if waiting to be brought into life, but it *is* alive, and furthermore, it knows I'm looking at it. It's just letting me look at it. Something about it is smiling, now, at my fear of it. It rises to the surface, and I cringe further back onto the bed and up against the wall.

Dripping, glistening, it lifts its head from the frothing waves, and rises, leaning its large head towards me on the bed. It's part-shark with the body of a snake. There is a plastic quality to it. Its shiny, gray snout lifts up with an awareness that shoots dread through my stomach. Lips pull back, and its teeth are unbroken rows of jagged white triangles in black gums, revealing a black throat rimmed in red. It leans towards me, using its snake body to push further up out of the water, getting closer to me, sniffing at me. A deep rumble comes from under the bed, or from the creature itself, and the hiss of the water grows louder. When I turn away from it to my left, I roll right into the face of another one staring directly at me. Its head is equally huge, gray, and seemingly older than the one lifting higher and closer. It opens its mouth and releases the same grumble. It's on the bed with me, half out of the water.

The walls rattle, and there is a deep booming sound coming from under the water, from whatever is outside of this room. Boom, boom, boom, boom! Something slams its body into the walls of the house, and I know that I'm in a house, now; that they're trying to bring it down, sharks slamming their heavy bodies hard into the foundation. I'm slick with sweat, as the two snake-sharks stay arched above me, daring me to move while the pounding increases. This is happening somewhere, I tell them. This is really happening, right now. I've lived this. I've known you before.

Ma's voice is what wakes me, screeching my name, *Reese, Reese, hurry up, come downstairs, come downstairs, hurry!* I stand from the bed onto the floor, and I'm hit with the slippery feeling of low blood sugar. I peel off my shirt and put on a clean one, then head downstairs to see why Ma Eldrige is calling me.

Guilt might be the last failsafe indicator of someone who is fully human. I distinguish full human beings from those that are not entirely human by this emotion. I do not determine it by their organic, physical form. I no longer look at a person and think, well, that's a human being because they possess a particular body, a *human* body; but, if I can discern an emotion in them like guilt, for instance, then I know that I am seeing a real human.

Outside, in the back of the house, I watch Ma pace in a half-circle, her jittery hands moving from the center of her chest, to her neck, and her face is pure guilt. Although, why this guilt is so profound a force in her is a mystery to me. Her house has split apart from a corner of the foundation to the roof, and it looks like someone painted a giant black stretch of lightening down the white, wooden siding, a black zig-zag. It almost looks comical.

The ground around this specific corner has also split open—a jagged explosion of muddy earth tossed back to reveal several layers of color underneath in the stark moonlight, shining bright and cold. The tree, visible from my window, has been uprooted, and leans back from the ground. Stringy roots shoot from under it, like a plucked hairbrush; the darker parts are clumped in solid, black mud, some of which dangles from the roots closest to the outside of the tree. Its branches lay flush with the ground; a possibility that might never have occurred to anyone living here during its existence, and it lays like a felled animal, leaves scattered silver in the light above. The forest behind the house is a silhouette, and the rest of the property is invisible in the dark. Stars can only be seen near the darkest parts, like sharp signals.

Ma paces. She mumbles to herself, and moans. Tambourine stands between us wearing a yellow and black striped tank top. His arms hang at his sides and he stares up at the house, silent. Ma's frantic movements increase, but no one says anything.

What am I going to do? What am I going to do?

Finally, I say, *Ma, look, can you call somebody? Do you have insurance?*

No one I can call, Reese.

Do you know what might have caused this?

Where were you just a minute ago? You didn't feel the ground shaking us to pieces?

I was sleeping—

Another earthquake. Biggest one we've had this year. And my insurance doesn't cover damage caused by them. My god, is my house leaning?

Ma, there has to be someone you can call that can help.

No one will help me with this. Not here, she says and walks away from us into the dark far out behind the house. I follow Tambourine inside. In the kitchen he shows me where I can make tea. I observe the house anew, seeking in it the changes wrought from the outside. Does it lean like Ma said it might? Is it crooked, now, slanting at a perceivable angle? Part of me senses that it does. The maroon tiles in the kitchen glimmer under the low, yellow glow of the stove light. Tambourine takes over my shoddy job of making tea and moves rapidly throughout the kitchen grabbing cups, and pouring the water. He joins me at the table. We sit there in silence for some time before either of us says anything. His face is drawn, weighted. His gaze is frozen on his cup. He looks like he is on the edge of admitting something, but holds himself back.

So tornados and earthquakes, I mutter.

He nods his head.

I guess they're pretty bad out here.

They get worse at night.

How long have you been having them?

A while now.

You guys are being swallowed by your own land. Surely there's someone who's looking out for the people here.

They look out for themselves.

That makes sense, unfortunately.

I guess Ma won't be back for a while.

She does this when she gets mad. Goes far out there.

I can't say that I blame her. Watching your home crack apart like this would do it to anyone.

She's a bit helpless.

Really?

Well, yes and no.

Do you think you'll stay here? After you graduate—or finish your studies, I mean?

I'm gonna be homeschooled. But I don't want to be. I know homeschooled kids, and they're fuckin' weird.

I never thought about it, but I see your point.

And no, I don't want to stay here. I want to get as far as possible from it. When I can. When I have money, or something. Why don't you answer your own question: would you stay here?

I'm just traveling through.

Everyone is.

Maybe you can answer something for me.

What?

Why does Ma make so many leftovers?

He shrugs.

When people come through here, how long do they stay, usually?

A few days, he says, sometimes longer, like you.

Anyone stay more than that?

Yeah, but they're gone eventually.

Where do they go? Do you know?

Ma has contacts all over. She sets them up, sends them off when they're ready. Sometimes they come back, sometimes they don't.

That simple?

I guess. I don't pay much attention to it. I mean I try to steer clear.

Any idea who these contacts are, or where they are?

No.

When Margaret was here, do you remember what she was like?

He lifts his head, and the expression on his face tells me he genuinely wants to provide me a real answer.

I saw her twice only.

He looks at me directly, and I encourage him to go on.

I saw her in the living room. She was sitting on the edge of the sofa. She had wild, curly, gray hair, and she seemed peaceful, not scared, not like others that come through here.

What about the second time?

I saw her upstairs in the bedroom Ma set aside for her. She was standing at the window touching the plants. She smiled at me.

Why didn't you talk to her?

I don't know. That kind of niceness is scary.

What do you mean?

She seemed like she had no hate in her, like none at all. I haven't ever seen anyone like that in my life. Everyone got some hate in them somewhere, just under it all. Some got enough to kill.

That made you afraid?

How much niceness you been exposed to, cause I bet you an' I have different experiences.

He looks down, and I feel a mire of shame rise up in me. My face blanches and emptiness eats at my stomach. I try to recover by saying: *Everyone has shit in life.* But, it's lame, and he knows it.

Maybe everyone has shit in their life, but some have more of it than others and, anyway, I don't want to talk about it.

He pauses. *Do you think our house will collapse? Like in the night, when we're sleeping?*

I don't know. I'm wondering the same thing.

I mean, how are we supposed to sleep when the ground is doing that?

Might be a while before we can.

What if our house just slides all the way down? In the night. And we don't hear it or see it cause we're asleep, pressed under it, and then we die?

I wouldn't go that far.

What if another one hits us? A bigger one than the last.

Tambou—Do you have a nickname? Something else you go by?

You can call me Tam if you want. It's shorter.

Okay, Tam. What's the worst thing you can reasonably say would happen? What could you do about any of it?

I could lose the only place I have to live, for one. What kind of question is that? Someone not far from here just got crushed when their house went down from the quakes, and the bridges in the cities are crumbling; there's a lot of bad that can happen.

I just meant what you can control.

I don't know anymore. A lot of this is manmade.

That is correct.

You know what I saw the other day? On TV? Shark soup. People are killing thousands of sharks in the ocean so they can have them in a soup.

I've heard of this.

Why would anyone want to kill an animal so they can eat it in a soup?

I don't answer, but he continues.

We're like the sharks, now. And the ground is eating us. I guess that's what you get when you shit where you eat.

Great saying.

Shark soup. All of those animals killed because some rich fuckers think they're ingesting the power of the ocean.

Some people embrace the stereotypes they're handed. For those without an identity, it's like something readymade.

I know. Look at Oklahoma.

Maybe one day you'll be able to do something about all this.

Or maybe there's a parallel universe, and the sharks are getting revenge.

You're very wise, Tam.

July 18:

The sky over the house is cloudless, and the sun is a hot, white eye over the property, and the trees lining the back of it. The wind has stopped, and heat rises from warm, red soil. The humidity underneath it is like a threat, occasionally teasing at the brief, dry air.

From where I stand, near the edge of the forest where Tambourine took me last time, I see Ma walking around the back of her house with two inspectors. The inspectors are like gray slashes next to a tiny, hunched Ma Eldrige. They move around it, making notes, squatting and peering up at the giant crack in its façade. The interior has been scrutinized, and they are doubtless that the house is in fact leaning a slight percentage to the left.

Ma's body conveys devastation, a gaunt, hallowed stare in every expression, as if she's being pushed slowly through a vise, crushed and strangled. She barely notices me, or Tambourine. Annoyed with her, and the inspectors, Tambourine takes a long walk to the town. Why he does this is never really clear. Except, I can only surmise that it's his way of being by himself; in the house, neither of us is ever really alone when Ma's present.

Now that she's distracted with the inspectors, I decide to take my new map, the one drawn by the stranger pissing near the burned lot on Stone Street, and go back into the woods to find the place he drew. Two different people, two different maps. I step into the trees aware of anxiety notched right in the place under my heart—I don't want this to lead to another burned lot, and no answers.

At the riverbed, I see our old footprints, Tambourine's and mine, faded and sealed with new mud and dead leaves. I follow them, and something ricochets through me, a crackling at the back of my skull; it's the weird sense of following myself all over again, a parallel; this is evidence of me at a particular point, and now I'm hitting the same exact point, but for different reasons, and the anxiety in my chest boils into a kind of dread. A parallel, I'm certain, that connects to something much larger.

Up the side of the embankment, and over to the other side, and I'm standing back at Tam's tree. I marvel at its blackness, how saturated it is with liquid, soaked through and glistening. Moss on the knuckles of its hiked and bulging roots appears stagnant, as if it can't grow any thicker due to the deep wetness of its bark, which is slick, and reminds me of snake skin. I reach out to touch it, wondering how it will feel in my grip, if it will pour sap with the slightest squeeze. When I do, I'm shocked by its hardness, the brittle, dry feeling under my fingers, and my dread doubles. There is something unnatural about it, and this realization comes right when I notice the hole where Tambourine keeps his letters. It is sealed with a massive rock choking the space. The width and density of it is too much for Tambourine to lift with his slender arms and limited range of movement; I wonder what caused it, or who.

I back away, looking up at its black, bowing limbs, at

the leaves glowing deep green, and march further into the forest. Eventually, the ground levels out, and the land appears to stretch in directions that offer no differences—just trunk after trunk after trunk, and grass struggling to grow under a dense canopy. Birds call out around me, their echoes among the quiet skittering of other animals ruffling the underbrush. I walk for about ten minutes and find a muddy road of sorts made with tire tracks, and some gravel, although it's scattered poorly throughout, and the road itself seems to have remained here by sheer default of how many times it's been travelled; however, it doesn't appear to be of use recently.

I don't know which way to go, so I take it up to the right, closest to where the man drew buildings on the map, and it starts to rise along a slight hill which, at the crest, I can see a row of A-frame houses that look oddly like ski lodges, or cabins from the 1970s. There are four nestled awkwardly amid the rest of the forest. Tiny porches with small railings and three steps lead down to the muddy road. The windows facing me are dark. The trimming on the roof is a faded maroon and the doors—once bright orange-yellow—have washed-out with time. Leaves clot portions of their slates, and only two of them have chimneys. The design of the rooftops allows the edges to reach almost to the ground, like a box set under two leaning cards. The furthest of the four from the road has a round dent in its roof like a giant thumb pressed into it, causing it to sag. Water drips from the canopy above me, from somewhere behind the row of cabins. Otherwise, it's quiet. I look again at the map, and this location seems to match-up.

I walk up the last part of the road to the first cabin. The smell of leaf-rot and mildew pours from its small, enclosed porch. I move up its steps and attempt a knock on its faded door, and feel ridiculous for doing so. Nothing is here. I try the knob, and it doesn't move. I step down and try the next one, and it's the same.

The third one, however, opens. I slide the front door back, slowly revealing soaked, beige carpet turned black in some corners, and a tiny, cramped living room with a wooden, country-style coffee table. Magazines—crinkled from age and dampness—are stacked underneath its glass top; a few boxes of dominos are adjacent to them. Light from outside comes through the sliding glass doors covered in mold. They lead to a grimy back porch. Flush with the back wall is a brown, bloated sofa from some time in the 1980s. The whole interior is made of fake wood paneling. The kitchen to the right has red-orange countertops. A plastic, green frog magnet is stuck to the side of a yellow refrigerator halfway between the counter, as if it's hiding there and peeking out next to a stack of unused paper plates.

A hallway with four doors extends from the living room; one door at the end, and two along the right-hand side. The one closest to the front door, I assume, is a coat closet. I start to move down the hall, and I hear a moan, suddenly, a deep, low-voiced moan coming from one of the two doors at its end. The sound is throaty, or agitated, and there's something vaguely sexual about it, but not pleasurable sex, something muffled and fearful. My throat and mouth become dry and my chest aches from my heart slamming, as if someone were yanking on it through my ribs with a hard wire, rendering me breathless. The moan escalates. Has someone been squatting in this place, or is this the genuine home of a person stashed at the far back end of this hall?

I step quietly towards the door, and lean into the corner, waiting to hear where the sound is coming from. Something slams into the door on my right, hard, like a ball, and I jerk back. There is some murmur of conversation behind it, and the softer tones of a television with the volume turned down, then movement again like someone adjusting themselves on a bed, sheets scraping, and the moan repeats.

H-hello? I try. There is no response, so I attempt it again and then turn the knob.

In the open the doorway, light from a window across from me illuminates a room painted Pepto-Bismol-pink. A small closet with an accordion door in the right wall leads to a brown wall-length desk stacked sparsely in old children's books, and crayons. On the beige carpet—cleaner than the carpet in the living room—is a pile of blankets, light-blue, white, and yellow, and they're spooled around a television my parents might have had in their kitchen in Florida, but in the 1990s—compact with a VCR attached to its bottom.

The long, gray body of a person stretches across a twin mattress on the left side of the room. The mattress is set into a part of the wall that recedes. It was clearly meant to accommodate a bed of this size. The body is almost too big for it, however. The legs reach to the furthest corner.

They're the color of old clay, grayish and dimpled. The feet are huge, and the toenails on them stick up yellow, long, and thick. I cannot tell if it's a man or a woman. White shorts ride up high on their thighs, which look even more dimpled and ashen. Their shirt is also white, but too small for their torso, and it lifts to show the blank, gray expanse of their stomach.

Their chin and throat is a similar color, but there is no definable jaw—just a throat rising up into a face with a hole in it, where dark, purple lips form a suggested mouth. The cheekbones cave inward, as if their face has wasted. The pallid skin is in high contrast to the choppy, black hair sprouting off their scalp. Their eyes are equally black and watery, and stay thoroughly connected to the events on the television. They don't appear to notice me at all, their eyes moving side-to-side, rapidly, and then another high-pitched moan rolls up from their open mouth, a protestation to something in the muted show. They do it again. Their arms are almost too long, it seems, with broad, masculine hands, the color of which is nicotine-yellow. They move them, as if they're heavy to lift, then place them onto their stomach and crotch, where they start to rub themselves, like they're trying to put something inside their skin.

The moaning starts to escalate, and some words follow, unintelligible at first, but gaining clarity: *Mmmmm m mm mm momm mmmy mmmooommy mommmm my my, tuuuucchhes tuuuuuuuches tutches mmmmeeeeee.*

I catch one of Ma's little, yellow bowls protruding from a darkened corner under the bed with bits of corn, and other dried up food, encrusted around its plastic edges, like tiny pies. I begin to back out of the room, slowly closing the door. But before I can completely move away, I try to stop the wave of anxiety in my chest, and the feeling of cold up my spine, and I'm not entirely successful until I am back in the woods and the house is no longer visible on my path.

JULY 15 / MA'S CONFESSION:

Ma asks me to join her in the living room with the curtains drawn back, revealing a brightly lit front yard, the dirt drive, and the empty road. She eases into an old chair filled with down feathers and sits across from the place I take on the couch. One of the old gas lamps has been left on, and it sputters orange light up the wall behind her. Her accent is mostly gone when she speaks, her voice adopting a sudden, strange clarity, as if she's been this other person the whole time, and the guise nothing but a thin tissue positioned casually to the side.

I suppose, Reese—I suppose I should start by apologizing to you; that's what everyone wants, right? An apology. I'm assuring myself that they still work because I don't have much by way of restitution for you. And you deserve it. If anyone deserves it, it's you, so let me start with that: an apology. And, in a way, you can see this as another version of that other meaning of the word, by which people derive an explanation of sorts, and I know that's what you're really after, isn't it? You can't go without one, and I wouldn't expect you to. Not after what you've seen.

Should I start with blame? That's where I want to start. I'm not entirely sure it's the right place, but it's where so many things begin, isn't it? Blame is easy. We're good at it, and I mean all people, not just you, but myself, and especially today; I mean, look at the new modes of discourse, blame everywhere! You remember Hester Prynne? Well, of course you do. I think of her a lot, and I know she's just someone we look to in a fiction story, but she's always been real to me because the scapegoat's the biggest part of how we exist and create, and make decisions about how a thing should be done. I've had to negotiate that myself a lot; you wouldn't believe it, but I have. Hester got stuck with that 'A', and a whole town that points its finger, condemning, hypocritically, because they're such, well, hollow people, Reese, carved through and empty of anything substantial; they're like animals reacting, the fear of disapproval of their cohorts right at the backs of their heads. So they punish others for the same crimes, and they let those go free who are manifestations of guilt; they do everything wrong because they're selfish, and where's the comeuppance in that? Where is justice, now? There's small justice and big justice, and then there's the justice no one sees or hears from; it's not in the public arena, the bully pulpit—it's just quiet and no one ever needs to know about it, and to me that's real justice, the quiet kind. There's nothing vigilante about it, either, because even that has a bit of show to it, a bit of theater for more approval that tries to say. See, I'm on the right side of things, and you aren't, and they say to themselves afterwards that this makes them better than you. Well, it doesn't, cause we all rot. And when you take away someone's route to superiority, to feeling *better than someone, then you reduce him; you take away his ability to hate, and that's the quickest way to do it. We all rot, and we all go down to the same place, and the rest is bullshit, if you ask me. But what I try to do here is a little bit rectifying. I try to help people get a better life, and maybe better mine in the process while I do so, and if that makes me a monster to the bastards in this shit town, then so be it. They're as much to blame, but they still point, hollow and animal-like, and do nothing. I took charge. I did something. And I know they're afraid of me because of it; that, and my connections and whatever else, but I doubled their fear once I made a decision. They don't have all the answers, they don't have proof, but they have the suggestions of things, and that's enough to send them spinning.*

You came at a bad time, and I don't know that there's ever really a good one, but you came looking for that girl, and you mean it with every part of you, and you stay here waiting for her, and waiting for her, and my guilt becomes like cement all through me. I get so heavy with it every time I look at you. I don't know why I ever thought you wouldn't find these things out; that you wouldn't somehow eventually have someone talk to you in town, seeing as you were with me, and then they led you to the right places; it was going to happen, it just was, but I had to think otherwise. I just had to. And Rick will always be mad at me for what he thinks I've done. He loved Sissy. He's right about what was done, of course, but he still doesn't know for sure, and that makes him angry. And people in towns like this—they've got very little besides anger and a childish need to get their way.

The people I mention, their names are Sissy and John Danforth. They lived in that house Rick sent you to the first time, you said. Their family has been in this town since my family and helped develop parts of it, although they were on the poorer side, and their father, Tate Danforth, was the resident religious man. He set forth many of the town's laws, and he started the church here, too, which has been closed for the last five or six years, but he started it, and the library, he helped with that.

Sissy and John Danforth were normal children. They were quiet sometimes, but they were a normal brother and sister, and they were good to their parents. And I struggle with this, but there is no other way to put it, no other way, than to say it, and that's that Tate encouraged them. He encouraged them. I found this out from Sissy later on, when she came to me out of fear, but not much I said was going to change what was going on, and Tate saw to that. He kept them closed in, away from the rest of the town, and their house became like a secret that everyone avoided. She told me it started because John hit the stage all men hit and asked his father for advice, and said that as long as it's a man with a woman, then it's okay. And before you point out the literality of his thinking, you have to understand, their religion moved away from standard practices to one that was off the map; they created their own form of Christianity that was more extreme than the Evangelicals, so it's my thought the literal thinking came from that, but it's also a perversion and rationalization. Regardless, Tate encouraged his children, and since they believed it was good and right, due to it being between just a man and a woman, they continued.

And that's when the first one happened. No one knew about it. She said it was dealt with behind closed doors. She said Tate beat her to pieces for aborting, told her it was against God, and she said after that she was afraid to say anything at all.

I promised her I'd go to the police, but she pleaded with me not to; that it would only make things worse, which is what you would expect to hear from someone like Sissy. It's trite, but then Sissy stopped coming around, and I never heard from her after that. And the police wouldn't have done anything, anyway; I know that, now. The chief was too big a fan of Tate to interfere, and that's all you need to know about that. Neighbors became aggressive the way animals become aggressive when they sense a threat on the border of their little community. They throw rocks at it, scream names, threaten it until it goes away. And that's what Tate did, he moved 'em. They took up residence out there in one of the houses you saw. They were out there for a good year before I saw Sissy again, and a number of years after that. She had lost all of her youthful weight, and was like a stick in a beige dress walking around the back of the house. I'd catch her, and sometimes invite her in, hoping to say something that would help because it was clear she was in pain and couldn't find a way out of it; but how can you help people who push back on the help? What can you do? I always acknowledged her; let her know she could come here any time. By this point, everyone here had an idea about what I do, and the help I give to others, but they did the smart thing, and minded their own, and I think this is because of what happened to Tate, Sissy, and her brother.

I went out there. What else was I going to do? I wanted to see what was happening to Sissy, so I took the path, probably the same one you took, and came with something I'd made to leave with them. It was pretense, but you can't just show up somewhere here with nothing when you plan to snoop, or else you're too known to them. So, I went, and I never got an answer at the door, the one that had lights on, but I was able to see through the windows, and what I saw was enough.

I started watching them, going out there regularly. I don't know if they knew, but that's what I did. The babies died, one after the next, stillborn, or alive for a while, and then dead soon after. She buried two of them out there. The other you know about, and yes, I found him, bobbing there still wrapped up in his placenta. She had hooked his cord to a part of the tree and set it in the ground there. It was raining, so he stayed afloat even though he was near death. I don't know how he stayed living, but that boy did. Sissy was mostly gone by then, just operating like she was in a dream, and couldn't be talked to; I don't know what she was trying to do by putting him there, but she did. I don't believe in accidents, or coincidence, and so I went and took that baby; I brought him here and took care of him. I got him going.

The one you found, I still bring him food. He was born about six years before, and I saw in my spying how they tended to him, feeding him always. They're brothers, but they don't know each other, and they don't need to know. I take care of them both. That's neither here nor there, but I knew this had to stop; this letting it go on like it was because of religion and how people in this place protect those who live behind beliefs, even if it causes harm to themselves and others; invented beliefs, *elaborated beliefs, all of it. It just couldn't go on. I wasn't going to let it go on, especially the quiet acceptance of the people here once it was out of their way, like it was less offensive somehow because as Tate said, at least it's only a man and a woman.*

So, like I said, I took care of it. I went out there, and I took care of it. All of three of them gone. The people here, they knew I had done something because no one saw or heard from the Danforth's again. That simple. There was just no more of them, and people stayed quiet around me; it's like they could tell I had made something happen that they thought about, but it horrified them. I can't understand how so little else seemed to. It's unimportant how I did what I did. It was done, and that's what's important. No more torture of Sissy, no more births, no more pain. I did what I had to, and I did what was right. And if you're thinking what I think you're thinking, then I'll remind you of good ol' Hester. Think about that long and hard.

I lied to you from the outset, about how I come to find you, and what I was doing that night. That man you met under the bridge, Quinton, called me on his cell phone to tell me some guy is asking about Margaret, and Quinton is kind of an in-between man down there, but he keeps his eye out for me in case people come looking, if you know what I mean, and so I gave him the order. Don't be mad, don't be upset, I had to have them take you down; them driving and hitting you was a warning, but then I drove up myself to take a look at you since I was down there myself, already helping another. And I saw you were no one of concern, just some guy looking for this person. I felt awful, Reese, and I tried to compensate by bringing you here. But—and this is the hardest thing for me—the worst of all this, is what I have to tell you, now. I know you will be devastated; and I know there's nothing I can do to stop that. But I don't have a choice, except to come clean with you. Margaret is never coming back. She's not.

None of them ever come back. That's a rule I have. If they show up, it's a fluke. And I didn't tell you that because you seemed so genuine and forthright, and like you needed something. Something I thought I could give you. I wanted to help you, too, Reese. And I didn't think that lady was the way to do it, and I'm sorry, I was wrong. I've been wrong. I did something I shouldn't have by lying to you. Having you here to help has been so nice, so good for me, and all of us. I thought maybe, after time, you'd stop wanting to find her and just stay here with us, and be like a father to Tambourine. How could I expect that of you? You were gonna go in search of her. Although, I will say, Tambourine loves you. He still goes out to that tree, leaving letters in it; I put a stop to that, too, though. He needs to find the path away from his childhood. I thought that might be you, but I suppose you'll want to leave now. Everyone does, eventually.

NIGHT:

I stand between the house and the felled tree, staring at its branches reaching like dead fingers into the cold moonlight. The multitude of chirruping crickets fills the space with gentle sound. The wind is still, and the humidity has dropped, so that the night has a quick coolness about it. The stars burn halos of silver against a dome of blue-black night. The lights on the side of Ma's porch leak dimly into the front yard, while those on the side and the back shine starkly near the corner, showing the aggressive, black crack in the side of the house. Somehow, it appears to have expanded as if it's splitting more, like a bit of rot that grew unchecked and gained control, taking its time eating, the house from the inside. Two deep, muffled pops erupt from somewhere in the crack, like boards snapping, but more abrupt, or it comes from Ma's window. My body tenses at the sound, waiting for more to follow, and when there's nothing, I sit down on the dry trunk of the tree, resting my hands on my thighs. The roots of it reach out into the air seeking something they can't find, mottled, and ancient. Looking at it, a sense of isolation threads rough filaments in me, a shard of abandonment I can't orient.

I hear the front door of the porch open and swing shut, a hard clamp over the slight chirp of crickets, then the shuffling of feet across sandy boards. Tambourine walks into the hard light on the side of the house where I sit. His black and yellow striped tank top is hitched at an angle over his collarbones. His tiny, oval face holds a sudden and unusual confidence, as if a full-grown man possesses his awkward, deformed body, and has been using it the entire time, using it to pull from people certain reactions. But I crush this thought, unsure, finally, where my sense of fear comes from, my distrust.

You're just sitting out here? He says this, gesturing at the house, as if to imply that there's nothing here to see.

Why don't you come in? You deciding what to do?

I tell him that I am, and notice a silver flash in his left hand. *What is that?* I ask. He lifts a gun into the light. It's polished to a high glimmer, and marks a clear spot between the house and me; I can't move.

What are you doing with that?

I've always had it. It's good for safety.

You just carry it around? To feel safe? You feel unsafe right now? Aren't you too young to own something like that?

No, I don't feel unsafe.

What did you mean by me deciding what to do?

Well, you're gonna leave, right? Especially after what Ma said to you. That's what I'd do.

How do you know what Ma said to me?

I listened on the stairs. I mean, she wasn't too careful. She knew I was there, she had to know I'd hear, or something.

I don't understand.

She probably did it so I would hear her, like telling you and me at the same time without having to do it again.

I suppose. How—what do you think, hearing all of that? You all right?

Look, he says, and tosses something at me, which I catch. A set of keys.

Why don't you take the truck?

I can't take Ma's truck, Tam.

Why not? She won't mind. After that, she owes you the truck.

I can't do it.

Yes, you can, and you will. Come on, take me with you. When you get where you're going, I'll drive the truck back.

That's a bit difficult, seeing as I don't know where I'm going.

One last thing, he says, and produces a black Moleskine journal bulging with papers bound with rubber bands.

What is that?

The location of your lady. Ma's record book. She keeps it here. So you know where she is, now, and can find her. He waits a beat to gauge my reaction, and when he sees I'm silent, says, *She's in New Mexico.*

For a minute, I stay quiet. I turn away from him and look at the ground, then off towards the darkened trees of the forest. There's a clinking sound, and my eyes return to the gun in his hand. He turns it in the light.

Come on, make a decision, Reese.

I should go say something to Ma, at least.

You don't need to say anything to her. She's asleep. Don't wake her up. She's fine. Better than ever, actually.

Yeah, I do need to say something to her. I can't just leave like that. I have to tell her. And I need to get my stuff.

I got your stuff already. It's packed on the porch.

His eyes hold the icy spark of the moon, the silver haloed stars. The gun keeps twisting in his hand, picking up slashes of light from the side of the house.

It's now or never, he says.

You'll have to put that somewhere.

Don't worry about me. Get your stuff on the porch.

I move around the side of the house, and find my things neatly packed. I grab them, comfortable only in their familiarity, and meet Tambourine at Ma's truck, where he stands waiting at the passenger side door. I go over to the driver's side, and hop in, throwing my stuff on the floor under the seat. I start the engine. Tambourine taps the glass of the window with the gun, and says to open the door, which I do after a moment of hesitation.

He crawls into the seat and puts on his seatbelt. *Good, he says, now, let's get the fuck out of here. Let's find Margaret.*

Okay.

Drive to the desert.

I back up and pull out, coursing down Ma's long driveway to the main road. As I speed away, I try to locate the house in the rearview, but it's gone, swallowed by all the dark around it.

PART IV: MARGARET— DESERT LIFE

How can I understand myself?…Of what matter am I made in which elements and foundation for a thousand other lives mingle but never merge? I go down every path and still none is mine. I have been sculpted into so many statues and haven't frozen into place…
—Clarice Lispector, *Obsession*

But the body is also directly involved in a political field; power relations have an immediate hold upon it; they invest it, mark it, train it, torture it, force it to carry out tasks, to perform ceremonies, to emit signs…
—Michel Foucault, *The Body of the Condemned*

THE GREEN MOSS HOTEL

A neon sign, lime-green faded to sickly yellow. A cluster of four cement buildings snug in the fold of a valley; a mountain rising behind it, like a back curved inward, brown and bald of trees. The two-story buildings have windows that face an empty, drained pool cut off by a chain link fence. The pool is painted with a worn, blue stripe around the rim. On its white, peeling floor is a two-day old corpse, facedown, like a piece of beige rubber glued to its surface.

All of the rooms are empty, except for the people staying in the building across from mine. The pool divides us. I've seen the others come and go from their rooms, shadow people, fast glimpses cut apart by lines in the fence. No one comes to remove the body. I watch through my window, observing its stillness. The sun is direct, no clouds. Everything here is lit in stark lines. For some reason, the neon sign stays on all night and during the day, buzzing. The sound is audible from the musty, brown interior of this room. The insistent tapping of the A/C is an odd comfort. The room is full of the perfected, chemical freeze found in most hotel rooms, piping air through rattling vents until it's like an icebox. My skin ripples with goose bumps, feels dry and taut under my fingers. I sit with my feet propped on the table, listening to it, my head leaning against the window. I have bottles of water on the floor. A man who comes from the office gives us bottles of water, and food, right at 8:00 PM, a single puce-colored tray left outside our doors. The food is made somewhere below, in the office or underneath it. No one's ever in the office, so I don't know where he goes when he disappears inside the place travelers would normally check-in.

I've got a quarter in my hand. I found it on the floor when I first arrived. I move it through my fingers, rub its edges. Whose was it? I wonder. How long has it been here, waiting, a glimmer caught at the edge of the bed? I tap its side in brief rhythms on the top of the table. I stare at the corpse. Its body takes on a lumpy quality as the sun lowers. A livid, desert-red slips around the edges of the other buildings, the tips of the mountains. The shadows around the pool grow into sharp, permanent shapes. For a moment, I can imagine this place as it might have been, years ago: hopeful families stunned by the possibility in its vacant locale. Surely the tiny man from the office has noticed the body by now. I imagine the others across me have also noticed it. Are they just interested in witnessing its slow rot? Or, is it negligible, like most things around here? This hotel, abandoned to the rest of the desert around it. No one's coming here. No one will see the corpse. No one that isn't shipped here to this way station.

The red light fades, and the sky goes black; the expanse of the desert stretches, and the hotel stands in its hollow silence. The four, dolphin-shaped lamps fixed at the corners of the courtyard provide the only lights, now. Their mouths and eyes burn the same strained yellow, each locked into a different flip or jump on peeling white posts. The navy blue of their fiberglass bodies has been eaten by sand and time, but the white, paisley shapes painted on their tails to simulate water splashing look untouched. They smile maniacally into the light pouring from their mouths. The cracked fiberglass reaches from the corners of their grins all the way down the dorsal side, and for some, cracks reach around the head to the black dot meant to represent a blowhole. Their eyes are like tempered, yellow coals, emitting faint trails of steam in the cold night air. One of them has a length of tail missing up its side. The interior is black.

We're allowed out of our rooms at certain times during the day. We take walks around the center of the hotel complex individually, unless you're with people, or share a room. Two of the three people in the rooms across from mine walk together, heads lowered, intent like mall-walkers. One is a young woman, possibly in her thirties, hair chopped short. She wears a dirty brown tank top. The man that accompanies her appears greased and shiny. His hair is saturated to an oil-black color. He has a rounded, hunched back. They speak in low tones when they make their circles around the emptied pool. They must have arrived together. They possess an idiosyncratic closeness as I watch them from my room.

Only a shape of the corpse remains now, etched in grime on the white surface. The man from the office must have finally had it removed. Yet, it's as if it still occupies that part of the pool. I spot the girl in the couple looking over at it a few times, probably curious about its absence. When she looks up at me, at my window, I shut the curtains.

When it's my hour to walk around the courtyard I move slower than I think I'm capable of, and it's a brief agony, the irritating inevitability of age and exhaustion, how we keep going anyway. I catch myself speeding up when I get near the door of the couple, and the single man in the room above them. He has only made one appearance, but nothing since. I'm afraid the girl will come outside and engage me in some kind of bone-picking conversation. The advice that was given to me is to trust no one I might meet here. They also give us rules: no contact with the others, no making of friends. But the girl does come outside, and I see that she's older than I previously thought, weathered. Her tan brow appears pulled. Lines around her mouth are like scalpel slices. Her eyes hold no wrinkles, but contain a heaviness in the way they move, a calloused quality the same as raw skin.

She sits in the blue, plastic chair between the door to her room and the grime-flecked window with its torn screen, and lights a cigarette with a lighter in the shape of a tiny goat horn. She watches me, and does nothing to disguise that this is her intent in stepping outside. Her dark eyes squint as if she's disassembling me every time I come around the corner. I train my eyes on the broken concrete, away from her, away from the dirty shape left by the body in the barren pool. My third lap, and she's on her second cigarette, less concerned with me, looking up towards the hotel sign, then her hands.

The sun lowers behind the west-facing mountains, producing a yellow halo over the top of it, a white sky. Sage clumped along its surface darkens, like old cigarette burns. A Coke machine buzzes on, light flickering sap-yellow behind a faded red sign. The next time I come around, she's standing at this machine getting a soda, which comes clattering down a plastic chute, her lithe body bent over to pull it out, then up again, and looking right at me. Before I make my turn around the corner, she sticks out her arm, halting me. She says nothing and cracks open her can. It creates a pop, like thick ice snapping underfoot. She takes a sip. We both look up at the buzzing, juddering sign; the sky has lost its white, and the mountains have lost the yellow crown from the lowered sun. Phosphorescent purple, and the dark blue of the desert night sky, replaces it. Stars shower over the hotel. The dry, empty coolness of the desert air moves between us, carrying the smell of burned sage, smoke, and the tang of pinion sap.

She looks at me, steps closer.

"You been watching," she says. Her voice is filled with a soft, confident Western accent.

I start to shake my head, but I don't know what she means, or what she wants. My impulse is to respond, yet I can't tell if she is attempting to reprimand me for something, or if she's just making an observation for the purpose of some needed conversation. She doesn't appear to consider my age; I must look old to her, but it doesn't seem to matter. I breathe as if I've run around the pool instead of walked. She drinks the rest of her Coke and sets the can gently on the ground, rising up to look at me again. The movement is smooth, and somehow by watching this I know that this woman has killed somebody. Somewhere in her past, a person died because she wanted it. I don't know how I know this, but it's clear to me, and I feel a queasy form of vulnerability loosen the center of my stomach. In the same moment, I also know she has no interest in harming me.

"The man in the pool," she says.

I nod.

"You been watching?"

"Yes."

"He was my brother."

"I'm sorry."

She stops and looks down. Her eyes fill.

"Do you know how?" she asks.

I shake my head. "No."

"No?"

I don't repeat myself.

"Be careful out here," she says. "None of us know for how long. None of us know who's watching."

She moves past me, almost brushing my shoulder. She smells of thick body odor, earth. I hear her snorting back snot and tears behind me. The thin, wooden door of her room opens. Sounds of a whirring fan, along with the vacuum-purr of the A/C, momentarily leaks across the threshold. Television light flickers blue over a wooden dresser. A man's voice mumbles something from far back in the room where the beds stand. The door shuts.

Later, when I'm in my room, I see the woman walk up to my door from my window. I wait for a knock but there isn't one, and then I see her return downstairs. When I go to open it, a folded piece of paper crushed between the doorknob and the jamb falls to the ground. I open it, and it says: *If you ever need my help, just come get me.*

At The Green Moss Hotel we are forbidden to step outside our doors after curfew (9:00 PM), and if we go further out beyond the property (to the hills, for instance), bordering the road facing the hotel, we could be shot. I wonder if this is what happened to the woman's brother. But, he was in the pool, so I am unsure what became of him, or if he was even shot. She is correct that we are being watched. This is something we were notified about early on before any of us are dropped here, bag over our head, blindly led by unknown bodies out of a car, up the gravel road, hands bound, then deposited in our rooms, our hands cut free, and the black sack we remove ourselves. Not everyone arrives the same way; some are dropped at night, and then picked up hours later, removed again, and shipped off somewhere else. These are intermittent moments, spread thin. For the most part, it is as if the hotel is outside of time. We have to wait until our Carrier comes for us. Once we have a Carrier, we're moved off with them, whoever they are, and we're bound to them for the rest of our lives. This is part of the cost of being "redirected," as it was put to me when the right people ushered me along to more right people.

I still think about Charlie.

Tonight, when the old man from the office brings me a tray of poorly cooked food, he lingers in the door with a stern expression. He wants me to know there is a serious development, and it is a privilege to get to hear about it.

"A man is looking for you." He stops, registers my reaction before continuing. "He is being held at her house. She is holding him, but she does not know for how long."

"Who is it? Does she know what he wants?"

The man hands me the tray, and shuts the door without another word.

After we eat our food, we are required to leave the tray outside of the door for pick-up. The man says it looks kindly on us if we place the silverware in the center of the white, ceramic plate, so I do. By now, the sun is down, and the desert night is thick, purple-black. Bug corpses sizzle and ping as they rebound off the feeble bulbs pouring light from the cracked dolphins stuck in eternal flips at the four corners of the empty pool. The sounds seem to ricochet around the buildings, emphasized by the great vacuum of the desert itself.

Tonight, I take a risk, too. Like the woman, I make a small transgression. I put her note in my pocket like an amulet, something that has energy; something that will keepsafe me, like a shield. Around eleven, after the man has come to retrieve his tray, I step outside of my door and stand barefoot on the warm concrete landing. The heat of it is a twig of familiarity jerking under my sternum, a familiarity that connects me to every memory of myself when I stood in warmth like this, my bare feet absorbing it, and then the scent of the heat moving through the metals in the rails that line the walkway. I root myself in it. I test the space, standing there exposed in shadows from the dull lights, the hollow quiet of the hotel. I wait to see if I will be shot.

My hands shake, and a brief, cool desert wind licks my skin. I feel my throat go to dry paste when I step forward, and get closer to the stairs. My stomach tightens, and I'm a child sneaking downstairs to spy on my parents, to look around the corner of the hallway to see them in the room without me, watching movies I don't get to watch, enfolded. The enfolding is the strangest to me when I see it, this closeness, and I'm getting away with two powers: I'm invisible, and I'm present. When I get to the bottom of the stairs that lead down to the pool, the main floor of the hotel, something picks at my intuition, and I've convinced myself I have sights on me, a red laser target right at my back as I move, naïve, unaware, ghostlike. I'm taking this for granted. I'm not heeding the warnings of the woman sleeping just a few feet from me.

I keep going, anyway, past the office with its lightless windows, past the car park, past the peeling, light-blue pole of the hotel sign. Pretty soon, I'm out beyond the circular drive and up on the curb of a median, filled with brown dirt, gravel, and cactuses, like balls made from sharpened tongues. I step off the median and walk into the street, and it has a different roughness on my soles, a different kind of heat. Between the median and the road, my heels and toes feel toughened, and I go all the way across the road to the base of the hill. I climb up its side with quick, feverish movements, as if I can't move quickly enough, and when I'm at the top of it, I turn around. The hotel is smaller than when I look at it from inside, a smallness that tries to appear innocuous. Its white exterior is part of a time that no longer exists. Voids carve through the spaces of its buildings. The sign, which seems bright from my window, is a tiny flicker of dissolved light in all this darkness. Standing here, I no longer feel part of it. I can see my room, my door, where I've been, and then I look away and up, around me at the dark stretching over the desert. I breathe it down as deeply as I can, as hard as I can, exhaling what's been put in me from the hotel, and its rooms. Thoughts of being shot from here—a sniper watching on the roof somewhere, perhaps—are gone. I lean down and scoop up a stone on the ground in front of me. I grip it. I'm almost certain there is no one watching when I decide to descend the hill and return to my room. When I slide quietly back into its controlled blackness, back to my bed with its thin quilts and rough sheets, I hold the stone in my hand, then up to my face to smell it. Early, before the light breaks fully upon the hotel, I get up and look out of my window at the hill I climbed. I feel as though I have made my own place upon it, a secret, a shelter.

Later in the day, when I take my walk around the pool, I hope that the woman will make an appearance, and talk to me. We can trade our transgressions against the hotel together. But she does not show. Her door stays shut, and the window is dark.

There is a clock in my room, which reads 2:14 AM. My eyes open, sleepless and expectant. I don't understand why I have woken, alert suddenly. I stare at the clock, smothered by the silence of the empty rooms around mine. I pull out old tricks to force myself back asleep; eyes open, eyes closed, eyes open, eyes closed, counting back from one hundred, counting back from 50, counting back from 20, counting back from 10. I hear two distinct cracks outside, somewhere across from me. Two hard pops, *bam bam*, and I start over from one hundred.

The next day when the office man arrives with breakfast, he is wearing latex gloves flecked in brown dots. He looks at me with a subtle kind of disappointment. He tells me that my Carrier has been found and will arrive soon. He has heard no more about the man looking for me. Before he shuts the door, I catch a clear look at the woman's window downstairs. One set of blinds is pulled halfway up the glass, and a woman is vacuuming inside, rolling the machine back and forth. The other set of blinds is yanked apart in the middle, as if clawed through, slats dangling from the cords. The glass has been cleaned, and hard chemical streaks glare in the sun. The woman and the man occupying it are not there, and I don't see them again. The man closes my door, leaving me with the tray.

I lie in the middle of my bed and hold the stone. I examine it for peculiarities, for specialness. These are things I want to attribute to it. It's round with a jagged, pie-shaped chunk missing from the side. It is the color of the dirt outside with offshoots of beige and hard clusters of orange-red. It's been kicked and thrown about, laced with scratches and white scars. It's like a stone on its way to becoming something, a geode, or a meteor with diamonds inside. What I hold in my hand is a petrified embryo. If I had the strength to crack it open, I believe I would find a secret in its center, right there. Luckily, I'll never know if this is true.

For three days, I do not leave my room. The office man comes at his regular times bearing trays of food, bottled water, and no messages. I do not even take my regular walk around the pool. I do not want to see the woman's room, her windows bared to the inside, blinds pulled all the way up, now. I'm afraid I'll see something. I'm not sure what I think that is, but it's enough that I keep my distance from it. It's natural to wonder if she was harmed, or worse. It's normal when you feel that you're the only one left in a place (I stopped counting the man occupying the room above hers long ago), and that, perhaps, you are being watched, like she said. Did someone see her leave the note on my door? Was my late night transgression a consideration? I worry that I did something; that if she was harmed, or worse, I have something to do with it. Part of me, a very strong, inarguable part of me believes that what happened to that woman was designed to punish me.

At 4:00 AM there is a hard knock at my door. The metal clasps, where a chain would go, rattles against the thin, cheap wood. The doorknob shakes loosely. I don't know why they don't just break it down; it would be so much simpler. I slide out of the covers and walk across the rough brown carpet to open the door. Instinctually, I crack it, and then widen it a little when I see it's the office man. He is standing next to a tall man with wide shoulders, a huge stomach and barrel chest. He's wearing a blue sport jacket and a black t-shirt underneath. I can't make out the color of his slacks. His face is black, and I can't see any of it in the shadows. His posture is rigid. He's performing a duty. The office man is also. He is facilitating it for this man.

A light rain starts behind them, smacking the barren innards of the pool, pinging off the chain link fence around it. The office man holds out his skinny arms roped in prominent veins. In his hand is a black sack.

"Put this on. Your Carrier is here. You're leaving."

I start to look for my shoes, and the stone.

"No. No, no. Unnecessary. Just put this on. You're leaving."

My breath stops somewhere in my abdomen. I can't get it to go further when I see that sack in his hand, and my tongue and throat dry up.

"Put it on," he says, impatient with me.

I take it from him. It's made of some kind of canvas different from the one I came here wearing. I slide it over my head, breathing a strange chemical residue, like the inside of a tennis ball. My breathing escalates in its blackness. I can feel myself thinning. I feel and hear the larger man move into the room. He grasps me gently to move me forward. His touch tells me he's practiced this; he knows what panic looks like, and he doesn't want to make it worse.

I'm led to the threshold of the door. I wonder if the office man is still there, observing the procession. My bare feet touch the rain-slicked concrete. I'm lead down the stairs, so I know he's taking me towards the road. The closer we get to it, his grasp becomes harder, less interested in my shaking. He's rough, now, so I drag my feet a little. I hear a car idling. A door opens, and I'm pushed inside it. I crumple into a large seat, which curves around the interior. I hold my hands to my chest, knees up. My eyes are closed, despite the sack. I breathe as if I'm underwater, as if I'm not being watched. I cling to the whirring quiet of the space. I listen. The car starts to move, and its momentum pushes me into the seat. There is movement across from me. Legs shift, a crinkle of paper, and something clinks.

A voice from a speaker above me: "Sit up. Sit up and take off the bag."

I hesitate. The sack has become a sudden refuge; taking it off has implications. Whoever's in front of me seems to understand this.

"Take of the bag, and sit up. Meet your Carrier."

The house is new, and I am conscious of my presence in it, like an acquisition. Upon arrival, I am immediately married to my Carrier; it takes place in the kitchen that night. The black bag that had been over my head is on the counter top, like a rag. I stare at it while vague paperwork is arranged, and I say, Yes, I do, to the man on my left. Part of the deal, they tell me. The suggestion is that I don't have to say yes; that I still have choices, but that I won't survive them if I refuse the marriage. My acceptance happens once I stand there with this sudden ring on my finger; I'm bone-thin, and draped in threadbare, unwashed clothes smelling of the hotel. I'm welded to acceptance, a past full of unknown, buried lives. I am made up of tiny histories. But they don't know that, the men surrounding me, my Carrier. They don't know anything. That is mine to keep.

SHOPPING

I have a dinner party to give at 8:00 PM, and I'm still out, wandering the plaza, looking at prints in a gallery near the Loretto Chapel. I have found an artist I like, and own three of his prints now, and purchased two of his larger paintings. One hangs in the dining room and shows an empty red chair in the corner of four white walls. The other hangs on the east-facing wall of the living room, a horse in the colors of purple and indigo grazing along the suggestion of a gray valley. It's just been six months, but upon my arrival in the first month, the gallery tells me that the artist is dead, and my attraction to his work grows. There's not enough of it. I want there to be more. I leave the gallery and stroll down the Palace of the Governors, swinging sacks in my hand with the new silver for the dining room table and the clothes that I will wear tonight. My heels clip succinctly along the ground. My ivory skirt is loose around my hips and thighs. The blue wrap—patterned in tiny, scurrying lizards—is draped over my shoulders, covering part of my chest and the silk, eggplant blouse I just picked up last week. My curls have gone full-gray, now, the strawberry tint faded from them, but they lift around my head in a spring-like bounce, appearing to compensate.

My fingers are already wreathed in silver, turquoise, jade, and amethyst, but I make it a point to look at the jewelry here, anyway. The long blankets spread out along the path hold black boxes and items placed in rows: crafted rings, necklaces, and stones representative of tribal symbols, shapes, and some that are new creations. The artists sit together behind their work, some holding children who move about restlessly. Others cover their faces with their hands when tourists try to take their picture, protecting their souls.

I don't find anything I want to buy, so I walk back across the street towards the La Fonda hotel, to the French pastry shop, and I grab a few glazed custard tarts for the buffet table where the spread will be. The fruit in them is arranged with sculpted precision, glistening like replicas. When I'm finished there, I find my driver, Mason. He waits for me reading a book in a corner café down the street from where he parked the Lincoln.

I meet others like me. There are a few in the surrounding neighborhoods outside of the city proper, neighborhoods like Eldorado, and some who have houses in the mountains close to Tesuque and Ten Thousand Waves. We do not meet up or have groups or discuss our lives. We are called Placements. When we see each other around town, we nod, we say hello, we talk for a minute or two, really pushing to absorb the roles we've been handed; and, in the back of the present, on the periphery, even, is a bit of our old lives, a piece of grit marring the performance. It isn't repression, exactly, but it's close. It's not a new chance at life, either. We aren't allowed certain things, and we have to obey rules, or there are consequences. Each Placement has different rules depending on their assignment, their Carrier.

The first for all of us is that once we occupy the home as the wife or husband of our Carrier, we can no longer use that name; we are to use their actual name. My Carrier's name is Oliver, a big man—over six feet in height with black hair slicked away from his forehead, which is shiny, and his face is long, round, and serious. When he's at the house, he moves with stern directness; his navy slacks whisper as he rushes through the large hallways, up the stairs, going to and from his makeshift office (the real one is elsewhere, and I have not seen it). His feet echo on the Mexican tile. He acknowledges me in passing, kindly, with the right amount of detachment. Do I need anything? How am I enjoying New Mexico? Should I require anything for the job I am assigned, to please tell him, or tell his assistant. Most of the time, Oliver is not at the house.

I have a monthly allowance of five thousand dollars. I can spend it however I want. If I try to leave, buy a plane ticket and go somewhere else, or visit people from my past, anything, it has been made clear to me that I will be shot, and later, dismembered and disposed of. I do not question this.

My first assignment is to decorate the house. I do this by moving throughout the city, selecting items at random. I accomplish it cheaply at first because I do not know how to spend hundreds of dollars on one chair, thousands on the right couch, a desk. But, I am given a separate credit card for these transactions and, eventually, I become adept at picking these things. I enlist shopkeepers to help me, and I ask for suggestions about the best craftsmen in the area. Soon I have a collection of original furniture filling the once bare, white spaces of the house, which feels like an abandoned art gallery at times: huge white walls, ceilings stretching to accommodate two chandeliers—the only things Oliver picked out himself—which are made of antlers stretching out in a spiked circle, slicing light across the walls.

The living room windows open to the city and the other houses cutting into the mountainside. We are higher up than it looks on the drive from the plaza. At night, the lights scattered throughout the black desert appear like gold dust. When Oliver's gone, and it's just me in the house, I sit with all of the lights turned off. I sit in total silence and dark, and I stare at the burning, gold-flicker meant to signify streets and malls and other people's homes, and it is the only time when nothing has ever happened to me, and nothing will.

My other assignment is to shop. Just shop. There is no other goal in this, but I am required to spend the money I have been given, and it becomes tiring. I have to buy something, multiple things, every day. I make so many friends this way, and many shop owners will do anything I want, even when I simply browse. After a while, I feel I've bought everything there is to buy, and then begin to purchase things I don't want, or don't think about much when I'm handing over money, because it is just part of the rules, so pretty soon I am accumulating items, some of which I see around the house and cannot recall why I would purchase such a thing. I spend hours in a pet shop one day with Mason, who helps me fill the trunk of the Lincoln: empty cages, fish bowls, dog toys. There is no dog. Oliver doesn't allow pets, so the cages are filled with the squeaky, rubber bones and chewable snacks in varying shapes. I sneak in a fish, fill the bowl with water, and add a plastic skeleton with a treasure chest, some multi-colored rocks. I spend hours watching him. He flits around the bowl uncertain of his new location. Dropped right in, none of it fazes him, his eyes wide, stupid looking dots, his mouth working mechanically. The skeleton is poor company for a fish. One of the rocks I placed inside forms a cave. He goes there often and hides. He peeks out once in a while, then drifts back. When he dies, which is rather quick, I empty the tank and throw away the skeleton.

I keep all of the accumulations in a back room at the end of a hallway near the living room. I never go in it except to deposit more things.

I am also required to give dinner parties at Oliver's request. He has them sometimes twice a month. Neighbors arrive, people from his business, of which I am only given the basics to hold standard conversations, if asked. Otherwise, I am not allowed to know anything. I am expected to laugh and feign a kind of naiveté, which works because none of the neighbors, the colleagues, the art dealers, the gallery owners, politicians, none of them really care. In exchange for all of this material, the house, all of it, I have to perform, so I do exactly that: Perform.

These people believe the tidy tales of a three-month honeymoon in Milford Sound, New Zealand, and our sparked meeting during a layover on the way to Province, France. I grew up in Martha's Vineyard. I attended Yale for art history. I am not Margaret; I am Diane. Both of our parents are dead, so that's an easy one. Offer trauma and everyone shuts up. Oliver, I know, has to perform a little during these nights, too. When he does, I feel like I have a partner.

Part of Oliver's job involves rocks, stones, gemstones. Poudretteite. Musgravite. Jeremejevite. Tiger's Eye. Black Opal. Fire Opal. Diamonds. My role in this involves a portion of the allowance I am given, as if he's cutting corners a bit, but it doesn't perturb me in the least. Sometimes I am handed instructions when I wake up. Mason kindly leaves them, typed and printed, in a stack on the bar in the kitchen. They list specific shops or locations on the outskirts, where I am to go and inquire about specific kinds of stones.

Oliver pays upwards of ten thousand dollars for some of them, which I arrange but do not pay for out of my own account. There is a separate one for these transactions. The smaller ones, ranging from a couple hundred dollars to fifteen hundred, I manage. When I come home with them wrapped snug in dirt-streaked cardboard boxes I must leave them in a sealed room. The door has a code, and it is made of glass. Inside are shelves holding stones spread out and labeled. The room's temperature is regulated. I have to inspect it once a week, and the door leading to it from the hallway is locked. I have a key and Oliver has a key. If any of the stones go missing while I am present, I will lose an ear for the first two. It goes up from there. Another rule.

The dinner party is a success, and more people attend than the last one, although it's less of a dinner party than I expected. People aren't sitting at the dining room table; a piece I bought for three thousand dollars made of hand carved walnut and oak, imported from Pavia, Italy. People set plates on it, some smeared with sauces from the buffet, withered orange carrot sticks nestled in puddles of white ranch and organic quinoa. The flowers in the center of it stand tall. White and yellow petals with pink centers showered in broken light from the chandeliers.

David, another Placement, arrives with his Carrier, Susan. It's unexpected and unusual for one Carrier to bring a Placement into proximity with another. I look at Oliver across the room. His face is flushed and his shoulders are raised while he watches Susan lead David around the room, introducing him to clusters of Oliver's colleagues near the kitchen bar, one of whom leans on the granite counter, his smug expression tilted up at David, who looks across the crowd and spots me. David smiles, and there's an unnerving amount of relief in it. His isolation is palpable through his arranged stiffness. A white bandage covers his forehead and thickens around the side of his head over his right ear. His appearance resembles a war veteran, yet it's comical somehow, and I'm surprised Susan brought him here, looking like this. His arm is draped around hers like a branch. Her red hair and poise is like a dagger in the room. She's taller than him, and she moves him around with the tension of a threat in every step, as if she's scolded him before arriving, telling him to be a good boy. A certain amount of fear is in the careful lifting of his feet. This is especially noticeable as Susan brings him from group to group, chatting, smiling, her bright white teeth gleaming. Without looking at him, she removes her arm, and he is set free for a minute. She has spoken without speaking: *Don't go too far, stay around here, stay close, if you want your treat, you'll do what I say, now go be a good boy*, which is when he drifts through a few of the older men in suits over to the dining room table to see me. Closer, and the bandage is not as prominent; it seems fussed with as if someone— Susan, perhaps—worked to blend it into the natural terrain of his hair as much as one can with a thick, gauzy bandage. He smiles at me with weariness, exhaustion. We have only spoken a few times when seeing each other out during our shopping duties. He usually goes to the same place and buys boxes of candles; the last time, it was an entire set of paintings from a restaurant wall. His emaciated body announces itself through the sagging clothes he's wearing, a blue sweater with a dress shirt underneath, some gray slacks. He won't look up at me, keeps his eyes on the ground, or on the door behind me.

"David."

"Hi, Diane."

I nod at the bandage, intimating concern as subtly as I can; people are always watching.

"Oh. Yes. Happened last week."

I scan the room for Susan, but I don't see her red hair, her demanding gait.

"Tell me," I say to him.

He waits a long time before responding. A server comes around with a tray of drinks. I ask him to bring me an ice water, which he does quickly. I hand it to David who drinks it. His bloodshot eyes are glazed.

"I took nothing," he says, shaking his head. "None of it. You know?"

I nod.

"I took nothing. But someone did take something. And she forgets things, too. She gets drunk and forgets and loses her own stuff."

He drinks more water, and I'm still looking for Susan. I don't want her to walk up, to catch him talking.

"It's all of the same shit she doesn't do anything with. Tons of it. She forgets what's there, what isn't there, thinks I'm taking it, stealing it."

His hand goes up to the wrapping around the side of his ear.

"It was done a week ago. A set of napkin holders went

missing," he says. "I was surprised it was her that would do it. Still am, and she used one of the knives I bought."

I try to look anywhere but at his head.

"You know what's weird?" he says, eyes widening. "When she did it, I was really peaceful. I could hear it going through the cartilage though. Sounded like I was chewing really loudly, but I couldn't hear her. Not at all."

I want to help him, and I want to leave. Eventually, Susan sees us across the room. She tilts her head, signaling to David it's time to go.

Mason cuts a deal with me. He completes my shopping duties for me on some days, and in exchange, I buy him things, lunch or dinner usually. His brown hair is pulled into a man-bun, and he moves with the elegance of a former dancer. His thin body is an asset in this way. He enjoys silence, and he is committed to the kind of silence his job requires; he's just supposed to drive me places, do some paperwork, but he's not supposed to make deals. I have been working on him slowly, smiling at the right moments, hoping he'll permit me to know what he knows. That sort of thing.

One of our arrangements is for him to complete the shopping duties early and return the items to the house; none of this is specifically stated as forbidden, so he does it without hesitation. He leaves me at various points around town, teashops, restaurants, parks, and then he picks me up and we drive together to places outside of the city, or up into the mountains, which is where we agree to go today. He brings food, gets a few things for the drive, and we spend the day this way. We're quiet in the car. What occurs inside of it is recorded, transmitted. The car itself is traced. Neither of us have control over any of it. But we're careful about the boundaries we push against. He's more careful than me in most respects.

He stops the Lincoln at a scenic parking space that includes a metal railing. The view looks down into a valley and across the rest of the city. Firs coat the sides of the mountain in bristling green rows. Mason sits on the hood of the car eating a sandwich. I walk along the edge of the lookout, running my hand along the metal rail. We maintain our companionable, mutual silence, our careful silence. It goes on for a while. Some tourists come and go, parking, getting out, taking pictures with their phones, then leaving until it empties, and it's just us.

I stand close to him by the car, leaning on the rail. He looks out past me at the lights starting to flicker down below. He holds his arms over his chest, his chin tilted.

"How long have you done this, Mason?"

He smiles at me, looks away for a minute. Have I crossed an unknown barrier? Are some questions forbidden, too? Questions I should know better than to ask. He leans forward.

"Seven years," he says, smiling. His V-shaped face catches the sun. The brown hair over his chin, combed like a fantastic devil's, shines bright yellow.

"How did you find it?"

"I just did."

What can I ask? What can I ask and get away with?

"I see," I say, feeling as though he won't let me get very far. I wonder if he knows I'm trying to get on a level with him, to secure an ally.

"How many of—how many Placements have there been?"

He drops his head as if he knew this was coming. Mason moves away from the car and gets closer to me. His voice lowers where we stand at the rail.

"There are many," he says. "There have been many."

"How many?"

"Does it matter?"

"No, I suppose it doesn't. What happened to them?"

"Different things."

"Are they still alive?"

"Some of them."

I wait after he says this, thinking what it could mean, deciding how this might apply to my place here, to Oliver.

"Okay. Help me out, Mason. What can I ask, and what can I not ask? What's forbidden here?"

"Well," he says, "this is."

Can I trust you? I want to say.

"Have any Placements got away?"

His expression says I'm pushing it.

"You've had this conversation before." I risk this, and he nods.

"Yes," he says, and his voice is regretful, despairing.

"What are my chances?"

He shakes his head; he won't go any further than this. Mason gets back in the car, starts the engine. I wait a minute before joining him. He has not left me with the same despair I heard in his simple answer. But, his refusal to answer my questions, their implications, is enough to know he is one form of ally, but he is only that.

On the drive back down the mountain, Mason pulls to the shoulder and shuts off the car. He tells me to get out. My chest cinches in on itself like a tight belt. What does he want? I step out and he joins me. He gestures to follow him a little way up the road from the car. He walks with the urgency of men who know they're about to commit a kindness by doing something that betrays a confidence, and puts lives at stake.

"Listen, you are Oliver's favorite. Don't try to fly away from that. Don't try for something else. Just let it be because there is nothing else. Do you understand me? There is nothing else."

I brush my hair back from my face and fold my arms as if bracing against something.

"Please, listen to me, this is the only time I will do this. You are asking me what I know."

My skin prickles in a wind that pushes around the corner. The clouds seem to drop, shifting to ash-gray over the pointed tips of firs.

"No life is perfect. What is so bad that you want to run from this one?"

I shake my head, not committing to anything, just listening to him. He puts his arms around me, and I smell his sweat.

"Just be Diane. Is it so hard?"

I start to ask him things and, anticipating this, he stops me, almost aware of my trajectory.

"Questioning what this is won't help you. What you're involved in. It's bigger than you. We're never going to know what it is."

DIANE / SUSAN

Mason is right, and it doesn't take long for me to accept this; that what he says is true: This is my life, now, whatever it is, with as much danger and as many pitfalls as any other, perhaps less so than some, and I know this, too. My life before isn't something that evaporates the way everything else has at the request of others. I know I am capable of living multiple lives with their varying conditions. This is what made me Margaret, and this is what will make me Diane. As I become her, as I become *this*, I find I am fluent in the art of mutation; the real talent of the 21st century is how well you can become somebody else, convincing yourself, not others. What other people think doesn't matter. It never has. So in lieu of escaping (my momentary burst of fight or flight upon seeing a fragile David worn thin, his ear cut off for transgressions I know he did not commit), I decide to go further inward, to become Diane all the way, making my own private deliverance to rescue David.

It is forbidden for a Placement to approach a Carrier, no matter how long the Placement has been a part of the community or lived in the house to which they've been assigned. This is one of the first things you are told upon your induction. There are punishments for attempting to elicit the attention of another Carrier, or to try to engage with them on a personal or friendly level. It is considered a breach of rank, and the Placement then becomes suspect for other potential betrayals. It also implicates the Carrier and puts them in a volatile situation; they are, likewise, considered suspect, and risk death as a result.

All of this makes it very complicated when I ask Mason to drop me off near the Plaza down the street from one of Susan's favorite restaurants and shopping areas. He's done the work for me, and sought out her schedule, an easy task for him completed through his connections with the other drivers; a simpler rule to break, apparently. He doesn't ask me why I want her schedule, and he does not hesitate to take me anywhere when I specify strange locations. When I ask for more research regarding Susan, he complies. In fact, he's quicker than usual as if he senses my urgency or intuits a plan. We make an unorthodox team.

Susan has lunch once a week at The Pink Adobe and drinks afterwards at The Dragon Room, next door. I'm told she conducts business there, sometimes alone and sometimes with partners. What work she does is also vague, and Mason can only find minute details, but that it has to do with guns among other things. I enter The Dragon Room and take a seat outside near the back. I order a Malbec, sipping it gently while I wait. A few people line the bar, but it's mostly empty. The lights strung above cross like shoelaces, and burn dimly in the afternoon light. I pull out some work of my own, the schedules, notes, tasks for Oliver, and begin to create an energy of business around me, or focus. I absorb myself in this activity, keeping my attention away from the entrance and the street, visible from where I sit. Soon, I am unaware of my location, of what I'm doing there. A couple of hours pass, and I have taken on an appropriate amount of tired body language, the pensiveness that comes with too much to do. I stand to stretch and get more wine.

Susan walks in about 45 minutes later than I expect her. She's in black. Her shoulders are bare, and her top blends directly into her skirt, which stops below her calves. Her shoes are pointed black pumps, and her red hair is like metal when the sun catches it, a bronze patina that appears unnatural. She walks towards the bar with the same directness, the same demanding push forward, and she signals the bartender, who I notice doesn't even have to say anything; in one fluid movement he stops what he's doing and prepares a drink specifically for her, and it must be what she always gets because she isn't watching him, but instead takes a seat at a table near the entrance with her back to the bar. She sets her black bag in the chair adjacent to her and leans back, tilting her face towards the sky. Her black sunglasses mirror the clouds. The fit of her shades around her eyes is so complete I cannot imagine them removed; that, if she did remove them, they would peel off, or tear skin in the process. The bartender comes out from behind the bar and places a glass of white wine on the table in front of Susan, talks to her obediently for a moment, and then returns to the bar. She stays in that position for a while with her head back, silent. It is minutes before she sits up and pulls the chair over to her, containing her bag. She digs inside it and retrieves black folders that she stacks in front of her on the table. She drinks her wine. Tiny sharp sips. And then she opens the black folders, flipping with sudden razor-focus on the materials inside. She notices nothing else around her, yet conveys an energy that she is aware of everything, and furthermore, that she's watching.

I sip my wine, trying to quell the burst in my stomach of adrenaline for what I'm about to do; frustrated that it is not helping me the way I thought it would. I begin to pack my things. I do it slowly, taking my time, slipping items into my bag with a bit of a pedantic quality, a bit of distraction. I slide the bag up my shoulder and approach the bar to pay my tab, and I leave, walking toward Susan's table.

I don't accidentally bump it. I don't drop anything, nothing so filmic and expected as that. I know she would think this was obvious, what I'm doing. It would implicate too much. I don't believe she would respond in any receptive way if I did approach her via an "accident." There are no accidents for people like her; I've gotten to know Oliver enough to know this about Carriers, despite the vast difference between the two of them. Instead of these passive strategies, I just say hello; a much bigger risk.

Her smile is like sculpted wax; lips coated in a clear, rose sheen that causes them to blend into the rest of her face, which is pale, and probably intentionally so. The smile is not a smile, but a fixed position for this part of her face.

It could convey anything, depending on the context, or the person looking at it. The expression of her mouth does not, in any way, communicate the standard that it's known for; that she is happy, or happy to see an acquaintance, or even kindness. It functions, machine-like, and protects her in the way that some amphibians shift skin, colors rippling into a mirror of their environments, coiled with eyes open, but invisible.

I try to reflect something similar to her; to disguise myself behind a quick guise, but I imagine she would pick up on this just as easily as if I had pretended to drop something to get her attention, rather than my polite hello. So I retreat to a form of unquestionable sincerity, a poise I hope she will respect. I wonder if she'll see my act of a polite hello as a risk worthy of consideration, not punishment. I want her to invite me to sit with her, and she does.

"Diane, right? Oliver's wife," she says, and leans forward, hand stretched out to me like a man. I shake it, and say, Yes, I am Oliver's wife.

"What brings you here? To The Dragon Room on this lovely afternoon."

"Work. For Oliver, I'm afraid."

"I've been hearing great things about you."

"You do," I say, uncertain, wondering if this is a transgression for a Carrier to tell a Placement what other Carrier's talk about when away from them.

"How are you liking the new house?" she asks, and sips her wine.

"I love it. It's phenomenal, the location. Oliver's taste in views is very strong. I'd like to see him add on to the back a little, maybe another bedroom."

"Oh, would you?" Her lips take on a disconcerting, amused smirk. It implies that I'm entertaining, a Placement who has taken such "ownership" of her house.

"Well, yeah, I would," I say.

"Another glass of wine?" she asks, pointing at the table, as if I have a glass in front of me. She turns towards the bartender, and signals. He nods his head and, a minute later, brings me another glass.

"I saw you when I came in," says Susan. "I figured since you're going to join me, you might as well have another one."

"Thank you."

She nods, then says, "I understand you've taken on quite a bit of responsibility for Oliver."

"I have."

"He trusts you, apparently. A lot. Considering what he does, and Heaven knows, he needs it."

I shift in my chair, sip my wine. She takes off her sunglasses, revealing green irises. Her smile is less sculpted, now. It's taken on an incongruent layer of compassion.

"I can tell you're nervous," she says. She reaches over the table, grabs my hand. "Don't be."

"I don't understand." I attempt this with a bit of genuine confusion. I know what she means, but I want her to explain herself.

"You have a right to be concerned about punishments, Diane," she says, settling back into her chair. "A right to be worried that something could happen to you. It was brave what you did, saying hello to me like that."

I nod and remain upright. I stay connected with her green eyes. This is Susan's way of saying she likes to cut out the bullshit. Does she want me to think she understands my position? What paramount deception, I think, to try to convince someone of empathy when the likelihood is slim.

"I think we're all impressed with you. Not many like you, to be honest. Maybe we could meet here again. Have drinks together, just you and I."

I work my smile to communicate to her that I am relieved, and that I would very much like that. I don't betray the chilliness I feel, the wall in me imperceptible to her, a quiet type of triumph.

"I appreciate you allowing me this," I tell her.

"Say nothing of it."

What's Oliver collecting these days? This is what I imagine Susan will ask me when I next see her. I have not heard from her or her assistant since our last meeting at The Dragon Room. Mason drives me out of Santa Fe to La Cienega to meet a new client, after which we will go to the small town of Madrid to meet the last client of the day. It's always this process, meeting clients in locations that don't make any sense. It's their way of circumventing any potential complications, or at least, that's what I understand. Some live in these places. Some are just go-betweens, and the real facilitator is somewhere else. Mason tells me La Cienega is a place of sociopaths. "Bad poets come from there," he says. "Rotten ones." When I ask him about these poets, he just laughs and turns the radio up.

The mountains are a blue, shadow-outline through the tinted glass windows of the Lincoln. The land stretches into a valley speckled in clumps of dark sagebrush. Houses break up the swatch of green, and clouds gather like ice floes clumping together over the mountaintops. The highway is smooth, and the car is quiet as Mason speeds towards La Cienega. I'm lulled in the back seat until we arrive, and he's forced to take an uneven side road through bare land spreading out around us. A crumbling woodshed is the only building until the land changes, and a small driveway splits off from the main street. It curves downward into an opening where a stucco house stands far back under two, large Aspen trees, and a thick weeping willow leans over the right wall.

Mason opens my door, and I step into the cool, dry air. A bird cries in the branches; the sound is like an animal choking, like it's being clamped in the mouth of a heavy, twisting vise. The house has large windows in triangular shapes spanning out in a row that faces the driveway. The rest of it is windowless; post-modern residual of late 70s architecture, as if the house is trying to shed an old skin, and morph into something more acceptable, despite its natural inclinations: Attempting to survive, to remain relevant.

Gravel and dirt crackle under me when I walk to the

front door. Ceramic pots, terracotta pots, and bags of soil are stacked around the corner near the entrance. Some are full of dead plants, and others are completely empty. One bag of dirt remains split. Dry soil is visible in the plastic. I wonder if someone started to prepare a garden, and stopped for some reason, abandoning the idea, leaving the materials just as they were when they first unloaded their car with them. Dead, crisp leaves coagulate around the porch, the creases of the walls, and scatter around the dirt path leading from the drive. I knock, and wait for the client. Mason stands by the car, his hands folded in front of him watching dutifully, protectively almost.

The door opens fast, a suck of air from the interior, and a sense of irritation behind the movement, as if the client has been interrupted and wants to hurry this up.

"Yes?" he says. He stands in a white tank top. His brown shoulders are greased with sweat. His black eyebrows lift at me. His mustache—a thin, black line over his lip—quivers. His hair is just as black and shiny.

"I'm Diane."

"Oh, yes. I'm sorry, please come inside. You caught me at a bad time."

"Did you receive the arrival message?"

"Yes, yes. I am distracted. I have other things."

"Well, I will be happy to get this done quickly."

"I have it in the greenhouse."

I follow him through a living room with furniture scattered the way the common room of a fraternity might be organized. Books and papers are strewn about on random surfaces. Cups and dishes clutter the corners of an unused fireplace. The smell is like a log of pinion wood, roasted along with other seedy, plant-based odors. The greenhouse is attached to the main property through a glass door with a wooden handle. He takes out a key and opens the door, leading me inside its humid, perfumed warmth. I watch his hulking, rounded back as he moves down the gravel paths through aisles of greenery spilling over, brushing our arms.

We arrive at a planter full of succulents. Their color is bold in this light, pastel, almost turquoise-green bursting through fine, felt-like hairs of some and the spinal, thorniness of the others.

"It'll take me a minute," he says. "They're in here." He then gestures at the box of crammed succulents.

"You buried them in the planter?"

"I *planted* them in the planter."

"Will it take a while? To dig them up?"

"Yes. You can walk around if you like."

He operates on the succulents with a thin garden shovel, cutting around them with surgical precision. He lifts each out of the dirt like an organ, and places them in a dry, plastic pan next to the planter. I move around the room, breathing in the raw scent of plant matter, soil and mildew. The fragrance in the humidity is overpowering, and I begin to feel lightheaded. I walk over to a table of crimson orchids, a fern, a group of mustard-yellow daisies. The color of the leaves, the deep green of them, echoes the strength of the scent. It's as if the plants will choke us out of their spaces, even if it takes a while. On the ground under one of the tables is a rotted dog corpse. The center, where its belly would be, is eaten into a black cavern, while its flank is still covered in clean fur; from initial sight, the dog could just be sleeping. I can't see its head. Just a neck that ends.

"Here we go," says the client. He holds in his hand a small cellophane bag of diamonds. "This is them."

I walk over to him and take the bag, and I reach into my purse retrieving the payment, which I hand to him while avoiding his glare.

"You have a dead animal lying under a table over there. I wasn't sure if you—"

"I'm aware of him, lady. He'd be somewhere else if I wanted him to be."

I nod, and start to follow him back through the greenhouse, through the glass door, and back to the front where Mason is waiting.

Another dog, the same spotted color as the one under the table, comes padding up to me, panting. I reach out to pet him, and the client slips a hand into his waistband and removes a pistol. He aims it at the dog and pulls the trigger, one quick pop, showering me in bright stipples of blood, as red as the orchids in the greenhouse. I back away, quick, shaking and wiping at myself, moving towards the Lincoln. Mason rushes to me, arms out.

"Fuckin' bastards!" The client screams at the dog, lying as still as the one under the table, now. "You think you can come around here? You think you can come around here?"

Mason helps me get into the car when the client tells me, matter-of-factly, that the bloodsuckers will not get to him, and that these—he gestures at the dog—won't leave him alone.

When Mason backs out of the awkward driveway, the client waves. The gun in his hand twinkles in the sun, and he smiles like a generous neighbor who is delighted to have received my visit, sweet-natured, and placid. He shouts to have a wonderful day and, unaware, steps into the vibrant scarlet pool forming like a lip around his toes.

Back in the car on the highway, Mason pulls over to the shoulder, and stops. He supplies me with a wet cloth that I use to wipe off the dog's blood, and he pours me a Scotch from the tiny bar set in the back of the Lincoln. I sip, and its warmth shaves the chill off of me. The glass is heavy in my fingers.

"Do you want to skip Madrid for today?" he asks.

"No," I say. "Let's get this shit over with."

"Are you sure? You just witnessed a pretty horrible thing at close range."

"Don't worry about me. I've seen plenty in my life."

"You were shaking earlier."

"Get in the car, Mason."

Susan calls on a Saturday. She leaves a message and asks me to meet her at The Dragon Room at seven. I tell Mason, and get ready.

At the last second, Susan calls and changes plans. She wants to meet at a new restaurant on the Plaza. They make guacamole at the table right in front of you, she says, and the salsa is addictive. Mason drops me at the corner, and I enter the restaurant, searching for Susan on the second floor. She sits near the balcony. The center of the Plaza is visible through its doors behind her shoulder. She's reading a menu and smiles softly when I approach the table. The low lights and the open French doors remind me of the French Quarter in New Orleans, and I have to suppress the surge of pain that comes from the memory: My old place of living, the Margaret version of me.

Our table has three tea candles lit in a clear glass cup on a midnight-black tablecloth. They're scented, and the room is like a church, flooded by the aroma of frankincense. Even Susan appears calmed by it.

She places the black menu to her right and pulls her chair forward. Her top is molded to her torso, form-fitting, and her shoulders are bare under thin straps. It is deep, navy blue and contains material that catches the light in a slick shimmer. Her hair is behind her ears. Her face is paler than usual, lined with unusual restrained vulnerability, but the green of her eyes is like glass, a heavy emerald. Her ears stick out a bit from her head with her hair pushed behind them, an odd look for someone like Susan; it makes her humorous, somehow, as if some part of her body is betraying her, sliding in a bit of self-deprecation to take the edge off, and she's unaware of it. I feel as if I'm a beneficiary of this humor; that I'm meant to have some silent fun at her expense. I wonder if David catches her in these moments, if he singles out her flaws, the cracks seemingly unnoticed by her, and chuckles, savoring it in rooms away from her, freed by it, maybe.

Susan has ordered wine for us, and we both sip at our glasses tentatively, neither speaking much until she looks down at her lap, and her expression changes. Her sculpted features have let go for a moment. It's as though she wants to allow me a secret of hers, and I wonder if it's a sudden, propulsive need to confess a buried conscience, but I'm doubtful, and when the expression evaporates in the flicker of the candles, my doubt is confirmed. After the waiter comes to take our orders, she leans a little further in, and an alien grin reveals her long teeth. It goes fast, and her teeth are once again cloaked behind her waxy lips. She's staring at me, now, observing me, and my reactions to her. The lizard smirk she's so good at appears, and her cheekbones gain unsettling sharpness. She sits back into her chair, lifts her chin, and looks around the room.

"My mother was a witch. A real one," she says, and laughs. Maybe this is what she's been building up to, a confession about her mother, another kind of conscience, perhaps. I wonder if, in some way, she's embarrassed for admitting this. If she is, it doesn't show.

"She would bring home things to us, my siblings and I, and we would get stories for each one: a stone, a feather, some herbs, all of the standard shit witches are into."

I lift my glass, and she follows suit, drinking with me. I hold onto mine intimating that I'm listening, and for her to continue, to push forward with her mother-narrative.

"I don't know what you remember about your mother," says Susan, "but mine had an answer for everything. Not in a controlling way, but in a metaphysical fashion, you might say. She taught us the cards, the rituals of magic, spells, that sort of thing. I cast a spell on a girl once. At school, in the sixth grade."

Susan waits a moment to see how I'll gauge this, and I just provide a lukewarm smile, something passable.

"I don't know if it worked," she continues, her voice flat. "But, the girl tripped and fell that day, and broke all of the teeth on the front row of her mouth. Taking credit for it got me through the rest of that year. I hated that school. Have you ever read tarot cards?"

"I haven't, although I know what they are."

Susan shifts in her seat. She's bored with my answer. Did she want a compatriot, someone to live nostalgically with her, while she revisits cubbies of spell casting as a middle school kid? Maybe I am disappointing her.

"What did you learn from your mother? What sorts of specific things?" I offer this question as a form of compensation, to show I'm still interested, and to keep her from jettisoning my place in her company; a position she no doubt believes is earned. She waits a minute before answering, filtering, I assume, what she will reveal.

"I think the most important thing I learned from my

mother was how to set the tone of a thing: yourself, a residence, a meeting. That, I learned first. The second thing I learned from her—and only a few things were worth remembering next to all of the smudging and oils—which is that people will always fail you."

"Did she say why that is?"

"Not necessarily, but she did point out examples. And it's true. People are often disappointing. They take advantage; they walk on others; they refuse to be there for you when they should be; I don't think I have to explain this for you to understand. I assume you've been through enough to know this yourself, Diane."

I avoid responding to her subtle dig at my Placement status, a reminder; most Placements come from trauma of some kind, terrorized pasts.

"I suppose," I tell her. "But I wanted to hear it from you."

"I don't have much of a new spin to be honest. I mean, do you agree? The massive disappointment people usually turn into?"

"I agree with you."

"Hard not to," she says. Her eyes catch the glow from the candles.

"Do you still use what you were taught? The lessons gained from your mother?"

She just smiles, then looks to her right for a moment, distracted by a couple in the corner in the room. She squints at them then looks back to me.

"Tell me, what do you think about people? I mean *really* think."

"I think that they mutate."

Our plates arrive, and we both devour the food on them as if drained from each other and our conversation. Susan's face becomes flushed. Her mouth looks as if she's drunk bags of wet carrion; its fullness is glutinous, and her eyes gain a slightly lurid, sleepy expression.

"Mutations," she says, sipping her wine. "Explain that."

"Well, I guess it is its own form of witchery," I say, cutting the meat on my plate, appealing to the memory of her mother. "People are inconsistent because it benefits them. They shift, change, mutate. They are never themselves."

"How do you know that?"

"That they are never themselves? Because that would require constancy, and a commitment to some kind of altruism."

"You're saying people aren't naturally altruistic?"

"I'm not saying that, but it is difficult to bet on."

"What advantages are there to altruism, then?"

"Altruism to the self has many benefits. Social altruism is a bit more difficult to pin."

"I wish I had you as my Placement. Not David." Susan grins at me, and her smile is fueled by wine and some appreciation for what I've said. She seems to want me to know she means this, and that it's important.

"What's wrong with David?" I ask, and my heart drops, a quick, sudden pull under my sternum. Have I just made an offense? Will I be punished for asking her about this?

Is there a rule for this kind of inquiry? I feel prepared to counter, to defend myself; she did offer it up, after all, the subject of David. I can't be held entirely at fault. But, the longer she sits in silence, the more I understand my position of defense is not for me, but just David. Did she intuit this?

"Let's not talk about him," she says. "He's where he is, and it's where he needs to be, and that's all anyone needs to know about." Her voice is like a sudden wall, a stone in her throat nothing can move past. "Although it's not easy talking to someone without any ears."

She sighs at this last bit, exasperated, as if it's a type of bureaucracy she's had to unravel, spanning days. So, she carved away the other one, I thought, depriving David of his full hearing, weakening him further. I nod that I understand her, and she doesn't break from looking at me. I drink my wine.

"I want to know something," she says. "How do you feel about some witchery on your part?"

"I don't know what you mean." This comes out harder than I mean it to, colder.

"Well, don't look at it like that if you don't want to."

"I still don't know what it is you're discussing."

She smirks. "Are you close with Oliver?"

"Close enough."

"I'm curious about his room. You know the one?"

"What about it?" I choose not to feign ignorance with her, not at this point.

"What's in it?"

"I can't answer that. You know that."

"I do. You're right. But I know you better."

I don't respond.

"I want some pictures. I'm just curious what he's got locked-up in there."

"I'm not unfamiliar with curiosity," I say, and a smile broadens my face. A flicker of surprise crosses Susan's features. Is she questioning my propensity towards obedience? On our first meeting at The Dragon Room, she made a point to alert me to the satisfaction with my behavior from multiple Carriers. Was this what she meant, my perceived obedience to this role? Was she fighting against a certain amount of disappointment from me?

She drops her napkin over her plate. Bony scraps poke out from under it, glistening in the candlelight. I sit up and look at her.

"I've got something better." She responds to the notes of conspiracy, betrayal, and shamelessness I work into my voice, like weaving threads. I conjure up the friend she's always wanted, and I tell her about a deal I'm conducting soon for Oliver. I tell her there's no reason she shouldn't benefit from it.

"Give me the details next week," she says, placing a stack of bills on the check and handing it to the waiter, who walks away to a brighter room behind us.

I give her a date, and I can tell something in her snatches at it. There's something almost contractual about her voiceless response.

The waiter brings her change, then leaves again.

"I should have you to my house sometime," she says.

"I'd love to see it." As I say this, I find myself struggling with speaking. My voice sounds cautious at the edges of my words. I've been granted access to a new level; a kind of currency for the deal I mentioned. Her eyes stay level with my face, and I don't see a change in them, so maybe she expected this.

She returns to the topic of her mother. She says, "I should have elaborated earlier, I'm sorry. I just realized this."

"I felt what you said was clear."

"It's a woman thing, you know. This thing about mothers."

"It is, I agree."

"But, there's so much to that, to what she said; setting the tone of a place, of a person. I find there's so much truth to what she said."

I gulp the rest of my wine.

"A witch's home is always cozy." She says this more to herself, than to me. But, she says it as if it's a maxim of comfort, and that I should derive comfort from it also, the way people will say *this too shall pass*, she says, 'a witch's home is always cozy' is a phrase crafted by her mother, and one she abides.

"A witch's home is always cozy." She says it again, meditating, raising her fingers to her collar bones, lips upturned.

I smile at her.

"This way," she says, "anyone who stops by will always think it's safe."

Monday of the following week I ask Mason to get me maps of the entire state of New Mexico, and not just road maps, but also topographical ones, detailed ones, and anything he can find that isn't produced by a computer. I study them for hours, making notes, and then ask him to return with more, specifically covering the areas of Diablo Canyon, White Sands, and the Painted Desert. I begin making notes on all three: mileage from Santa Fe, exposure, distance, temp variance, access. I get a call from Mason when I'm in the middle of finishing some notes, and he tells me Oliver is dead, a heart attack on the plane on his way to Japan.

"The lawyers are coming to see you," he says. His voice is clipped, full of business. "I'd get ready if I were you. Wear a suit."

When the Carrier of a Placement dies, the Placement inherits everything, just like a real marriage. All of which is forfeited, and the Placement is shot, if anything is revealed to anyone on the margins of the community. If the Placement deviates from the set narrative in any way, it is as if the Carrier never died, and they inherited nothing. Everything is the same, except the Carrier is permanently removed. Placements are not allowed to have relationships, post-death. We cannot get remarried. We cannot flirt. We cannot indulge. We are not really free, but the feeling of it is close.

Later, when the paperwork is signed and the lawyers leave, Mason stands in my kitchen eating an apple. His smile is sexual, boyish.

"How does it feel to be a rich woman?"

"Mason. When you're done eating that, I need more maps."

"You're only the third, you know."

"The third what?"

"To make it this far."

"A man died. I don't know how much that has to do with my agility."

For a moment, the air changes.

"Why does everyone think in terms of games?" I ask. "Can't they think larger than that? Is that the best everyone's got?" As I say this, I'm grinding my jaw, staring down at a grid of the White Sands.

"Well, regardless, it's all yours now."

"Maps, Mason."

There are days when the notion of unfairness becomes a splinter in all of my thoughts, preventing any others from coming forward, unscathed. Maybe this is because it has so much to do with justice, ideas of what should or should not be 'just', or righting wrongdoings. Hypocrites are usually the first on this list. Then, there is our new, 21st century society, and the sort of electronic, social lawlessness pushing through the cracks; verification of the legitimacy of others through apps and sites, things I am not allowed, and the one thing for which I am grateful in terms of the rules here. I don't have to be verified through apps and sites to achieve my legitimacy. I exist as I am.

Relationships and boundaries are no longer sacred things, either; everyone's disposability is incisively facilitated through rendered code, a single click. The illusion is made manifest. Mason tells me of the many dates he goes on that fail, and the arbitrary deletion of friendships overnight, the endless holy worship of profiles and profiling.

When I learn about it from him, I see a return to old brutalities dressed up in algorithms. Scapegoating, mobs, vindication, all of these are human luxuries. Some are better achieved away from the electronic bully pulpit; this refined digital gallows with access for everyone. Some vindication can only be had in nature, where it's rooted, where it happens on a cellular level, skin-to-skin. There are choices in how one conducts it, what rituals will be involved, if any.

I'm thinking about these rituals when Mason makes arrangements with Susan's assistant for me. He tells me about David's new losses this week; all of the fingers on his right hand have been removed. Susan claims to her assistant that she has discovered more missing items. Confident David has taken them, a tireless search around her house has begun. Susan speaks with me briefly, says that the end of the week works well for our meeting. I tell her I haven't received confirmation on the location yet, but I will know soon.

"Perfect," she says.

She tells me she's exhausted, and is going for a massage; the July heat is getting to her. She says David collapsed during the cuttings, and requires an IV. He isn't responding. She says she's getting tired of him. She says he is too needy.

The arrangement is for Thursday. Mason drives to Susan's house outside of Santa Fe to pick her up at 7:00 a.m. Her home is u-shaped, the same orange-brown stucco of the other homes, but with no garage. The center of it contains a tiled water fountain, which ejects a single line of water over a bed of smooth, obsidian rocks. Palms, ferns, and cacti in varying ceramic urns encrust the brick walkway leading to the front door, which creates a layer of coziness. Two wooden benches flank both sides of it, and rectangular turquoise pillows lean against their wooden arms. Wind chimes hang to the right of the door, unmoving. Mason keeps the engine running while we wait in the circle drive. I check for signs of David, although I don't know what I expect to find from the car. I imagine he'll come to the door with her, and that she'll usher him outside to say hello in the guise of politeness, the way you introduce a child to a relative you haven't seen in a while. But, this does not happen, and Susan comes walking out of her door in a black dress, large black sunglasses, and black pumps.

She slides into the Lincoln and asks if she can make a drink. I gesture at the console. She grabs a glass, dumps ice into it, and pours a Scotch. She says she's nervous, and sips. I pat the back of her hand, tell her not to be nervous; that Mason has got us covered, and that no one will know of the transaction, or that she's even with me.

"Good. That's a relief. So, how is the widow, these days?" says Susan.

"More than fine."

"I imagine, since you now own the business."

"I do, among other things."

"You'll continue operating it for Oliver?"

"Well, not for him. But, yes, I run the business now."

"That's great, you're almost a colleague, Diane," she says. "Where is the location? You never told me."

"Oh, I'm sorry. I meant to have Mason get that to you. It's my fault. The location is in the White Sands."

"The White Sands? The monument? Why there?"

"I don't know. The client was very specific. Said he would only meet there. There wasn't much negotiation."

"What the hell are you buying?"

"Not me, him."

"He's buying from you? Why the change?"

"It's one million dollars for the largest black opal stone on the market."

"Oliver didn't have that on the market, did he?"

"No, of course not. I'm not talking about *that* market."

"How big is it?"

"Like, half of a cantaloupe."

"Congratulations. Impressive. That's unheard of."

"Thank you. I think it will be a successful transaction."

"Have you dealt with this client before?"

"No. He's new. Got a hold of me through older channels, but knows of my work. So, he's interested."

"Oliver never mentioned him?"

"Oliver never mentioned anybody."

"Where do I come in on the deal?"

"I want to give you half. To reinvest in other properties for me, other items. Are you interested?"

"Absolutely. What's my percentage?"

"I thought forty percent. How does that suit you, Susan?"

"Suits me just fine. You're about more than a colleague at this point."

"I'm flattered."

"Why bring me along for the business side of it though? You could have just gone on your own, and let me know later. I would have said yes, Diane."

"Because I thought you wanted to go along for the ride, see how it's done."

"I still don't understand why the White Sands. That's a ridiculous distance for him to make you travel."

"Less people. Less coverage. No cameras. No problems. I don't know, but I do know from experience to humor the client. Go where he wants to go, and the transactions are usually flawless."

"We have a drive ahead of us."

"Yes, we do."

The drive to the White Sands takes three hours with Mason's speeding, rather than the full four. We stop twice to get food, gas, and so Susan can smoke a cigarette. When we're not talking, she sleeps, or she stares mutely out of the window at the stretch of desert along I-54 and I-70. She takes off her black pumps and rests her bare feet on the edge of the seat. Occasionally, she checks her phone, but returns to look out of the window, indulging in an unusual passivity. A meditative expression forms around her eyes. There is an uncomfortable lightness about her that emanates the closer we get to our destination, as if she's capable of being an altogether different Susan.

Mason guides the Lincoln past the White Sands Welcome Center and down an adjacent road where he parks. Susan stretches. She reaches for her shoes.

"I wouldn't wear those if I were you," I tell her.

"We're going further in than this?"

"About six miles in. Walking. Can you handle it?"

"Oh, you've got to be kidding. Six miles? What the hell am I supposed to walk in, Diane?"

"I figured you would need different shoes. Mason picked some up. He got us enough water, bags, hats, sunscreen, everything we'll need."

"I don't know, Diane. Waiting here in the car might prove a bit more fruitful for me."

"It might, you're right. But I'd like to consider you a part of the transaction. To see it."

"I've seen transactions. Don't you think walking out there for that long at your age is a lot to handle? Has that not crossed your mind?"

"It will be much harder for me to part with the percentage I offered you if you decide to stay here."

I fold my hands together. I look at her, channeling a stern mother in place of her own so she knows I mean what I say. She's quiet again, and pulls into herself on the seat like a spider cringing before a slow building flame. She touches her face, her lips.

"Well, here's a side to you I couldn't have predicted. Let's see these shoes."

BLACK SPITTING, THICK-TAIL SCORPION

The dunes are smooth waves. White bellies, one after the next. I can't help but think of how they mimic snow. The sun hits the ground in a hard glare against the white, and my sunglasses grow greasy on the bridge of my nose. I tug on my large sun hat so that it tilts lower, creating a shadow over my face, a veil. Mason makes sure everything is working properly, the backpacks that contain water with hoses for us to drink from. Expensive looking things made for extreme hikers, adventurers. Our faces are slathered in sunblock, and Mason carries the black opal stone in his pack along with the other materials.

We are half an hour into the walk on The Alkali Flat. The trail is set apart by markers. Susan is a few feet ahead of me, and Mason is on the tail end. I watch her making uncertain but committed steps along the path. She wears also a sun hat and black sunglasses that engulf her face. The hiking shoes are a humorous contrast with her slim, black dress, and the hiking backpack, a mix of beige and hunter green lined in red piping, clips and straps. She holds the small plastic hose to her mouth most of the time, drinking a consistent stream of her water supply, despite Mason's warnings to ration. We anticipate this and let her do it anyway. Further warning will intercede or provoke hyper-vigilance, if she's capable of that. Best to just let her be. Observing her quiet willingness to stay on the path, uncomplaining, has me questioning the shoes. She's never appeared more relaxed. Does she always wear black pumps?

Around fifty minutes into the walk, Mason tells us we've covered almost half of our six-mile trek.

"How is that possible?" asks Susan, turning to look at him for a moment, then back out to the rows of white dunes.

I guess he might be fudging it a bit, a little less, a little more, but it doesn't matter. He knows that. So do I. Approximation is what counts. We need to be at least six miles in. The wall of mountains facing us is purple-black, like a shadow of broken bone, a reptile spine against the white, rippling belly of the desert floor. Stony-blue thunderheads form a tattered crown at the edge of the peaks. Sweat leaks down my sides, and my heart hammers. My shoulders feel burned in the sun.

I turn around to check on Mason. He could be any young hiker used to this environment with his boots, rust-orange shorts, and green T-shirt. His blond hair is pulled back into its standard ponytail, and his arms swing with light frivolity, like someone who doesn't know me, or Susan, someone who just happens to be on the same path in the desert. I find myself wanting this for him, and turn back to look ahead of me. Susan's figure moves further ahead than us. She resembles a mark, a black blemish.

After an hour, Mason says we're getting closer; another thirty to forty minutes and we'll be far enough out, close in proximity to six miles at least. Susan asks to stop. She wants to rest. So we stop and sit down, all of us quiet for a moment. She leans back on one arm and stares out at the dunes, her face squinting in the light. Her cheeks are flushed, stippled red. Her throat shines with sweat, which she wipes at with her hand. She drinks more of her water. Her shoulders slump. She drops her head back between them. Her original composure is lessening in the heat. Her limbs wilt the longer she sits.

"Jesus," she says, moaning. "This fucking heat."

Neither of us comments.

Mason appears unaffected by the increase in temperature. He seems to have adapted. He sips at his water hose. I can't see what he's watching because of his sunglasses, but I want to. He catches me staring at him, nods, and the nod is an invitation to get started. And he's right. I know he's right. I nod in return to signal that I agree, let's move on.

We stand, and Susan groans, shifting her backpack. She looks at me with complete exasperation, as if to say why did I agree to this, but I trust you. I acknowledge it the way a friend would.

"Come on. You'll survive," I tell her.

We walk for another twenty minutes when Mason says we're at the crossing point. We have to veer off from the markers. So we trek left, walking deeper into the dunes, sliding down the sand and moving with cautious agility. Small cacti reach up in corners at the edges of the sandbanks, some in clumps of faded grass. The thunderheads grow thick and divide the sun, showering the white banks in dappled shadow, which turn gray, then purple. Alien coolness sweeps across us for a second, a phantom wind, and its gone as soon as the clouds part again, releasing the light. Susan turns around to look at us.

"Keep going!" Mason shouts, pointing.

I look at him.

"We're almost there," he says, lower. "Close enough, but almost there."

"Then let's stop. This is good enough."

"You sure?"

I nod, my mouth dry. "Yes. I'm sure."

"Susan!" I scream. "Come back! We're here!"

She waves and then returns to us over the short distance she walked. Mason takes off his pack and sits on the crest of the dune. Susan starts to do the same thing.

"Susan?" says Mason.

"Yeah?"

"I know you want to sit, but can you stay standing? We need to keep an eye out for the client. He'll be coming from that direction. Diane and I need to prepare the stone, the paperwork."

"There's paperwork?"

"If you see anyone approaching in a red jacket and a black hat, that's him."

"Wearing a jacket in this?"

"Here," says Mason, handing her a pair of binoculars. "Use these. If you see anyone or anything, tell us."

She lifts them to her eyes, turns her head.

"This is incredible, Diane. I feel less blind looking through these."

"That's good," I say. "I'm glad to hear it. Very glad."

Mason pulls the black opal stone out of his pack. It's wrapped in a pillowcase. He twists the pillowcase until it's tight with the stone snug at the end of it. He stands, testing its weight. His lithe body is quick, certain. I watch him silently, as if we've caught an animal and don't want to frighten it away while it crawls into our camouflaged snare. I freeze as he moves up to the correct distance, right behind her. I expect her to turn, to look back, to confront him and unfurl an outrage directed at both of us, but she doesn't. She just continues scanning the dunes, binoculars held firmly to her face, hand on her hip.

He inches forward, the wrapped stone hanging from his hand, which he lifts, swings, and launches directly into the back of Susan's head. One smooth snap of his arm, and the stone connects. There is a crisp popping sound when it hits, and Susan collapses, sliding the rest of the way down the dune where she lays in a black puddle, splayed, her hair thrown up around her head. The binoculars stay in her hand. Her backpack slumps to the right of her shoulder.

Mason moves quickly to her, and I join him.

"Let's hurry," he says. I don't respond. I squat down and check the water in her backpack.

"She's got about a cup left."

"Good."

I touch the back of her head and feel around the crown.

"No blood. Any bruising, you think?"

"If there is, that's fine. That's why I brought this."

Mason takes a plain desert rock from the bottom of his pack and wedges it into the sand behind Susan's head. The effect is that it's always been there, part of the scenery.

"Is she still breathing?" I ask.

He tests her pulse, her breath.

"Yes," he says. "I told you, I know what I'm doing."

"I believe you."

"Ready for the next part?"

"Do you think it's necessary?"

"I don't know," he says. "She'll wake up disorientated. The sun is pretty hot. She doesn't have enough water, so she'll die from dehydration most likely, but on the off chance—do you want to take the chance that she might—"

"No, No. No chances, you're right. Get it."

Mason unzips a side pocket on his pack and frees a clear plastic tube a little bigger than a tube of toothpaste. Inside the tube crawls a black form, its armored body alert, ready.

"Okay, get down and hold her mouth open so I can get this inside."

I gently clasp Susan's chin and open her mouth, which lowers like a catatonic's. She doesn't move. Mason slides the end of the plastic tube between Susan's lips, pushing it in far enough so that the end is near her throat.

"Hold it steady. When I pull on this lever, the bottom will release. I have to push on this plunger to force it out. Do you understand?"

"Yes."

"Okay, once it's in, shut her mouth quick, and hold it there."

"Okay, just do it."

"Here we go."

Mason pulls back on the black cord lining the side of the tube, opening it inside Susan's mouth. He presses the plunger, slowly forcing the scorpion's squirming, plated body down the tube and into her throat. It's tail flexes, flinging its thorny, black needle-tip against the plastic.

"Go on, you bastard. Get in there."

The plunger stops. The creature disappears somewhere inside her mouth. Mason slowly slides the tube out from between her lips. As he does it, I gently press her jaw up, closing it. My hand against her chin looks like a lover's, as if I am admiring the line of her jaw, her face. Her eyes are static.

"How long should I hold it?" I ask.

"Let go, and see what happens."

I remove my hand faster than I mean to, thinking it might come crawling out of her. I stand next to him, watching. Her mouth stays shut. Nothing presses against her cheeks from inside like I thought. There is just stillness.

"Now what?"

"It's probably scared and figuring out its cozy new home."

"How do we know it will sting?"

"We don't but these guys spray from their tails."

"Is it doing that?"

"I saw it start to ejaculate when I depressed the plunger. Some liquid is still on the side of it. If anything, it's rampaging in there, looking for a way out."

"What can we expect?"

"If not the sun, and the waterless environs, paralysis and pulmonary edema from what she's swallowing."

"When she's found?"

"These animals aren't uncommon out here. In the desert."

"So she got stung. She fell."

"Yes. It's done. What do you want me to do with this?"

Mason lifts up the black opal stone wrapped in the pillowcase and sticks his hand inside it. He holds the stone into the sunlight. Fragments of sun scatter like glass on the sand; ignited, the opal's colors shower our faces, bursting upwards and across the blank dunes.

"That's yours now. Put it away."

"Why did you bring it, if you weren't going to show her?"

"I anticipated she might ask to see it. But she didn't."

I catch a brief smile on his face before its replaced with his perfunctory seriousness. He rewraps the stone and stuffs it back into his bag. We check ourselves, re-strapping our bodies, making sure we have all of our things and walk back towards the Alkali Flat Trail, the red markers in the sand, silent like before, Susan's body is invisible behind us, hidden by the arching dunes. I let Mason walk ahead. A horrible weakness begins to spread through my hands and up my arms. My legs feel carved through. I'm cold.

Mason turns around. He stops.

"What's wrong?" he asks, cupping my shoulder. "You're shaking. Hard."

"This—this is just not me."

"What isn't? Do you need water?"

"This is just not me. Doing that to someone, even her."

"You need to relax. It's done. You know why you did this."

"How long before David inherits?"

"Probably a while. They have to find her first, announce

her death. Then the lawyers. It won't go as quickly as yours, but soon enough."

"How long before she's dead, do you think?"

"By the time we reach the car, I imagine. Let's go."

I refuse to walk. My feet feel roped to the earth, stagnant, entrenched. Between him and Susan's body, I am anchored, a place split in time where moving forward will split me again. Mason enfolds me, and I catch the scent of his body, his sweat. He holds me as we walk, and his arm is an unwavering bulwark along my shoulders, the feeling of it radiating deep love and protection. He doesn't let go of me, even as I start to cry against him.

"I'm sorry."

"You're fine, Margaret. We're almost there. We're almost there."

I know that this isn't true; the path is long. He knows this, too, but it feels good to hear him say it anyway.

VAUGHN, NM

Roadwork forces us to take a detour off I-54 through the town of Vaughn. Mason cruises down the main road. Buildings labeled as diners and hotels are boarded, sealed. Their fronts are peeled to the raw wood underneath. Some of them appear to lean into each other. Trees have grown huge around their sides. Weeds sprout tall through concrete cracks in old steps. Doors hang. Abandoned commercial buildings with red and white painted logos faded to smears stare out at empty parking lots. The lines that once marked their parking spaces are almost transparent. A sign advertising the Ranch Way Motel in a bold, red rectangle with a yellow arrow curving up and around it, points back at the tiny shuttered buildings. It's next door to a café that is also closed and has a sign that hangs at a slant, as if trying to be seen on its own merit. Weathered white letters on a red background. In the distance, a brown field, clouds building. Mason finds a single, operating gas station and pulls off the road.

"Getting gas," he says, and steps out of the car.

I sit up and stretch my legs. My feet knock over Susan's black pumps on the floor of the car. I stare at them as if a body should be there, or that she'll come back to retrieve them. They take up a prodigious amount of space somehow. Their color appears richer, as if made with something else altogether. I'm afraid to touch them, to put my hands on them, scared that some of it will rub off, coat my fingers, seep inside.

They're an invitation.

I have to remove them, the last of her. This is evidence. I see Mason through the station window moving around the aisles, grabbing things, taking his time. I reach over, fighting the recoil in my stomach, and grab hold of Susan's black shoes. I clasp them by their heels in my right hand and get out of the Lincoln. I make sure Mason does not see me. I want to be alone while I do this. I want no one else to be a part of my miniature burial. I walk a few feet away from the station towards a ramshackle alley made of crumbling garages with bent doors, half-sealed. A few other unmarked buildings stretch beside them, all painted gray. Their doors lacking knobs with glass painted thick-white. Rusted cans, debris, and nails cluster together in cracks filled with heat-dried weeds, cinderblock stacks and old tires. Beyond the buildings at the end of the alley, trees bloom like weeds, unchecked, smothering the structures, and pressing them further into age. I get to the end of the alley, set on dropping them somewhere around the tree in a bucket, a trash barrel, maybe, whatever is there. There is a danger in being too romantic about this.

I turn at the edge of what was once an auto-parts store, more than likely erected sometime in the early fifties. The glass entrance and windows are soaped over. A tiny bell hangs from a tattered red string attached to the door handle, its bronze eaten to scratches, and covered in a dense mold color. On the north side of the closed store the tree creates shade over a dirt yard filled with yellowed leaves, mulch, and chunks of rotted bark. The branches above are laced in worm webs, silken nests clotted in the grooves, as if spoiled cotton candy unspooled from somewhere deeper inside it. Sap-stink, like stale post-sex, rises up from the mud.

Then, there's the truck. A blue pick-up truck idles a few feet in front of the tree, just outside of its shadow. Through the back window I can see the shoulder of someone lying slumped against the driver's side door, just the round edge of it where it slopes down to the neck. The engine struggles, and must have been sputtering like this for a while, burning through whatever gas is left in it. I move slowly up the side, the shoes squeezed in my sweaty hand. My stomach tightens. I get up to the window; the thrumming, staccato rumble of the tired engine is louder. The glass of the windshield and passenger window is smeared in dirt, streaked in filth, and chunks of red matter. When I get closer, peering down inside the cabin, I see the body of a boy lying across the seat next to a man behind the steering wheel, as though he collapsed there. The man's head is pressed against the corner of the door, and the window. His forehead is cratered, a black hole over his right eye. The skin of his face is pale, blue-green, like the color of a vein. The boy's skin is the same color under his black and yellow tank top. His face is covered in dried blood like tar. I move around the front of the truck and look through the other window. On the floor, at the man's feet, is a gun just out of reach from the boy's limp hand. The seat in the cabin is soaked black, and the boy's head is turned slightly downwards. His shoulders appear tiny, as if squeezed inward by invisible fingers. Born that way, I thought.

I walk towards the truck bed, back towards the tree, cold all the way through. It has Oklahoma plates. I leave it where it idles, the two bodies decomposing quietly, like two brothers sleeping after a long drive from somewhere. This is how I choose to think of them. The idling motor becomes a tiny hum the further away I get, and I realize it was always there, just underneath the stripped silence of this town, the abandoned storefronts and garages. Even before the town. Waiting for me to find it there. It stays with me as I walk. I pick an arbitrary nook between two buildings and drop the shoes, no longer concerned with any kind of ceremony, or burial. I leave them, and it is as if they were nothing, powerless baubles. What I found in the truck has overridden them, and I feel as though I'm being followed by what was there; that in some way I was led here to this, led inexorably to it: the shattering of a person's heart; the seeking of something and forever seeking it without recompense.

Back at the Lincoln, Mason stands at the curb near the main road smoking a cigarette while the pump fills the tank. I avoid catching his attention and get into the car. I curl into myself on the seat. I listen to the thudding of the gas pump as it works, echoing the idling engine of the truck hidden back there down the alleyway. I see the boy, his arms spread out towards the man as if seeking to be embraced.

Mason finishes his cigarette, and fills up the rest of the tank. He says nothing when he gets into the car, except that we'll be back in Santa Fe before dark. He asks me if I want anything, if I'm hungry. I don't respond, and he starts the car, pulling away from the gas station and back onto the road. I stare out of the window, my hand clinched over my mouth, woven to a new kind of coldness.

When we reach the limits of the city, the sun is mostly gone; the world is a blackened thing. The sky is orange-red. It appears like an incision over the mountain crests, coating clouds like liquid. Then comes the dissolution of the sun. It is quick, then, that the mountains are no longer visible, and the earth no longer a defined space.

The dark is a form of suspension, and all of its beasts make a home in it.

PART V: MASON

Awakening, you transformed our mundane human language…Everything in the world was transfigured, even simple things like basin and jug…We were led who knows where, to cities built by magic…
   —Mirror

THE STORY OF THE BOY
ON CATHEDRAL COVE

Margaret's funeral is on a Saturday. My wife, my children, and myself are the only people to attend it besides David. The house is quiet, and the children are solemn in their response to it. When they ask how she died, I tell them she grew old, which is what she did; it's as simple as that. The century is closing, and this story has found its way to me through my wife.

January: Cathedral Cove, New Zealand. A fourteen year-old boy (who remains nameless in the report), takes a surfboard to the beach every day, and has for the last two years. He swims out into the waves during the afternoon, as well as the night. He is always in the water, his mother says. His father is dead, but his mother has supported him in his adventures, his seeking of the waves. The boy has struggled, but over time grows adept at tackling the water.

His brother says that he will watch him from the cliffs, his body propped on his board, just floating in the sun. He will not come into the house, and most of the time has to be dragged away from the cove. It is during one of these nights that the boy becomes restless, and his older brother asks him what is wrong, why he's so upset. And the boy tells him, he says it is the closest thing to space, that it is space that he dreams of. When his brother asks him why this is the case, the boy tells him that he has known space, has been in it before, drifting and floating. He says he remembers the planets, the gasses bursting around him, the stars showering the blackness, the aloneness of drifting. That he remembers clearest. *Why would you want that?* His brother asks, and the boy says it is not a matter of wanting; it is just something he has been before, an astronaut, an explorer. He says he remembers being this person; that he remembers his life ending in space, drifting forever. His brother, dismissing him, still goes to the cove with him every day, sometimes watching from the cliffs, or the beach.

It is at sundown one day that he notices fins surrounding his younger brother who paddles on his board. Looking from the cliff, he can spot innumerable shark bodies circling him in the water. He begins to scream, to try to help his brother, certain that he will be killed if something isn't done. Then killer whales approach, and the sharks disperse, although some remain, but there is no attack on either party, no fighting or killing amongst them, and this is so strange that he goes to get his mother. She brings her friend, and others start to arrive, too. When they return, the circle of sharks has grown, and the boy lays on his board on his stomach, with his arm in the water, touching the noses of them as each one breaks through, just for a moment, then they dive back down. His mother is crying from terror, and the neighbors cluster around her, equally disturbed. *What is he doing?* Screams his mother. Get out of there! Get out of there! But the boy does not hear them.

Eventually, the sharks leave, diving down and away, leaving him to paddle himself ashore. His mother is frantic, taking him to the house and lecturing him all night. His brother could not sleep from her incessant, vehement speeches. Finally, he does fall asleep, and returns to the cove again, this time to see his brother doing the same thing with the same circle of sharks. His mother and the neighbors have returned, beside themselves with horror. Unperturbed, the boy continues to pet the sharks. Soon, the news stations discover this, and the reporting begins, worldwide. The boy's visitations with the sharks don't seem to have an end, and the boy's mother exhausts herself by the end of the week, and lies sleeping in their flat, attended by friends.

His brother stays, keeping an eye on him with a few other onlookers. He observes it when all of the sharks vanish except for one, a great white that continuously circles his brother on the raft, poking its nose up occasionally, and then propelling itself away. The older brother thought he could detect a mysterious familiarity between them. Why does it not kill him? He wondered. Why does it not leap up out of the water and swallow my brother, chewing him to bits, taking him apart, and leaving only his board, and a blood-slathered beach? Why does this shark not act like a shark? Drowned in his confusion, he hopes that his observations from his perch on the cliff will reveal to him an answer. The shark's huge body swims guardian-like around his brother's tiny brown form. Its large fin draws a barrier around them, its black eyes visible from here.

Late at night, when the boy is at home, and his mother is asleep, his older brother confronts him. He says, *Why do you do this? Why do you scare everyone, especially our mother? Do you have a death wish? First, it's space, and now you are petting sharks? Can you explain yourself?*

The young man is quiet for a long time before answering his brother, but when he does he says, *The shark is my lover.*

Your lover? What do you mean 'your lover'?

That shark is my greatest love, brother. We have known each other before.

How can you love a shark?

I do not see a shark like you see a shark. I do not see like you. We found each other. Be happy for us.

He gestures to indicate the two of them, their house, the sky and the cove, the ocean and the stark moon above it. He does this as if to say, *Do you see? Do you not understand?*

Amidst this, a miracle.

ACKNOWLEDGEMENTS

My gratitude is unlimited for those who helped me on the adventure of writing this book. I am extremely thankful for the advice and direction from Dr. Reed Bye early on in its development. Anne Waldman was not only instructive in her inspiration, but also supportive in our brief pow-wows together. Laird Hunt helped me find what was important in a story and what to leave out. Sun Yung Shin, who has stuck by me as a writing comrade and friend, keeps me going when I want to give up, and who championed this book from the start; thank you for being you, and for arriving at Naropa when I did. Rikki Ducornet was largely instrumental and crucial to my growth as a writer, and the impact it had on this novel through our conversations, alongside the incredible journey in the many workshops we had. Dr. Sara Veglahn not only changed my writing path, and my perception of what writing is, indelibly, but became a mentor too few of us experience. I have endless gratitude for Shawnie Hamer, a brilliant poet and educator; without her incisive feedback and utterly selfless reading of my manuscript, it wouldn't have some of the right notes in place. I am lucky to have her as a colleague, friend, and writing comrade. I also need to communicate my gratitude for the general community of writers and friends, both at Naropa University and around the globe, who took the time to support me with this project. Writing is often an exercise experienced in a vacuum; the support of this community helped me survive it.

References

Alighieri, Dante. *The Purgatorio.* Barnes and Noble Books, 2005.

Foucault, Michel, and Paul Rabinow. *The Foucault Reader.* Vintage Books, 2010.

Lispector, Clarice, Katrina Dodson, and Benjamin Moser, ed. *The Complete Stories.* New Directions, 2015.

Sweeney Todd: The Demon Barber of Fleet Street. Directed by Tim Burton, performances by Johnny Depp, Carter H. Bonham, Alan Rickman, DreamWorks Pictures, 2007.

Mirror. Directed by Andrei Tarkovsky, performances by Margarita Terekhova, Anatoliy Solonitsyn, Mosfilm, 1975.

van Lommel, Pim. *Consciousness Beyond Life: The Science of the Near-Death Experience.* HarperCollins, 2010.

Blake Edward Hamilton holds an MFA in Creative Writing from Naropa University. His work has appeared in World Literature Today Magazine: Windmill, NPR, South Broadway Press, and Bombay Gin Literary Journal, among others. He is the author of the poetry collections, *All Through Your Multiple Selves* and *Move In Silence*.

www.ingramcontent.com/pod-product-compliance
Lightning Source LLC
Chambersburg PA
CBHW010842190726
48286CB00012BA/2946